Also by L.M. Vincent

Novels

Final Dictation
Pas de Death

Nonfiction

The Dancer's Book of Health
Competing with the Sylph
In Search of Motif No. 1

Saving Dr. Block

L.M. Vincent

Bunbury Press
Manchester, MA

For Jack, of course.

Chapter One

It was the end of April, a sunny but cool spring day, and bursts of wind off the plains were chilling Howard's skin, penetrating his T-shirt and gym shorts as if he were wearing cheese cloth. The choosing of sides had just begun, and Chris Beaman and Ryan O'Hearn, big surprise, were the self-appointed team captains. He shifted from one leg to the other to fight the cold.

"Pick yourselves captains and divvy up into teams," Mr. Saunders always commanded, sending them off to the playing field while he did whatever he did in the gym office. Probably he just read "Sports Illustrated" or "Motor Trend" with his feet up on his desk and rubbed the long forehead indentation where the discus had struck and split his skull when he was in college. Saunders had never gone into detail about the accident, which likely meant that he hadn't just been in the wrong place at the wrong time, but had done something really stupid. No great intellect, that Saunders, but maybe he had been sharper before the blow to the head.

Howard wondered why Mr. Saunders couldn't just state the obvious, uphold the time-honored food chain of junior high gym class, and tell everyone that Chris Beaman and Ryan O'Hearn would be the captains. The trauma of the missile crisis still a fresh scab, Howard couldn't help but imagine a team of Russians playing with Cubans. Admittedly neither Chris nor Ryan, both already thirteen years old, physically shared much in common with a pudgy bald guy with a mole or a black bearded cigar smoker with a green cap. But in any case, in such a scenario would commies other than Khrushchev and Castro end up as team captains? No way, team captains were inevitable.

In theory, flag football was not supposed to involve body slams and tackles, but Chris, Ryan, and the rest of the top-of-the-heap *shagetzes* in the class liked to throw their weight around. Sometimes, especially during the winter or when the weather was bad and they had to stay inside and play dodge ball, class seemed less like gym and more like a pogrom. That was it, Howard realized with satisfaction—they were like Cossacks, Chris and Ryan were.

Only the three of them left in limbo now, always the same three—himself, Mike, and Stinky. Chris and Ryan made a big deal out of deciding on the dregs at the bottom of the coordination barrel, as if it conceivably made any difference. The three were superfluous, just trying to stay out of the way and scurrying like pigeons if anyone of either team came too close. Still, on and on the captains agonized, twisting the dagger of humiliation, straining to differentiate gradations of physical klutzdom. Howard could count his blessings again. If Chris and Ryan were Nazis instead of Cossacks, all three of them would have been picked right off the bat and send directly to those showers.

They were friends, the trio at the bottom tier, and not just from being foisted together as rejects in gym class. Howard was closer to each than they were to each other, bridging the cultural divide between the Jew Irwin Devinki—or Stinky, as he was known even by people who liked him—and Mike Hunsacker, who was pretty much a gentile. The notion that Howard was a literal and figurative intermediary, some indeterminate cultural hybrid, was not lost on him.

Stinky was clearly Jewish, even if you didn't know his last name, but Howard had not only inherited the fair complexion of the Polish forebears on his father's side, but his father had changed his name after the war from something long and ending in "-sky" to Block. So Howard could pass as a gentile, and choosing the path of least resistance, did so at every opportunity. But navigating the religious divide was confusing. Howard didn't feel completely Jewish but couldn't feel gentile either, and his discomfiture was intensifying with his looming Bar Mitzvah in June. Bar Mitzvah boys were not supposed to be cultural straddlers, stuck in some nether world of stunted assimilation; they were supposed to be Talmud-thumping, regular army Schlomos.

"This is tough, but I'll take 'Old Yeller' shorts," Chris finally decided.

That meant Mike Hunsacker, whose gym shorts were in truth quite yellowish. His mother, evidently also a gentile, sent him to gym class without bleaching his shorts. Stinky was a natty dresser and would never dream of wearing yellowing gym shorts, and Howard's mother saw it as a bad reflection upon her capabilities as a mother if Howard's shorts were not routinely bleached and pressed. After all, he was Dr. Block's son and had to make an impression. If a pair of gym shorts started to turn, like fruit on the wrong side of ripe, she immediately donated them to charity and bought Howard another pair.

"What a *putz*," said Stinky, under his breath. The "old yeller shorts" line had been used before, often—or in nearly every gym class at least once—but Chris still thought the moniker was original, clever, and incredibly funny.

Mike began running over to Chris's line of recruits and clumsily removed his T-shirt. He snared the shirt collar on his chin and flailed about for several long seconds, face covered, skinny arms waving, legs stumbling and directionless, like a drunk double-amputee spider. Stinky tucked in his own shirt, trying to camouflage his midriff. He was hoping to be chosen next, Howard knew, which would make him a "shirt" and not a "skin." Not exposing his overhanging belly meant a lower level of mockery about his jiggling flab. While Stinky sucked in his gut in as best he could, Howard adopted a Jerry Lewis pose, turning his toes in and partially bending his knees so he looked spastic. He didn't mind so much being a "skin," at least not as much as Stinky.

The ruse failed.

"Okay," said Ryan to Chris, with a disgusted, over-exaggerated sigh, "we'll take Block if we have to, but you get the fat Jew."

Howard exchanged glances with Stinky before slowly walking to his team. Stinky hesitantly pulled off his shirt, bracing himself, and trudged across the field, lagging behind his teammates.

***

Howard and Stinky left the school building with hair wet from the recent shower. Stinky had slicked his curly black hair back as smoothly as possible, but without Brylcreem, strands were beginning to meander obdurately with drying. He pulled out the waistband of his black Sans-a-belt slacks and tucked in his white polo shirt. Then he kneeled to pull up his thin ribbed calf-high socks—like Howard's father wore—and straightening, shimmied as if snuffing out a cigarette butt to readjust his feet into his Florsheim tasseled loafers. Not penny loafers, of course, but a more formal-looking pump. Were he a man of fifty, Stinky would be considered a spiffy dresser, but the effect was somewhat jarring given that he was not even thirteen.

Primped and straightened, Stinky cleared his throat. He had something on his mind, something with gravitas, which he couldn't just blurt out without first being presentable.

"How come *I'm* the fat Jew?" he asked.

"You're not fat," parried Howard, "you're husky."

"You know that's not what I meant," snapped Stinky. "They think you're gentile."

Howard didn't respond. The statement led in all sorts of directions, and Howard didn't want to go down any of the roads. He stood at the mental crossroads warily and said nothing.

"No reason to advertise, I guess." Stinky replied for him.

Howard wasn't to blame for being fair-complexioned and having a straight nose that didn't demand attention. Stinky had his parents' olive skin and a beaky, show-off of a schnoz like his father. If anyone was to blame, it was them. Howard hoped that with time Stinky would grow out of his huskiness and grow into his nose.

The appearance of Mrs. Devinki's green Buick turning into the circular drive provided a welcome change of subject.

"There's your mom," said Howard unnecessarily. "Guess I'll see you there."

"Today's Thursday, isn't it."

"Yep."

"Shit a brick. Need a ride to *shul*? My mom can take you."

11

"I rode my bike," said Howard.

"What? Your mom let you?" Stinky shook his head in astonishment.

***

Howard felt an independent soaring spirit on his green Schwinn 10-speed as the wind hurtled through his hair. He passed the row of waiting school buses and happily absorbed the jolt of going over the curb when he could have pedaled just a bit further to the graded cut of the drive. Then he looked over his shoulder to confirm the way clear, and ventured into the street. The wind billowed his hair momentarily, as if the Lord were signaling approval. Howard Block was in the street. He was free.

Howard's previous bike, though also a twenty-six incher, had no speeds at all, and worse, pedal brakes like a kiddy cycle. Howard had acquired the Schwinn used from a schoolmate in secret negotiations with saved allowance money and stunned his mother by proudly showing up on it one afternoon. Jeanette had reluctantly accepted the purchase, fighting both the hurt that her son had denied her involvement in a significant adolescent milestone and the fear that a tenspeed—in some circles referred to as a "racing bike"—was extremely dangerous, especially if not ridden on the sidewalk. Since his mother knew little of bikes, Howard assured her that he would only use one speed at a time. And for show, he always rode on the sidewalk until a block away from the house, beyond the range of maternal surveillance.

While he was coasting along a relatively straight patch mid-way home, Howard checked his watch. Odds were that his mother was checking hers as well. Jeanette had not totally reconciled herself to the notion of Howard riding his racing bicycle home, since God-forbid he could be hit by a car (in this scenario, the car had to careen out of control and jump the sidewalk) or collide with some reckless and wild gentile bicyclist (who, paradoxically, would be riding on the sidewalk despite such wild recklessness). When Jeanette was able to get a grip on herself during these moments of panic, she clung to a deeply felt spiritual confidence that Howard would be okay, just as she had sensed that her cousin Freida Kaplan would survive her hysterectomy, and told her as much.

But just in case, Jeanette was rifling through drawers and checking countertops in multiple rooms in a frantic attempt to accumulate coins for the *pishka*. Housed in one of the kitchen cabinets, the *pishka* was a rectangular blue metal bank with a white Star of David imprinted on the front. The accumulated coins were picked up at regular intervals by volunteers and donated to Jewish charities through the United Jewish Appeal. Jeanette's blue box was always full, weighted from her efforts to bribe fate and ward off evil through charity. Howard did not resent the ritual of the blue box. A benign superstition as superstitions went, the alleged protective powers of the pay-off allowed Howard more latitude and privileges than he otherwise might have been permitted. Like leaving the house.

With great relief, Jeanette reached her coin quota by locating a dime and three pennies under a seat cushion in the den. Remarkably, Jeanette's forays for coins always proved fruitful, as if coins in the bottoms of drawers and under seat cushions had the capacity to replicate like laboratory mice. In her distracted pursuit, she never stopped to consider the phenomenon. Counting silently, she dropped the coins into the slot in the top of the box. Howard would return any moment now, and wasn't it silly to think that Howard's bike ride home was any more dangerous than a hysterectomy?

Howard crouched in the racing position for the final straightaway before the curve off High Drive as it merged into 67ᵗʰ Terrace where, just below the crest of the hill, he returned to the sidewalk six houses away from his own. Dutifully on the sidewalk the rest of the way, he coasted up his driveway, gradually coming to a stop in front of the garage.

Jeanette was waiting in the doorway before he got there, gripping the blue metal box in her left hand. She wore a housedress but her face was fully made up with a cabinet's selection of cosmetics. A quick change of clothing and she would be ready for anything, ready to be seen anywhere.

"You ride your bike and what happens? We're late."

"I didn't think it would be safe to ride too fast," Howard said.

"Smart boy," said Jeanette, obviously pleased with his retort. "Anyway, I put money in the *pishka* so you wouldn't get in an accident."

"When are you going to stop with that? You don't need to give money to charity to protect me every time I ride my bike! I'm almost thirteen, Mom!" Howard feigned indignation out of some sense of pride and duty, not anticipating his protest making any difference, nor really wanting it to.

"It wouldn't hurt," said Jeanette. "And it's for a good cause. The United Jewish Appeal plants trees in the desert. Someday there will be a forest in the Holy Land where there used to be sand."

Howard didn't buy the tree argument for a second. Maybe a few saplings here and there, but the bulk of the money had to be going for weapons. Howard had yet to see any indication of a Sherwood Forest near Haifa, at least not from the pictures he saw on the news, or from the few synagogue friends who had made the Pilgrimage and told him about the barren landscape.

"Well, I hope they're saving some of that money to buy water."

"Don't show disrespect, Howard."

Howard bristled. What if he stopped planting those coins in the drawers and under the seat cushions the night before he rode his bike? What would she do then, huh? Empty-handed and desperately in need of coins for the *pishka*?

"Sorry," he apologized, perspective showering upon him. Wherever the money went, it was a small price to pay for being able to ride his bike in the street.

In spite of chastising Howard for his lateness, Jeanette found the time to make him a snack, consisting of a neatly cored and sliced apple, three slices of American cheese, and a handful of Wheat Thins, all placed carefully in a covered plastic container.

"Do you have your *Haftorah* book?" she asked, snapping the lid on the plastic container.

Howard patted his back pocket, from which protruded the top third of the approximately thirty-five page pamphlet, folded lengthwise. The blue booklet, his constant companion for weeks, contained all the blessings and other materials he needed to know for the big day.

Assuaged for the moment, Jeanette said nothing further until she was backing the 1958 two-toned turquoise and white Chevrolet Bel-Air out of the garage.

"Next time I'll just pick you up from school," she said.

"We'll make it. . . there's plenty of time."

"We shouldn't be rushing in this traffic."

"It's not all my fault if we're late, Mom. You didn't have to waste the time to make me this snack."

"Of course I did," she snapped. "Don't be ridiculous."

That settled, Howard avoided engaging his mother in further conversation, occupying himself with his snack. And then, while folding a slice of cheese to fit a Wheat Thin without overlapping the edges, Howard spotted the rear side of two blonde girls walking together along Ward Parkway. One was just about his own age, and the other, likely an older sister, had entered the young woman phase, sixteen at the very least. Howard hurriedly began to roll down his window in anticipation of peering back for a frontal view, as they looked enticing from behind, both wearing just above knee-length tight skirts—the kind that sexy secretaries wore in the movies—and sleeveless blouses.

Howard cranked down the window to the very bottom, tilting his head to catch the wind and readying himself for whatever feminine visual feast awaited.

"Shut the window," his mother said.

"Just a sec—" he stalled.

"Shut the window," she repeated, "you'll catch a draft."

They were now just passing the girls. He needed to concentrate.

"It's okay, my hair's not wet," he shouted over the wind whooshing in his ear.

He focused on the younger one. He couldn't remember ever seeing her before, and she definitely didn't go to his school. She was beyond really cute, she was foxy, and from the brief and distant glimpse, he didn't see anything in the way of complexion problems. Even from such a distance and at nearly thirty-five miles an hour, she was clearly a babe.

16

"For me, then," Jeanette was saying. "Shut the window. I'm getting a chill."

Howard didn't register her voice.

"What?"

"I just got my hair done. It's blowing out my hair."

Howard slowly closed the window, squishing his face against the glass for a final look.

"Aren't you going to finish your cheese and crackers?" Jeanette asked.

"I'm done," said Howard. He was no longer concerned with bending cheese slices to confrom to his crackers, as that activity had been supplanted by a different preoccupation. He and the babe had made eye contact, and the world seemed like a very different place.

Chapter Two

The synagogue language lab, employed exclusively for Bar Mitzvah preparatory training, occupied one end of the largest basement room of B'nai Jeshuran Synagogue, an unassuming space with a low pock-marked ceiling of acoustic tiles and linoleum flooring. Except for Bar Mitzvah receptions and the occasional B'nai Brith social or Purim Carnival, the space was the exclusive domain of Cantor Benjamin Birenboim.

The set-up that awaited Howard and Stinky twice a week—along with other twelve-year-olds in different stages of their training, depending on their birthdays—consisted of study carrels accommodating up to eight pre-teen captives who listened to recitations of their Bar Mitzvah services, pre-recorded by the Cantor, with appropriate pauses for vocal repetitions. The lessons required individualization because each student was assigned a different *Haftorah* selection, thematically related to the particular passage from the Jewish Holy Book—from the actual Torah scroll—that was to be read on that specific Sabbath.

On the Cantor's tapes, each snippet of Hebrew chanting was repeated over and over again, moving ahead with snail-like pace to the subsequent parsed phrase. During this process, most of the boys habitually checked their watches, unconsciously reassuring themselves that time was not standing still.

***

Despite maternal concerns and admonitons, Howard arrived on time that Thursday, refreshed both by the snack and his sweet memory of the girl. Nonetheless, all of the other boys were already settled in their carrels, and Howard felt guilty for being late even though he wasn't. Crossing the room he acknowledged Stinky, impatiently drumming his fingers in Carrel 8, with a barely detectable raising of eyebrows. The gesture spoke volumes. He and his friend were in this together, another ordeal to suffer through, and Stinky already looked bored and hungry.

Howard stood outside the open control room door and watched as Cantor Birenboim, headphones securely in place, reached up to position a tape onto one of the wall-mounted tape recorders. Howard couldn't help but fixate on Cantor Birenboim's arms, which were hardly those of a rabbinic scholar.

Those forearms were formidable, muscular and hairy and usually exposed, as Birenboim tended to roll up his shirtsleeves as far as they could go without cutting off circulation to his hands. There was a blue-collar quality to this craggy-looking man in his late thirtes, with his unruly coarse black hair, except for the black horn-rimmed glasses, which conferred a softer but nonetheless Semitic Buddy Holly look. Despite his daunting physical presence, the imposing baritone had never been known to raise his voice above standard authoritative discourse, except when his liturgical chanting called for a dramatic fortissimo. But Benjamin Birenboim still looked like someone who would beat the holy crap out of you if you scratched one of his Billie Holiday LPs. No one in his right mind would mess with the Cantor.

Howard looked beyond the arms and peeked into the control room, the personal lair for this devout audiophile and electronics buff. No one dared to cross the threshold to actually examine the room's contents, the Cantor's privacy so implicit that he never bothered to lock the door. Measuring roughly six by ten feet, the room contained eight high-end Wollensak reel-to-reel tape recorders inset across the length of one wall, mounted custom speakers, an electronic control panel with an array of knobs, dials, switches, and indicator lights, and an enormous microphone. Floor to ceiling bookshelves lined the opposite wall, housing rows of previously recorded tapes, manuals, electronics textbooks, and trade magazines. Soundproofed with the door shut, the room allowed a panoramic survey of the carrels through a large double-paned glass window.

Already, the reels of the first two recorders were spinning, transmitting the Cantor's recorded voice to Danny Becker and Bruce Dworkin, both May Bar Mitzvahs. Hunching in their carrels, they leaned forward on both elbows with their palms cupping their leather earmuffs. Danny, tone deaf and always off-pitch, was mimicking the Cantor as best he could. By the time all eight reels were operational, the cacophony would be overwhelming, like the racket of wild animals in the jungle at the approach of the Great White Hunter.

The Cantor turned his attention to Howard just long enough to hand him a set of headphones.

"Number 4," he said.

By the time Howard had found the right page in his *Haftorah* pamplet and plugged in his headphones, his tape was already running, emitting the hiss of the twenty-second tape lead. The real-life Cantor was moving on, preparing Recorder 5 for Bobby Weneck, another June Bar Mitzvah stationed kiddy-corner from Howard on the opposite end of cubicles, while the disembodied recorded Cantor was commencing an interminable two-hour session with Howard Block.

The static ended. Howard took a deep breath. The taped Cantor also took a breath, and exhaled into a pitch pipe, producing A flat below middle C. Pitch thus established, the chanting began.

"*Dibre Yirmayahu. . .*" sang the Cantor. Pause.

"*Dibre Yirmayahu. . .*" responded Howard.

"*Dibre Yirmayahu. . .*" sang the Cantor again.

Howard felt Stinky's shoe on his foot. Being across from Stinky was a good draw and could provide needed diversion, which became more crucial with each passing minute. Both slipped out of their loafers and began playing footsies. After a brief interlude of restrained horseplay, Howard pulled his foot back and put his shoe back on. They had to pace themselves. Class had barely started.

Stinky had yet to be wired in. He leaned back into his chair, lifting the forward legs off the floor, and peered around the cubicle to check on the Cantor's progress. His *yarmulke*, the mine canary warning of the impending tipping point, fell off. Startled, he jerked his weight forward and plopped the front legs of the chair back to the floor. Hurriedly, he bent down to retrieve the *keepa*, kissed it reflexively, and replaced it tenuously on the back of his head.

An hour or so later, the tapes continuing to advance onto their take-up spools, Cantor Birenboim was leaning back in his desk chair reading "Popular Electronics." All the boys were now slumping to varying degrees in their chairs, some resting forward on crossed-arms as if attempting to take a nap, some twisted sideways, others slouching so far forward in their chairs that only the tips of their tailbones made contact with the seat. Fatigue and diminished enthusiasm were evident in the haphazardness of their singing. Still, there was no relief or slowing down or faking it, since every carrel was wiretapped and could be penetrated at will—eavesdropping as simple as a flip of an unseen switch. Which explained why Cantor Birenboim always kept his headphones on—who could tell if he really was reading "Popular Electronics" or using it as a decoy while he listened in?

***

Howard had intermittently done more of the footsie thing with Stinky and wasted several more minutes peering at light reflection patterns from the crystal of his watch when Stinky sent a note by floor delivery. Howard was able to slide it with his feet to within arm's reach, all the while responding to the Cantor's melody cues.

". . . *nawve lagoyeem nutateechaw*. . ." droned the Cantor.

". . . *nawve lagoyeem nutateechaw*. . ." Howard rebutted distractedly.

Howard looked over his shoulder to confirm that the Cantor was otherwise occupied before slowly unfolding the paper. In block lettering, the note said: "How about a rind?"

Howard quickly glanced back at the control room to make sure the coast was clear, took the pencil from his pocket, and scribbled underneath:

"Are you *meshuggah*?" He folded the paper, dropped it to the floor between his knees, and slid it forward on the linoleum as far as he could reach. Eating, drinking, and gum chewing were verboten in the lab, but pork rinds in an orthodox synagogue in the presence of the Cantor Birnboim was beyond brazen. Howard felt Stinky's foot caress his own, pedal transmission complete.

Undeterred by Howard's response, Stinky painstakingly opened the green book bag at his feet and exposed an already opened bag of pork rinds. He reached down and took a handful. Howard could sense what was going on by the smell and became ill at ease.

The next message came soon. Frog-legged, Howard reached down for the note as he was singing one of his favorite melodic passages, a showy cadenza that included the highest note in his *Haftorah*. He repeated the phrase three more times before the Cantor moved on. Then he opened the note and read:

"Last chance! They really take the edge off!"

Howard was preparing an appropriate retort when something catching his eye took his breath away.

Yakov Bettinger, Director of Education at B'nai Jeshuran—which amounted to being Principal for the Sunday and Hebrew Schools and encompassed the training for Bar Mitzvahs—had entered the basement from the entryway across the expanse of room. He was heading toward the control booth on a path that would take him past Bobby Weneck in Carrel 5.

Howard tried to kick Stinky under the partition, but missed and slammed his shin on the bottom of the paneling.

Although teachers and adults referred to the Principal as Mister Bettinger, or rarely Yakov, all the children and young adults universally knew him as simply "Bettinger." The single appellation provided impact. The television gunslinger Paladin, for instance, was simply that, although Danny Becker, who was kind of a dummy, once argued with Howard and maintained that Paladin's first name was "Wire." There was no argument, though, over Paladin being one tough customer, and nearly as tough as Bettinger.

Howard, heart racing, frantically scribbled in large capital letters: "BETTINGER," breaking his pencil lead during the crossing of the second "T."

"*Va a baim vuh he nai. . .*" Cantor Birenboim responded.

"*Va a baim vuh he nai. . .*" Howard quavered back, cutting the timing of the measure from 4/4 to 2/4.

Bettinger was a short and stocky man in his late forties who had emigrated from Poland as a teenager before the war. He always wore a dark suit, jacket unbuttoned because of an overhanging belly, and a thin tie of a dark solid color. His eyes were narrow-set and beady, he had a thick moustache, and his nose was hard to describe because no one paid much attention to it, being distracted by THE MOLE. Technically a nevus, the raised growth was high on his left cheek, about the size of a quarter, and sprouted hairs that diverged like a floral arrangement crammed in a small vase. THE MOLE drew the eye and was a fearsome thing and tellingly, Bettinger chose not to have it removed.

Bettinger crossed over by the control room and waved to the Cantor through the glass. He was making his appointed rounds, walking his religious beat, a part of his job to which he was well suited. Naturally inclined to nose around, Bettinger unexpectedly dropped in on classes, eyeing the proceedings and silently nodding, an effort at reassurance that never succeeded and only made everyone, including the teachers, squirm in their seats. The Cantor, however, only momentarily lifted his eyes from the magazine he was reading.

Howard kicked so hard under the partition that his chair hopped. This time he made contact. Stinky misinterpreted the signal, though, assuming Howard was initiating an aggressive round of foot play. He kicked back gamely, then withdrew both his feet to the neutral corner under his chair, postponing the match until he finished his pork rinds. He procured another handful from his book bag.

Howard, with a half-backward glance at Bettinger, reached down as if to pull up his sock, and crammed the note between his toes. Then he swept his foot under the partition like a windshield wiper, to no avail, since Stinky had his ankles crossed under his own chair. Desperately, Howard kept playing minesweeper.

Bettinger was coming his way, so Howard turned and began chanting with increased passion. Then Howard felt Bettinger's hand patting him on his back. Turning toward him and managing a sickly smile, Howard nodded and kept singing so he wouldn't have to engage in conversation. The brief encounter, though, was enough to give Stinky the heads up. Spotting THE MOLE from over the carrel, Stinky disposed of the remaining pork rinds by jamming them into his mouth.

Bettinger continued his rounds of the carrels. He stopped for a moment behind Stinky, listening to a somewhat garbled rendition of his Torah reading. Then he sauntered on, apparently not noticing anything amiss.

Howard could not remember the last time he had breathed or swallowed and felt hungry for air, as if he had been swimming underwater. His mouth was full of saliva, but oddly enough when he tried to swallow, the effort felt foreign to him. It took a couple of tries before success.

Stinky, his oral cavity stretched to capacity with partially masticated rinds, leaned back slightly in his chair to scope out Bettinger's movements. The Director of Education wisely had walked past the tone deaf Danny Becker and stopped again to listen at Bobby Weneck's enclosure. His back was to Stinky as he nodded in rhythm with Bobby's singing.

Stinky leaned back further, as far back as he could without his *yarmulke* falling off.

Bettinger suddenly turned and lunged at Stinky, who choked as he fell backwards out of his chair. Chunks of pork rind exploded from his mouth.

Pandemonium ensued, with Bettinger red-faced and screaming.

"PORK RINDS?" he screamed. "A JEW EATING PORK RINDS IN THE HOUSE OF THE LORD?"

Put that way, indeed it sounded bad.

All headphones were quickly off and the room was silent. Stinky had managed to get to his feet and was struggling to escape, but Bettinger had him by the ear.

Howard saw that this was not pretend rage, but the real thing. Bettinger wrestled Stinky ineffectually for a few seconds, almost spinning him around as if they were playing blind man's bluff, and ultimately settled again on Stinky's ear, which he held with a pincer grip as he dragged Stinky away. Stinky was crying and blathering, tears streaming down his face and moistened pork rinds still being propelled from his mouth like projectile vomit.

"PORK RINDS? IN THE HOUSE OF THE LORD?" Bettinger reiterated, spewing spit droplets like a wet sneeze.

Cantor Birenboim stood in the doorway of his control room, magazine in hand, and indicated with a sweep of his arm that the lessons for everyone else should continue. Then he shut the door, sat back down, and began fiddling with knobs on the control panel as if nothing had happened.

The boys at their carrels were still stunned, but no longer at a loss for what to do. They deliberately put their headphones back on and leaned forward to retreat into their shelters. Howard was standing, though, staring at Stinky's *yarmulke* lying inverted on the floor a few feet away. He forced a swallow.

Howard had never witnessed such rage. The rage of men in wartime, the rage of the insane ranting, the rage of the self-righteously religious. This was Moses slamming down the tablets, not acting out for effect, not trying to make a point. Moses, like Yakov Bettinger, had been really pissed off.

The rage terrified Howard.

And even more so Stinky, poor Stinky, who had wet himself, peed all over his Sans-a-belts.

Chapter Three

Jack sawed aggressively at his pork chop, one of his favorite dishes after scallops and lobster tails. Being Jewish had never put a crimp on the Block family diet in any fashion. Not only did they not keep Kosher, but hardly a day passed in the Block household without pork of some kind. Jewish dietary laws, viewed as a quaint custom irrelevant to modern life, were flagrantly and guiltlessly ignored. Paradoxically, numerous non-ordained Eastern European superstitions were preserved and passed on essentially intact, at least on Jeanette's part.

Normally a rushed eater, Jack was clearly in transit. Briefcase at his side, grey fedora placed within reach on the table, he would head back to the hospital for evening rounds one final time before the workday officially ended. Even then he remained a slave to emergency calls that happened with the unsettling regularity of randomness. In the meantime, he haphazardly drizzled his chops with Worcestershire sauce

"There's ketchup, if you want," said Jeanette.

Jack's absent nod was silent, but ample validation. Dr. Jack Block would never be wanting for ketchup on the kitchen table, or anything else, as long as Jeanette was around.

"Howard got so many wonderful gifts today, Jack," she continued, filling the silence that only bothered her. "All your patients are sending him gifts already."

Jack kept eating while Howard rolled his eyes.

"Howard," she persisted, "you're keeping a list of all the presents, right? You'll have all those 'thank you' notes to write. So many gifts! Irv and Sadie Weinstein sent something today."

"That's nice," said Jack. "What did they send?"

"Another thesaurus!" Howard moaned.

"Something different." Jack pursed his lips together for a momentary wry smile, a brief pause in the cadence of his chewing.

"A beautiful one," said Jeanette, "with the tabs on the side. And you wouldn't believe all the gift certificates from Jack Henry's!"

"What do I want from there?" complained Howard. "It's an old man's store!"

Jack didn't seem inclined to come to Jack Henry's defense, so Jeanette did.

"We can get you nice slacks, wool ones. Custom fit. Plaid with nice cuffs."

Howard was glum and becoming more so. "Wool itches," he said.

"No hard cash?" Jack asked.

"Not much."

"A real shame." Jack shook his head sympathetically, in synchrony with his chomping.

Jeanette was embarrassed, as if non-family members were privy to such a conversation. "Honestly—but Howard, tell your father the news!"

Howard was toying with his food.

"I got my Bar Mitzvah speech today."

"You memorize it yet?"

"Very funny, Dad."

"He just got it *today*, Jack," said Jeanette.

"You don't want your pork chop?" Jack asked Howard.

"I'm not very hungry." He needed to swallow. He took a sip of water to make it easier.

Jack stared at him for a beat, then speared his son's pork chop and worked it off the fork onto his plate.

"The speech sounds like the rabbi wrote it," said Howard.

"Well, the rabbi *did* write it, didn't he?" Jack was dousing the chop with more Worcestershire.

"Of course he wrote it." said Jeanette, "Show it to your father, Howard. It's wonderful. . . very scholarly. . . very rabbinical."

"I'll look at it later," said Jack. "I have to get back to the hospital."

Howard had been stewing, his glumness turning into rebelliousness. He decided to lay one on, punch below the belt.

"Bettinger says it's a sin to eat pork."

Jeanette was silent. She gave her husband a meaningful glance, which he missed, since he was swirling a chunk of pork chop in the thin brown sauce. Some of it dripped down his chin as the meat went hurriedly into his mouth. He wiped his chin with the back of his hand and spoke with his mouth full.

"I would imagine so." He chewed. "For him, it *is* a sin." He chewed some more, deliberating. "For me, it's a sin to eat *rare* pork."

He swallowed, wiped his face with his unfolded paper napkin, and pushed his chair away from the table so he could stand up. The chair made a pronounced screeching sound on the linoleum. Jack put on his fedora and adjusted its position.

"Pork is fine as long as it's well done," he continued. "Like your mother cooks it. Jews should never eat undercooked pork."

Then he winked at Howard and made his exit from the kitchen, turning back at the entrance to the den for his final words.

"Don't take Bettinger too seriously, boy. He's just doing his job. And let me know if he gives you a hard time. . . the next time he's in my office I'll tell him that big mole on his face is pre-malignant."

"Jack!" snapped Jeanette, as she rummaged for loose change in her apron and scurried off for the *pishka*.

***

Later, upon his father's return, Howard was able to get in a few words with him in the upstairs master bathroom, the only reliable safe haven free from his mother's lurking and intrusions. Howard, certain of total privacy only when Jack Block was moving his bowels, had recognized the opportunity for paternal quality time at a very early age.

Jack was sitting on the stylishly rose-hued toilet, pipe in mouth, perusing the latest issue of the "New England Journal of Medicine" when Howard knocked. Without waiting for a reply he entered and hopped onto the pink tile countertop, his accustomed perch for conferencing. Then he waited for the standard greeting from his father.

"Can't anyone take a crap in peace?" Jack asked. When Howard was smaller, he would throw a smile his son's way, reassurance that he was only joking, but no longer was there a need.

"Well?" he continued, looking up from the journal.

"I'm having trouble with the Bar Mitzvah stuff," said Howard.

"Can't learn your *Haftorah*?"

"That's not it. It doesn't seem to mean much. It's supposed to be a really big deal, but—" Howard forced a swallow.

"Maybe it's not a big deal in the way you expect it to be."

"You never go to *shul*," accused Howard, "and when you do, you fall asleep."

Jack always kept a book of matches near at hand. He relit his pipe before responding, then dropped the spent match between his thighs into the toilet bowl, pushing his genitals out of the way. Howard could hear the faint sizzle when the match hit water.

"When I was your age," Jack began, "I kept kosher and was observant. You know that. Until I went off to war. After that, I looked at things differently."

"Why?"

"Why?" Jack considered before speaking further. "Well, a large part of being Jewish, boy, is defining yourself as a Jew. Traditions and dietary laws set Jews apart from the Gentile world. That's their purpose really." He paused for a couple of puffs and blew the smoke out with a breathy whistle. Howard liked the smell of his father's Cherry Blend under any circumstances, but especially when it masked the smell of shit.

"After the war," he went on, "I didn't feel I needed to define myself as a Jew anymore."

"How come?"

"I guess," Jack replied, "I figured the rest of world would do it for me."

Jack unrolled some toilet paper, the cue that the conference was near ending. Howard stared blankly across the small space at the shower curtain, thinking about what his father had said. He became aware that his mouth had filled with saliva and he needed to swallow, which he managed with some difficulty.

This captured Jack's attention.

"Sore throat?"

"No," said Howard, "I'm fine."

Jack arched forward to wipe, clenching the pipe between his teeth.

"Anything else, boy?"

"Well. . . just that Bettinger caught Stinky eating pork rinds in *shul* and Stinky peed in his pants," Howard said matter-of-factly.

On the surface Jack appeared unfazed, and Howard didn't pick up on the fact that his father was taken aback enough to stop in mid-wipe before regaining his composure.

Jack flushed the toilet. Howard was oblivious to the sound, thinking that pork rinds and Bettinger weren't that big a deal compared with World War II.

Standing up, Jack lifted up his boxer shorts and then pulled up his trousers.

"Well," he said, taking a deep breath, "that isn't something that happens every day."

***

Something was going on that Saturday, because Jeanette Block was placing even more emphasis than usual on the urgency of a man-sized breakfast. And she was taking too many of those deep sighing breaths again. Howard surreptitiously glanced at her over the rim of his glass of orange juice as he drank. Appraising too long, he inadvertently finished off the juice. Glass empty except for adhering pulp along the side, a mistake.

"More juice? I can squeeze you some more."

He shook his head.

"Fresh squeezed," she added, a revelation, as if there were any other kind. Everybody knew that vitamins were leeched out of canned or frozen juice; for Jeanette to provide anything but fresh-squeezed was a dereliction of maternal duty.

"It will only take a minute to squeeze more."

"I don't need any more."

"You need to wash down your food with something. You could choke, God forbid."

"I have my milk here. I'll manage."

"You have enough?"

"If not, I'll get more." The bottle was beside him on the table.

"It's been sitting out, it's warm."

Howard reached out and gently placed the back of his hand against the bottle, the way his father would feel his forehead for a fever.

"It's still cold, mom. It's okay." Pre-empting further discussion, he took a healthy gulp from his milk glass.

"Oh, I almost forgot the left-over ham from last night." She trotted to the refrigerator from her expectant servant stance beside him at the table. "It's honey baked. You need a slice."

"I've already got bacon with the eggs, Mom."

It was seven-thirty, and Jack Block was long gone, up and out by 6 a.m. for early hospital rounds, even on a Saturday, preceded by breakfast in the hospital cafeteria. Howard, occupying his father's customary chair at the kitchen table, had been presented with a bowl of Maypo, a plate of bacon and a sunny-side-up egg with raisin toast, milk, and of course, fresh-squeezed orange juice. As his father's surrogate, he had the privilege and the curse of being waited upon by Jeanette. The overattention was enough to take away his appetitie, but he ate and made predictable conversation, all the while under a watchful eye, being scrutinized for early signs of choking.

Howard sliced a thin square of butter and spread it onto his raisin toast. He tore off a corner and perforated his treasured yolk with the sharpest edge before sopping up the yellow goo efficiently, like sponging spilt milk. He swallowed the morsel but couldn't completely savor it.

"Why don't you sit down and eat, Mom?"

"I already had my breakfast. Now eat."

"No you didn't. You're lying."

"I never eat breakfast," she said distractedly, and then took a sighing breath. "I'll eat something a little later. And anyway, dinner will be early tonight. Your father has a meeting."

The distraction was thus revealed.

"What kind of meeting?"

"You know—just a meeting. An office meeting. With the partners."

"Here?"

"Yes, here. At seven. We have to be done with dinner and have the kitchen cleaned. And I need to make some little— you know—treats. Or," she sighed, "maybe I'll just pick up a little something at Wolferman's."

Howard nodded as he chewed on a strip of bacon, feigning disinterest. All would be revealed in time. Howard would overhear bits of conversation after the meeting, his mother peppering her commentary with Yiddish. *Not in frent of de kinder.* But Howard was becoming facile with understanding Yiddish, particularly dirty words, and secrets in the house were impossible to keep. He'd find out soon enough.

"I'm spending the day with Mike Hunsacker, Mom."

"Good. I'll take you."

"I'm riding my bike," he said firmly.

Jeanette felt martyred. As if the office meeting weren't enough to worry her. Now she had to worry about traffic, reckless drivers, hidden curbs that popped up out of nowhere, kidnappers, and a host of other potentially threatening obstacles that could confront her son in the span of twelve suburban blocks.

"It's no trouble. I'm going to the store and it's right on the way."

"No it isn't. And I'm riding my bike. I'll call you when I get there."

"I won't be home."

"Ada will be here. She'll give you the message."

"And we have to be finished with dinner before the meeting."

"I know, you said." Inwardly he groaned. He had just became conscious, for the first time that day, that he had to swallow. He took a swig of milk. "I'll be home no later than six."

Howard took another small sip, just enough to help him swallow again. "I promise. No later than six."

"Mike's a nice boy," Jeanette reassured herself, high praise for a gentile.

"Yes he is."

"A sensible boy."

"Yes."

"Doesn't do dangerous things."

"No," said Howard, underscoring his agreement by shaking his head, utilizing his neck's full side-to-side range of motion.

Danger was relative. Mike Hunsacker's family went camping, fished from a small boat without wearing life preservers (just floatable seat cushions), and his father had a workshop with power tools. A table saw, for instance, that could take off your hand at the wrist. Mike was a Boy Scout and carried a pocketknife. He had once singed his eyelashes trying to manufacture a contact explosive with his chemistry set. He also had numerous pets, including reptiles and rodents. Howard did not consider these dangerous things, at least not in the real gentile world. But to his mother, had she known, the whole bunch of them were *meshugennah*, living on the edge. Only by luck did they not poke an eye out or contract rabies.

Howard stood up from the table anticipating, and reached into his pocket.

"I'll put money in the *pishka*," said Jeanette. Then she furrowed her brow. "But I don't think I have any change."

Howard was already counting the coins retrieved from his pocket. "I have eighteen cents."

"I just need eleven cents," Jeanette said, taking the money, "and I'll owe it to you."

He handed her the change and started to clear off his place, putting his utensils in the empty cereal bowl and stacking it on his plate.

"I'll do that, Howard," Jeanette said, managing to carry both glasses, and plate with bowl and utensils to the sink without loosing her grip on the coins.

Their maid, Ada Lee, would arrive soon and take over from there, transport the glasses and dishes from sink to dishwasher. Ada, a forty-something black woman who bused in most weekdays from 39th and Paseo, and occasionally on Saturdays when the need arose, did the dishes, cleaning, scrubbing, vacuuming, and laundry, all of the more physical chores over which Jeanette served in a strictly managerial capacity.

"Let me at least get you a snack for later," said Jeanette.

"I don't really need. . ."

But Jeanette was already rummaging in the cupboard.

"Maybe some sunflower seeds," Howard suggested.

Too late, since his mother had already scavenged a snack-sized box of Sun Maid raisins. As was her habit, she opened the top of the box, held it under the tap, and ran a torrent of cold water through it. She shook the excess water from the box as if she were shaking down a thermometer, and for good measure, patted the box with a hand towel.

Reluctantly, Howard took the soggy box of raisins, put his arms around his mother, and kissed her on the forehead.

"Good-bye, Mom," he said, adding pre-emptively, "I'll be careful."

During such tender moments between son and mother, respites between generational intolerances and impatience, Howard was reminded of her complex and contradictory nature. She was forty-four and attractive, with a smooth complexion and dark hair turning gray in a cirrus cloud pattern. Just beginning to thicken at the waist, she was always smartly dressed, as her status as the wife of a physician required. In keeping with this, she never betrayed her roots in poverty to outsiders, for whom at casual glance she seemed a sophisticated and well-off modern American woman. Nonetheless, she would spit whenever passing a cemetary and surreptitiously, but habitually, position her thumb between index and third fingers to ward off the Evil Eye. Within the cloister of house and extended family, in fact, Jeanette Block showed little to distinguish herself from a nineteenth century peasant woman in a shtetl in the Ukraine.

"Be careful," she said, and might well have added, "Watch out for Cossacks."

Howard closed his eyes heavily. She couldn't help herself, telling him again to be careful even though he had just said he would. He felt an attack of rebellion coming on. But at what could he protest? The superstition and neuroses of impoverished Eastern European Jews? The scars left by the Holocaust? The happenstance of living out of context, a Jewish family in the Midwest trying to assimilate? Not wanting to seriously postpone or jeopardize his departure, Howard settled on a more manageable topic.

"The Hunsackers drink canned orange juice," he said provocatively.

His mother shrugged and bit her lower lip.

Once before Howard had stubbornly challenged her on this issue and she had claimed not to personally know anyone who drank canned orange juice. The leaching of vitamins was a well-established scientific fact.

"If canned juice is so bad and unhealthy," Howard went on, "why do the juice companies sell so much of it? I mean, if the juice didn't sell, they'd stop making it, right?"

She sighed, resigned to the trials of motherhood, but Howard persisted. "Somebody's buying canned and bottled juice, lots of it. So who's buying it, then, huh? *Who's* buying it?"

Jeanette sighed once more before answering, before stating the obvious, before putting the matter to rest so her son would not bring up the topic again and they both could commence the day.

"The *goyim*," she said.

Chapter Four

On that crisp and sunny Saturday morning in April, Howard headed off in the opposite direction from his destination, awkwardly gripping the left handlebar of his Schwinn with three fingers while thumb and index finger pincered a soggy box of Sun Maid raisins. Old Mission Hills was his allure, with its winding and lush tree-lined streets and stately homes—his favorite place for riding despite the hilliness. No boring and predictable grids for passage were to be found anywhere in that prosperous section, where the rich could meander and stroll along the lanes and drives and cul-de-sacs.

Had Howard not been preoccupied with the vistas of his detour, he might have spotted her sooner. The younger of the two girls he had seen from the car on the way to *heder* two days earlier—that eventful day with Stinky—was walking down the front path of a large red brick colonial-style house. She was a knock-out in a blue print sundress with a strap that looped around her neck. Given her home base, she was clearly a private school girl, Barstow or Sunset Hill. Howard slowed down to a coast for a better look and watched as she bent down to pick up the newspaper. But when she glanced up at him, still kneeling and her dress inched up well above her knees, Howard pedaled away as if being pursued.

So dumb. He could have said hello or raised his eyebrows in a friendly manner, but instead, like an idiot, he had fled as if he had been caught looking up her dress. Hoping for a second chance, he raced around the block. This time he came to a full stop in front of her house, but she had already disappeared inside. Disheartened, Howard decided it was time to head off to Mike's. But at least he knew where the mystery girl lived.

He pedaled leisurely, alternating the raisin box between hands when his fingers began to cramp. The economic transition of his route was from the wealthy to the well-off to the more modest homes of Prairie Village. Mike Hunsacker's block was typical for the area, with single story ranch houses intermixed with the occasional bungalow and small two-stories built during the post-war housing boom, a good decade before the split and tri-levels and more expansive ranches of Howard's neighborhood.

Mike's house was a pale yellow two-story on a street with a lot of small kids. Howard pulled his bike into the empty driveway and slipped forward off the seat into a straddle. Mike was nowhere to be seen, so Howard looked expectantly up at the attic dormer above a second story window. The shades were drawn. A cool breeze gathered itself from nowhere, or everywhere, and rustled the hairs on his forehead.

Howard was lifting his right leg over the bike when Mike leaped out from a hiding spot behind a large juniper. Startled, Howard lost his balance and fell over, precariously hopping on one leg as if using his Schwinn as a pogo stick.

"SHHH!" commanded Mike. He was wearing a World War II army helmet—a war souvenir given to him by his father—aviator sunglasses, a discolored and torn striped T-shirt, and faded denims that were too short.

"Jeez," protested Howard, still stumbling and finally stabilizing himself with a grounded left hand and knee. Miraculously, the box of raisins was still in his right. "I wasn't saying anything. . . ."

"SHHHH!" Mike hissed ferociously. "Quick—with me!"

Howard clumsily disentangled himself from the bike, and not wasting time to use the kickstand, let the bike rest where it laid.

Mike, who took his war games seriously, had dived over the juniper and landed on the other side in a tucked roll. Howard casually walked around the bush and crouched beside his friend. With Mike Hunsacker, you just went with the flow.

In his makeshift bunker behind the juniper, hidden from both the street and the nearest house, Mike had set up a field center with a variety of army (or camping) supplies and paraphernalia. He picked up a two-way radio and began adjusting the dials. Howard watched, non-judgmentally, still holding the raisins.

"I guess I shouldn't have left my bike there, in plain sight like that," he said remorsefully, not enjoying the sight of his most prized possession prone on the cement.

"Too late now," said Mike. Then, into the radio, in a harsh whisper: "We have contact. Over. Repeat. We have contact. Over and out."

"You get that thing to work?" Howard asked. He took the transmitter from Mike, held it to his ear, shook it, fiddled with the knobs, held it to his ear again, and gave it back without indictment. Mike angrily tossed it into the grass.

"Useless. The Ruskies have been jamming the signal, those filthy Commies. A temporary setback. But look at this. . . ."

Mike craned his neck to both sides and deeming the situation secure, withdrew a magazine from the base of the juniper. He handed it to Howard. It was "Playboy."

"Whoa," said Howard.

Mike grabbed the magazine back.

"Intelligence has given us indications that somewhere in this magazine—somewhere hidden very deviously—lies the key to breaking the Russian-Cuban code." He flipped through the pages, with more concentration than casualness. "This may take a while to figure out. Want some Spam?"

He rummaged elsewhere near the base of the juniper and pulled out an open tin, with a plastic picnic spoon protruding from the meat product like Excalibur. Howard declined with a shake of his head, Mike took a spoonful.

"We don't have time for this now," he said, indicating the magazine in hand while chewing his mouthful. "It could take hours. Maybe longer. We've got the launch as our highest priority."

"Right," agreed Howard, without a clue as to what Mike was referring. Then he noticed that Mike was looking at the the box he held.

"Want some raisins?"

"Sure," said Mike, taking the box. When he lifted the lid, the soggy cardboard top peeled off in his hand.

"You can have the rest," said Howard, forcing a swallow.

"The box is all wet," said Mike.

"They were—I washed them," said Howard.

"Oh," said Mike at a loss, but immediately getting back on his own track. "Good thinking. You can't be too careful in this business. No telling how many good agents have been

44

lost because of poison-coated raisins." Then adding, puzzled enough to break character, "You really washed them, huh?"

In the midst of serious war games, how could Howard explain that Jeanette Block washed raisins in the box, just as one carefully washed all fruits and vegetables, and that he *always* had to contend with a soggy box? How does one begin to explain a soggy Sun Maid raisin box to a gentile?

"What if the code isn't in here?" Howard changed the subject in the most plausible tone he could muster, referring back to the "Playboy." "That would be some waste of code-breaker man hours, huh?"

"Too bad. Then we'll just have to look at all these boobs!" said Mike, grinning fiendishly.

Which both boys did for a few minutes, in the shade of the juniper, postponing whatever so-called launch had been scheduled. Then Mike packed up the magazine and the rest of his gear into a ragged burlap bag and, with the bag clutched to his chest, made a mad dash to the back porch door and the safety of his house. Howard joined him inside, as soon as he had circumspectly picked up his Schwinn, moved it from the driveway to the side of the house, and properly put down the kickstand.

***

Mike had an attic bedroom all to himself, and Howard had never encountered anything quite like it. With every visit, the room appeared more chaotic, like abstract art becoming more layered, nuanced, and complex. From a non-artistic perspective, the room was a complete mess, strewn with clothes, magazines, and model airplanes, as well as a miniature zoo of three fish, two turtles, a snake, an iguana, a parakeet, a hamster, and a white mouse. The dresser draw-ers were all open to varying degrees, with rumpled clothes crammed, protruding, draped, and piled. The smell was a cross between a horse stable and the junior high boy's locker room.

"I can't believe your mother doesn't make you keep this place clean," said Howard, his voice tinged with admiration.

"She won't come up here," replied Mike, still wearing his army helmet and sunglasses. "It grosses her out. So we reached a compromise—I'm in charge of my room and she doesn't ever check on it. Cool, huh?"

"Kinda smells."

"You get used to it. It's the worst in August."

"What about your laundry?"

"Mom does it . . . no problem, except, you know, I have to bring everything down to the basement, since she won't come up here, like I said. But enough of this idle chatter, we have an important mission. . . ."

"What's up? You haven't told me."

"Of course not, it's Top Secret. You don't have security clearance yet. For your protection. The Ruskies get a hold of you, you'd squeal like a pig."

"No, I wouldn't."

"Yes, you would. So I'm letting you in on a 'need to know' basis."

Mike began gathering components of an Estes Model rocket and battery pack from beneath clothes on his bed, and carefully placed them in the burlap supply bag.

"Spam?" he offered, pulling the can from the bag.

"No thanks," said Howard. Mike put the Spam back.

"Now check this out," said Mike. He walked over to his desk, pulled out a thin wooden dowel from the bottom drawer, and then proceeded to insert the dowel into what apparently was a drill hole in the wall behind the desk.

"You didn't notice this, did you?" said Mike. "The pattern of the wallpaper is great camouflage. Now watch. . . . "

He pushed the dowel further. Six or seven feet away from where he stood, a hidden drawer magically emerged from the wall.

"Jeeze, Mike," said Howard, I can't believe you cut a hole in your wall. . .what would your parents say?"

"They'll never know. Now look at this. He walked to the secret drawer, removed a small object, and pushed the drawer back into place. He proudly held an Estes Rocket nose cone.

"Check out this capsule. I just finished putting on the decals this morning."

Howard took the nose cone and read the stenciled "Capt. Yuri." He turned it over in his hand to admire the workmanship before Mike took it back and placed it in the bag.

"Before we go, we need to deal with this," Mike went on, indicating the "Playboy" magazine he had tossed on the bed. "We need maximum security for this, for obvious reasons. Where my sisters will never look." He picked up the "Playboy," looked at it longingly, then lifted the mouse cage and placed it underneath.

"I wouldn't squeal," said Howard, still smarting from Mike's earlier assertion.

"You can't be too careful in this business," Mike did his best to placate. "But we're almost all set anyway, and you'll see soon enough."

Mike went over to the mouse cage and watched the captive white rodent furiously running to nowhere on a rotating wheel.

"Incredible dedication," said Mike. "He really knows how to keep in shape." Gingerly he opened the cage and stuck his hand inside. Yuri the mouse climbed onto his open palm without hesitation. Mike stroked his back several times with his index finger and tightened his grip into a secure caress.

"A credit to his species," said Mike, picking up his duffel with his free hand. "It's time. Let's go, men."

The two boys walked to the elementary school playfield, only a couple of blocks from the Hunsacker house, Mike holding Yuri the entire way. Howard silently watched as Mike decided on the optimal launching site, set down his gear, and began assembling the rocket components, painstakingly readying the parachute. All the while Yuri was either safely corralled on the grass by an arrangement of supplies, or within Mike's gentle hold. After a caressing finger stroke of farewell, Mike carefully situated Yuri in the newly labeled nose cone of the rocket. Howard's eyes widened, but he kept quiet. Mike was intent upon his task and clearly wouldn't welcome any dumb questions. Besides, Howard had figured things out. This was a serious, live-mouse mission.

Howard noticed the few small droppings in Mike's hand but didn't comment. Mike, though, had seen that Howard had noticed.

"He's not afraid. This is just his normal shit time," he explained, pausing before adding, "You needed to know that."

Howard nodded.

Ignorant about the logistics of launching model rockets, Howard watched quietly as Mike set the rocket on the ground and made sure the selected spot was completely flat by getting down on all fours and sticking his chin to the ground like a golfer lining up a putt. He walked backwards to their observation post about fifty feet away, reeling out the wire that was attached to the battery pack. Once set, both boys lying on their stomachs, Mike secured the connections to the battery pack and began an appropriately dramatic countdown.

"5. . . 4. . . 3. . . 2. . . 1. . . ."

Mike flicked the switch and the engine of the rocket ignited and flared. "Lift off!" Mike cried.

The rocket launched magnificently, reaching toward the heavens in a straight upward trajectory for two hundred feet, then veered off at an angle, the chemical propulsion spent.

Mike, of course, was aware of the problem before Howard had any inkling that something was amiss.

"Parachute! Parachute!" he screamed, jumping to his feet. The army helmet fell backwards off his head to the grass.

The trajectory had taken the rocket to the other side of the chain link fence that separated the playing field from the school parking lot. The nose cone had not disengaged; the parachute had failed to open.

Mike was already running toward the parking lot, screaming, before the rocket crashed, nose cone first, onto the asphalt. Mike reached the chain link fence and began to scale it, with Howard a few paces behind. Once on the other side of the fence, they stared at the nose cone, completely crumpled on the pavement.

"Could he be alive?" Howard finally asked after what seemed to be a very long time had passed.

Mike, seemingly paralyzed until then, kneeled on the ground and placed his ear against the nose cone, listening for squeaks. He was ashen.

"You hear anything?"

"Nothing," said Mike, shaking his head.

"What do we do? Open it?"

Mike clearly couldn't bear the thought.

"Bury him," he said, voice cracking. "We need to bury him in the capsule." Mike untwisted the nose cone from the rest of the rocket and held the capsule to his ear, giving one more listen, praying for squeaks.

"A hero's funeral," he said, hearing nothing, a tear streaming down his cheek.

"Absolutely. You sure he's dead, though?"

"He's dead. Really dead. Killed by sudden deceleration."

"Like, the crash, you mean?"

Mike was non-responsive. "Not a word of this to anybody. Word can't get out. This would really make the Ruskies' day." He wiped his eyes with the back of his arm. They were already red and swollen, and his whole face was blotchy.

The boys didn't say anything to one another for the rest of the afternoon. They walked back to the Hunsacker house in silence, Mike carrying the rocket parts, and Howard handling the duffel and carrying the helmet. They buried Yuri in his capsule just behind the juniper bush. Mike made a cross marker with two Popsicle sticks tied together with wire, then they sat at the gravesite for a while. Eventually, without saying good-bye, Howard left Mike alone, retrieved his Schwinn from the side of the house, and rode home.

Head in his hands, weeping, Mike held vigil at the small earthen mound until well past dark.

Chapter Five

Howard didn't have much of an appetite for dinner, even though Ada had made her delicious fried chicken with mashed potatoes and green beans fried in bacon grease. He had eaten small amounts though, because swallowing came easier with food and milk to wash things down. During large segments of the day, fortunately distracted by the daily activities of his twelve-year-old life, Howard was not preoccupied with the accumulation of saliva and how to deal with it. But then, prompted by some unknown cue during moments that should have been occupied by random reflection, Howard would remember that he needed to swallow and that he had trouble doing it. During those times it seemed as if he had been suffering so for his entire life, and he wondered if he would ever have the blessing of absolute forgetfulness again.

His father's business meeting, occurring on the other side of both the sliding door and the closed louvered pass-through between kitchen and den, was about to provide him with some needed relief. Ada had agreed to stay late, since Jeanette was nervously playing hostess and too discombobulated to deal with anything else. So while Jeanette fluffed pillows and stood at the ready with a tray of soft drinks, coffee and tea, and cookies and small pastries from Wolferman's, Ada was assigned Howard's dinner and expediting his passage to bed, or at least to his bedroom, shortly thereafter.

"You've left room for some of my apple pie now, haven't you, Howard?"

"Sure."

"And there's some vanilla ice cream from the Velvet Freeze."

"Great," he gulped, looking away from her.

Howard sat glumly as Ada removed his dinner plate. He refilled his glass with milk from the bottle on the breakfast room table and strained to make out the murmurs of conversation from the den, interspersed, if he concentrated, with the rustling of papers.

He had been allowed to greet the men upon their arrival for a few minutes, enduring the indignity of compliments regarding how big he had grown and rhetorical questions about life in junior high school—the usual conversational fare of adults uncomfortable with children. He had even been asked about his stamp collection, an especially obnoxious query, given that Howard had abandoned it when he was nine.

Arriving nearly simultaneously, promptly at 8 p.m., were Dr. Ed Foreman, the most senior partner in the group after Jack, and the younger associates, Drs. Frank Lipsky, Morris Schlozman, and Harold Ginsburg. All were in white shirt and tie and blue or gray business suits, the same ones they wore to work every day before swapping the jacket for a long white coat. They were all Jewish, not by choice or coincidence—there were simply no mixed medical groups in Kansas City—and their partnership comprised one of three Jewish Internal Medicine practices. The fifth man, a lawyer whom Howard had never met before named Martin Oliver, wore a green twill sport jacket and was the shortest and baldest of all the men. Presumably he was Jewish as well, and likely a member of an all-Jewish law firm and a member of one of Kansas City's two Jewish Country Clubs. That was just the way things were.

"I used to collect stamps when I was a kid," offered Martin Oliver, once Morrie Schlozman had brought up the subject, a miserable and failed attempt at ingratiation.

Howard nodded and forced a smile, as if this was going to be the beginning of a long and beautiful relationship with a middle-aged Jewish lawyer.

A proud Jeanette had smiled broadly during the awkward pleasantries, viewing Howard's politeness as well-mannered charm that naturally reflected favorably on her skills as a mother. Jack, who characteristically also revealed pride at such moments but from a deeper well, was not smiling but standing, seemingly impatient, with furrowed brow. Howard had never before felt his presence a bother to his father, and the sensation was discomforting. Something unpleasant was happening that night, and Howard wondered what it was.

"What you waiting for now?" asked Ada.

Suddenly aware of the pie à la mode in front of him, and no less conscious of Ada's scrutiny, Howard picked up his fork and began removing a protruding slice of apple from the apex of the wedge. He was beginning to smell the cigarette smoke seeping in from the adjacent room, and the voices were getting louder. Ada knew, and Howard knew that she knew, that he was stalling. He strained to hear as much as he could.

Jeanette, standing by the bar as if she had a reason for being there, had no problem hearing. She was lurking, frankly, with no intention of leaving the room. Jack wouldn't ask her to leave, she knew, and the others would be too polite. She made no pretense of hostessing anymore.

"I'm forced to agree with Marty, Jack," Ed Foreman was saying. "I think it's the only way to go." Ed was tall and lanky, with the easy manner of a ladies' man, although he was married and had a couple of kids in high school.

Jack sat silently, grinding his jaw.

They all waited deferentially for the response from the senior partner.

"Bullshit," he blurted. "This is bullshit and you all know it."

"Now, Jack," Martin Oliver pleaded, ushering in a chorus of simultaneous dissent and supplications, a restrained chaos on the verge of escalation. Jeanette started forward, then stopped. This was not the time for more coffee.

"You ain't done with that pie, yet, Howard?" Ada proxied her vocal contribution to the argument in the other room. "I'm fixin' to leave soon and I don't wanna leave this kitchen a mess for your momma."

"Not yet. Almost," said Howard.

"You should be up to your room by now."

"What's going on out there?" With no answer possible, since Ada was as much in the dark as Howard, he got up from the table and walked across the kitchen.

"I'm not done with my pie," he said as he brushed by her.

Once across the kitchen, he turned his back and leaned into the counter and quietly lifted himself up, then shimmied on his butt until he was sitting next to the pass through. Deftly adjusting one of the louvers, he shifted his head to get the best view possible of the room.

"Something's going on out there," he whispered.

"Nothing but a bunch of adult business talk, and no concern of yours. Now finish your pie if you're gonna."

"In a second," he said, as Ada shook her head in resignation. Jack was talking animatedly.

"She was comatose when she came into the ER, for Christssake! Who the hell could know what medications she was on?"

"No question about it, Jack. You did the right thing," said a conciliatory Ed Foreman. "I'm personally convinced you saved her life, but that isn't the point—"

"They don't have a case, Jack, but why take a chance when—" That was the lawyer's voice, immediately interrupted by Jack.

"And every one of you—every single one of you—saw her on rounds the next week! All of you! And no one put her on Valium! Am I right? Ed? Frank? Morrie? Harold?"

From his vantage point, Howard only had Frank Lipsky and his father in view, and he could see that Frank was averting his eyes from Jack, as likely the others were.

Martin Oliver was speaking again, leaning forward on the sofa intently.

"My advice—and I'm your lawyer and that's what you pay me for, right?—is just to settle out of court."

Jack was well beyond reasoned lawyerly advice.

"Bullshit!" He voice was quite loud now. "I'm not admitting any guilt. . . . "

"Jack, don't look at it that way. Don't look at is as an admission of guilt. We all know—"

Ed interrupted. "We all think it's best if you just settle this out of court, Jack. For everyone."

"So you've already discussed this amongst yourselves? Before coming over here? What? You had a separate meeting of your own before coming over here?"

"Calm down, Jack." Harold Ginsburg tried to placate him.

But Jack was not about to be placated by anyone, particularly his *nebbishy* junior partner.

"What kind of chicken shits are you?" Jack managed a snort of a laugh. "I brought every last one of you into my practice. And this is what I get? You betray me like this?"

"Jack, let us explain," said Morrie Schlozman, and things quieted down for the moment.

Ada meanwhile felt that she should at least make the attempt, even if unsuccessful, to get Howard back to his pie. Then, later, she could honestly say, "Why, Mrs. Block, I tried my best to keep him away, but Howard would have none of it!" She couldn't go anywhere, anyway, not without walking straight through that den, which she wasn't about to do. Ada instead walked over to the kitchen work desk, where she had placed her purse.

"Come on over here, Howard," she said, not anticipating success. "Did I tell you that my Junior turned sixteen last week? Jus' got his driver's license."

"No, that's neat." Howard's eyes remained fixed on the louvers.

Ada wiped her hands on her apron and opened her handbag.

"Come on over here. Let me show you his picture. All these years I've been working for your momma and you've never met my Junior. Come on and have a look. Lookee here. I got his latest school picture right here."

56

Torn, but politeness winning out, Howard slid off the counter and walked to Ada, who was holding out the photograph.

"He looks kinda like you," Howard said, not quite knowing what do say about the light skinned black face with a long and narrow nose. Ada had said she was part Cherokee, and Howard thought he could see a resemblance, although a younger version, to Michael Ansara, who played Cochise on the TV show "Broken Arrow."

"He's a sophomore at Paseo High School. Junior gonna be a junior!"

"My Mom went to Paseo High," said Howard, the upper middle class doctor's son unexpectedly finding a point of life intersecting with a black domestic, although a rather tenuous one.

"That a fact?" asked Ada, amused. She thought more and then laughed outright. "There hasn't been a white face there in quite some time. Ooo-wee!"

"I'd like to meet him," said Howard. "Junior should come over here with you some time." But Howard didn't really want to talk about that at the moment, that much was clear. He kept looking toward the louvers.

"He'd like that, too. You through with your pie, now?"

"Not quite," he said. And with them both knowing the score, Howard went back to the counter and resumed his prior position at the observation post. Ada sighed, and tried to make herself busy with a washcloth and a sparkling clean stainless steel sink.

Things on the other side of the louver were heating up again. Howard had never seen his father in such a state. His face was red, and he was grinding his jaw and making twitching movements with his neck and shoulders. Howard was scared, worried that his father might work himself up to a stroke or a heart attack.

". . . we're getting sidetracked here, gentlemen," Martin Oliver was saying. "The main point here, Jack, is that the suit is being brought against you individually, not the group. And my best advice is—"

"Bullshit!" Jack completed the sentence for the lawyer. "Your best advice is bullshit! There is no negligence! There is no malpractice! No doctor in the world would agree that—"

"That's where you're wrong, Jack," interrupted the lawyer, his voice rising even above Jack's. Suddenly the room became quiet. Jack, sensing the heartfelt conviction of his adversary, looked pained and perplexed. Martin paused, as if all the words spewed into the room were particulate matter that needed some time to float down to the floor and settle before any more could fill the air.

The lawyer took a deep breath before continuing. "They have a psychiatrist who maintains that drug withdrawal directly led to a psychotic breakdown. We don't want to get into this. It's much easier—"

"Psychiatrist?" demanded Jack. "What psychiatrist? You didn't tell me anything about this psychiatrist!"

"Chad Huntley," Ed said flatly.

"Oh, for Christssake! Huntley!" Jack shook his head in disbelief.

"He's out to get you, Jack," Ed continued. "There's no sense in jeopardizing the partnership by fighting this thing."

"Easier to hang me out to dry, is that it? You *momzers*! Get out of my house! I don't need any of you!"

Howard could see that his father had risen from his chair and was storming around the room like a raging bull. He slammed down a sheaf of papers on the coffee table, unsettling some cups and other dishware. The partners and Martin Oliver saw no point in hanging around and were themselves surprised at the fury they had unleashed; Frank Lipsky actually looked quite fearful. Jeanette was clinging on to the counter of the bar, as if about to faint. The men hurriedly gathered their things, Jack continuing to scream a string of obscenities. Not satisfied, he followed them to the door like a furiously barking dog, invectives continuing to pour forth. Frank Lipsksy actually stumbled on the heels of Morrie Schlozman in their rush to escape.

"*GUTEH FREIONT FUN VEITEN!*" Jack screamed. "*GEY EN DRERDE, YOU MOMZERS, YOU!*"

He slammed the door and tramped up the stairs to the bedroom.

"Jack, honey, wait!" wailed Jeanette, trailing behind him and now sobbing outright.

"I think I best be going now," said Ada.

Both she and Howard were trying their best to ignore a moment of monumental awkwardness. For the twelve-year-old and the family maid, it was unexpectedly easy. She didn't offer to console him, and he wasn't expecting her to try.

But Howard was stunned. He had never seen his father like that. And now his mother had broken down as well. They were both upstairs behind the closed door of the master bedroom, sharing something from which he was completely excluded. What was he supposed to do? What could he possibly say?

"Yes, I guess I be going," said Ada.

Howard, suddenly realizing what he had witnessed, looked at her, eyes wide with amazement.

"Ada," he said, grabbing both of her arms, "my Dad spoke Yiddish! Did you hear that? He spoke Yiddish!"

***

Outside the house, the expelled guests congregated in the driveway.

"What the hell was that he just said?" asked Harold Ginzberg.

Frank Lipsky, the only partner somewhat knowledgeable of Yiddish, answered, "A Yiddish expression meaning 'You are better friends at a distance.' You get the gist. Then he called us bastards and told us to go to hell."

"I got that last part," said Harold.

"Face it," said Morrie. "We're cowards, we let him down."

"You're doing the right thing whether you're cowards or not," said Martin Oliver. "Good night, gentlemen. I'll be in touch."

"He'll get over it," said Ed, trying to reassure the younger associates. Ed and Jack went way back, the former having been an intern at the University of Missouri Medical Center when his current older partner had been Chief Resident.

"Maybe," said Frank, "but he sure as hell ain't gonna forget it."

***

The break-up of the meeting had been surreal to Howard, like the culmination of some sort of performance. The entire cast had exited abruptly and dramatically, leaving an empty stage. Howard stayed in the kitchen, pretending to finish off his slice of pie, which seemed to have taken on the regenerative properties of Prometheus' liver. Ada had gone nowhere despite what she kept saying, and was clearing the dessert plates and cups and saucers from the den. Both were waiting for any of the actors to reappear upon the scene.

Finally Jeanette came downstairs from the bedroom, pale and eyes swollen from crying. Howard heard her footsteps on the stairs and miraculously finished his pie. When she entered the room, he was sheepishly standing next to the kitchen door. Jeanette pretended nothing had happened, and Howard pretended along with her, stifling his instincts to console her. His mother then assumed a new role in a straightening-up pantomime, rearranging accessories on the coffee table and slightly repositioning the armchairs by mini-slams with her thigh. Howard moved from the door to the bar, where he could survey the entire set.

If Jeanette were perturbed that Howard was still down-stairs, she didn't show it. She was trying to organize her thoughts, which for her were even more disorganized than usual. Howard could see her lips moving in either an internal debate or a rehearsal of what to say to her husband. Jack, however, did not reappear, remaining behind closed doors upstairs.

"Is Dad going to the bathroom?" Howard asked, hoping for a conference opportunity.

"He's going to bed, Howard. He's got hospital rounds early in the morning."

"Everything okay?"

"Sure. Everything's fine. I'm just going to pick up a bit down here." Then, to Ada. "Ada, honey, don't bother putting those dishes in the dishwasher. Just leave them in the sink and I'll get to them in the morning."

"Can I help?" Howard didn't really think there was any-thing for him to do, but offered anyway. Noticing from his vantage point that there were scattered copies of documents left on the floor behind the sofa, he casually made his way around the room.

"That's kind of you, dear, but you just go upstairs and go to bed, and don't bother your father."

Howard, now behind the sofa, placed his palms shoulder-width apart on the top of it and leaned forward on straight arms. He slowly rocked back and forth, in an hypnotically repetitive movement, an old man praying in the synagogue.

"I guess I'll just go to bed, then," he said to his mother, who was not listening. Without betraying movement below his waist—therefore unbeknownst to both the preoccupied Ada and Jeanette—Howard used foot skills mastered in the Bar Mitzvah language lab to maneuver every single piece of paper that was on the carpet until all had vanished underneath the couch.

***

Howard, wearing his pajamas and lying stiffly in his bed like a corpse, could hear murmurs of conversation between his parents in the bedroom behind the closed door. He strained to make something out, but couldn't. Ada was long gone now, and all the lights downstairs were off. Howard wasn't sure of the time, but had been waiting impatiently for his parents to stop talking. He was getting sleepy, and the muffled voices seemed an endless conversation.

Howard couldn't wait any longer. He snuck out of bed, slipped through his half-opened bedroom door, tip-toed past his parent's bedroom, and crept downstairs to retrieve the papers.

Much later, and after his parents had somehow managed to fall asleep, Howard read through the papers with the aid of one of his father's disposable penlights—a pharmaceutical company give-away that was meant for looking down throats. Certain words and phrases were cornered in the cone of light like a trapped criminal trying to escape along a wall. Howard took notes in a small memo pad.

***

Howard spent the next few days in a fog, his routine unchanged. Jeanette continued to insist on a nice full breakfast before school, typically ham or bacon and eggs with toast and jam, ignoring his supplications for simple cold cereal. Classes at school seemed interminably long, but fortunately homework could be dispensed with in an hour or two, so academics weren't much of a distraction. Tuesday and Thursday boasted the same miserable lineup of seventh period gym class—flag football would be played for the rest of the year, a testament to Mr. Saunder's laziness—followed by *heder* after school for himself and Stinky. After the pork rind fiasco, Stinky didn't dare play footsies anymore, let alone engage in note passing. He had been grounded for a month and was really glum. Even his appetite had been affected. Mike was equally sullen, still in mourning for Yuri.

Both of Howard's friends seemed older and defeated, broken in spirit. As for himself, he was increasingly preoccupied with his father's legal difficulties, poring over the documents every night for pertinent details and nuances to add to his memo pad, which he now carried with him at all times. Overall, there was plenty of time for reflection, which meant ample time for Howard to dwell upon his swallowing.

Howard had seen little of his father, who was leaving early and working late, and during their brief moments alone he couldn't bring himself to ask about the lawsuit. His swallowing seemed to be getting worse, but he had no intention of revealing the malady to either of his parents, particularly with all that was going on. Given how his mother overreacted to health matters, suffering in silence had definite advantages.

But unfortunately he let his guard down shortly after snacking on a box of Sun-Maids. She finally caught him unsuspected in the midst of a transient grimacing contortion, and the game was up, just like that.

"What's the matter with you?" Jeannette shrieked in alarm.

"Nothing. I'm having a little trouble swallowing," he said, cursing himself for not being quick enough with something like "That last raisin caught in my throat." So she interrogated him until both were exhausted, eventually squeezing it out of him. She took his temperature and plied him with hot tea, Campbell's chicken noodle soup, and Aspergum. With nothing left for her to do but worry, she kept vigil until Jack came home. For more than two hours they sat on the sofa together, Howard trying to watch television as Jeanette watched him.

Both responded with a jerk to the sound of the electric garage door opening. Jeanette straightened her housedress as she heard Jack's footsteps coming up the stairs. Howard took the opportunity to get in a good, unobserved swallow.

Jack entered with his briefcase in one hand—which Howard knew to be full of patient charts awaiting dictation—and his portable Dictaphone in the other. He wore one of his navy suits and a lightweight plaid fedora. Placing both his cases just outside the door at the top of the steps, he kissed his wife and smiled at Howard.

"*Nu?*" he asked.

"Howard can't swallow."

Dr. Jack Block raised his eyebrows as if learning something new. His wife had, in fact, called him several times at the office to keep him apprised of his only child's infirmity. A patient man, he had yet to roll his eyes.

"So, you're having some dysphasia, boy?"

"Speak English, Jack!" Jeanette snapped.

"Trouble swallowing, boy?" Jack patiently rephrased the question, which Howard had clearly understood the first time.

"I already told you he couldn't swallow! Weren't you listening?" Jeanette interrupted.

He continued addressing his son, a well-perfected deaf ear to his wife. "Throat sore? "

Howard shook his head.

"Congestion? Nasal drip?"

Negative.

"And no fever," he said, palming his son's forehead for an instant.

"It's below normal. Below. He can't swallow," said Jeanette.

Jack carefully palpated for swollen nodes under Howard's neck, then behind his ears, and finally under his chin. The son saw the father's hands as precision instruments, always manicured, magical in their capabilities. They would touch and caress, they would diagnose and heal. They were the conduits from the physical to the spiritual, and through them the world entered Jack Block.

"Glands?" Jeanette's voice quavered.

Had he been a perverse instead of a practical and patient man, Jack Block could have continued to ignore her. Instead, he shook his head reassuringly—a deaf ear always having a time and a place, and certainly a limit—then reached into his shirt pocket for one of his disposable penlights, cuddled next to his Sheaffer. A few other lights, each an advertisement for a different drug, occupied the butter compartment of the refrigerator, minus the ones Howard had requisitioned for his own personal use.

"Get me a spoon."

"Can't you see without a spoon?" Howard implored, since the spoon pushing down his tongue always made him gag.

"I'll get a spoon," offered Jeanette.

"I don't need a spoon. Open wide, boy."

"Ahhh. . . ."

The doctor illuminated his light and perused the cavity from side to side, keeping the light stationary and altering his vantage by directing Howard's firmly held chin.

"Red? Strep?"

"He's fine," Jack concluded, pocketing the penlight. "It will go away."

"He's had it for weeks and it hasn't gone away! He hasn't been able to swallow for weeks!"

"Everything okay at school, boy?"

Howard nodded.

"And *heder*?"

He hesitated, then nodded again.

His father looked at him intently, features morphing into a slight, but very definite squint.

"Appetite okay?"

"Fine."

"What did you have for breakfast?"

66

"Just sausage patties and eggs."

Jack nodded thoughtfully.

"You or Stinky have any more run-ins with Bettinger?"

"No," said Howard.

"What about myasthenia gravis?" Jeanette interrupted.

"No, Jeanette. . . . "

"So what is it?" He had to be more specific, this greatest and most respected diagnostician in the world, a pillar of the Jewish community, with the largest practice in the city. He was Jack Block, after all, and she was Mrs. Jack Block. The question was simple enough. "Why can't he swallow?"

"It's nothing."

"Nothing? He can't swallow and it's nothing?"

"I think I feel better," Howard interceded to the air.

"Nothing." He looked at his wife searchingly, gauging his words. "It's going around," he finally said.

She sighed, exhausted with relief. "Thank God it's nothing!"

***

That evening, Howard finally managed a bathroom conference with his father.

He slid the pocket door open after knocking, closed it, and hitched himself up onto the counter. His father was vigorously puffing away at the Cherry Blend and reading his "New England Journal of Medicine."

"Can't anyone take a crap anymore in peace?" he said. "Hit the vent fan, will you, Howard? It's a little smoky in here."

Howard flipped on the fan; he watched as the previously directionless swirling smoke began to take on form and move purposefully toward the fan in the ceiling above the shower.

"Thanks. So how's your swallowing, boy?"

"Okay, I guess." He watched the smoke begin the travels from his father's mouth along its predictable route, like a swarm of determined bees. "I've been meaning to ask you about, you know, that business meeting you had the other day."

"It's nothing," said Jack. "A lawsuit. Physicians get sued all the time. So it's my turn, but it will be fine. The worst part is that the lice I have for partners want me to settle out of court."

"Why would that Stringer lady sue you, though? You're the best doctor in the world! And you saved her life!"

Jack looked up from the journal suspiciously. "How do you know her name?"

"Well," said Howard casually, "there may have been a couple of papers left over from the meeting. I was just helping to clean up and couldn't help but notice, you know, as I was throwing them away."

"I see."

"So. . . why?"

Jack shrugged. "It's a cockamamie thing. A woman comes in nearly in a coma and she goes home after three or four days—"

"I believe it was four," said Howard.

"Maybe you should be explaining things to me—" Jack stared at his son with the subtle squint that characterized sudden and intense cerebration.

"No, I'm sorry, Dad, go on."

"Okay, she left the hospital fine after four days. Then six months later she claims she had a psychotic breakdown because we hadn't kept her on her tranquilizer—Valium—during her hospital stay. A psychotic breakdown from Valium withdrawal, allegedly. Of course, when she came in, we had no idea what medications she was on, and after we had brought her back, she showed no signs of withdrawal of any kind."

"What about the psychiatrist guy Huntley?" asked Howard.

"Chad Huntley," said Jack. "The expert witness. This is where things start to make sense. A while back Huntley had a drinking problem. Maybe he still does, for all I know. Anyway, he was called up for discipline when I was Chief of Staff—"

"So he's out to get you!"

"Impossible to prove, but I'm sure he would jump at the chance to even the score."

Howard ruminated. "The other thing. . . You spoke Yiddish. I've never heard you speak Yiddish before."

"What do you mean, boy? Your mother speaks to me in Yiddish all the time. You know that."

"Just the dirty stuff she doesn't want me to hear, and I can understand most of that stuff myself." He paused. "But you never answer her back. I thought you understood it but couldn't speak it."

"Actually, I'm considerably more fluent at Yiddish than your mother, but I choose not to speak it. We live in the United States, not the old country. We're Americans. Yiddish is the language of the old country. That's not who I am."

"But you sure spoke it the other night!"

69

Jack hesitated, searching for the easiest way to explain himself. "Sometimes, I guess, you're not always who you think you are or want to be."

Howard did not give the answer the time or reflection it deserved.

"We just need to prove that Huntley is out to get you, right?"

"Huntley? Prove? Boy, all you have to worry about is your *Haftorah* and memorizing that Bar Mitzvah speech!"

Chapter Six

On the second Saturday following Yuri's catastrophic space flight, Howard finagled a way to spend the day with Mike, whom he considered a more suitable point-man than Stinky. Jeanette, poorly hiding her stress over Jack's legal situation, planned to do some shopping at Wolferman's and had decided to take Ada along, stopping for lunch on the Country Club Plaza at Winstead's Drive-In. Ada was always easy with a laugh and pleasant, non-threatening company; thus, she escaped her customary Saturday morning cleaning responsibilities with full pay. Naturally, Jeanette preferred that Howard join them, hoping to avoid the additional anxiety of him being off on his own for the day, very likely with that *shagetz* Mike.

"How about if Mike comes along with us?" Howard suggested, and his mother jumped at the compromise.

"We'll pick him up at noon," Jeanette said. "I like Mike. He's such a sensible boy."

The plan, so far, was going smoothly. Mike answered the telephone, and without identifying himself, Howard simply said: "New mission. Pick up at noon. Be ready," before clarifying with "My Mom's driving," and hanging up. The message was enticing, and Howard knew that Mike would cancel any of his plans for the day, if he had any.

The boys said little as they awkwardly sat in the back seat of the Bel-Air for the drive to the Plaza, the lack of privacy palpably constraining them. Mike, of course, was completely in the dark, and Howard had not exactly fleshed out any plan. With Jeanette straining to overhear anything they might say—not harboring suspicions but simply nosey—the boys made stilted and clearly artificial comments about school.

As they turned into the drive-in restaurant lot, Howard pulled out his memo pad with forced casualness. He gave Mike a knowing glance, then rifled to the last page with writing on it, that morning's entry. At the top of the page was written: "Discuss situation with Mike. 'Need to know' only." He snapped the pad shut before Mike had a chance to see anything else.

Jeanette had taken everyone's meal orders and was addressing the carhop, who stood outside the driver's side window, leaning into her hip, pencil at the ready. She was a career waitress, with at least a quarter century of service to the local restaurant and the varicose veins to prove it. Marilyn—Howard knew all the waitresses' names without looking at their name tags—wore the same style white blouse and black skirt that had been supplied to her on her first day of work, just after high school graduation, and was also sporting the same perky ponytail. The contrast of Marilyn's leathery and wrinkled skin with the bobby-soxer hair-do was bizarre and a bit frightening.

"Four double cheeseburgers—I'll have grilled onions on mine, please—three orders of fries and I'll have onion rings. Three Cokes and I'll have an iced tea with lemon."

"We need to talk," Howard said to Mike in an undertone, as his mother was occupied with Marilyn.

Shortly after ordering, Jeannette looked back over her seat.

"After lunch, Ada and I will be doing some shopping. I'll drop you off wherever you want. Where should we meet back up?"

"Mike and I want to hang around the Plaza longer. We can take the bus home."

"The bus?"

"I do it all the time, Mrs. Block," Mike reassured her. "You can catch the Ward Parkway bus just about anywhere. And there's a stop right at 67th Terrace and Ward Parkway."

"The bus?"

"That's my bus and my stop," Ada intervened, smiling slyly.

Marilyn returned with their meals with characteristic expeditiousness, hardly enough time to convince Jeanette that the bus ride home was not especially treacherous. Ada, somewhat boldly for a maid, vigorously played the role of advocate, which put Jeanette at a disadvantage and made her question why she had needed to bring Ada along in the first place. Once again, freedom for Howard meant undue additional anxiety for herself, maternal selflessness that did not come without a considerable price.

Meanwhile, Howard had noticed that three of the four meals were on plates—the fourth was paper-wrapped as if for take-out—and all but one of the beverages were in glassware. Naively thinking that Ada would miss such a slight, Howard quickly reached over Jeanette's shoulder and grabbed the paper-wrapped burger and the Coke in the paper cup for himself.

"These are mine," said Howard, wondering what the code was, how Marilyn could indicate a customer's race on her memo pad. He wondered if she put a small "N" or "C" in the margin. In any case, the system was pretty slick, and Howard was happy to confound it.

After lunch, Jeanette pulled the car over to the curb on Nichol's Parkway, the pre-determined drop-off point suggested by both Ada and Mike.

"This is where we can catch the bus back," said Mike, getting out of the backseat. "Thanks for the lunch and the ride," he added politely. Howard slid across the seat and followed him out.

"Are you sure you'll be alright?" Jeanette asked.

"I'll be home before dinner," said Howard.

Predictably, she asked if he had money for the bus fare and a dime for a phone call. Howard pulled a handful of change from his pocket to show her and returned most of it to his pocket before reaching past Ada through the window.

"And eleven cents for you," he said, with two nickels and a penny in his outstretched hand for the *pishka* as soon as she got home. While Jeanette looked down to pick the change out of his palm, Howard took the opportunity to force a swallow.

A car horn, bleating twice, forced Jeanette to pull away into traffic, distraction and anxiety about leaving her son trumped by the impatient driver behind her.

It was T-shirt weather, with a blue sky, scattered cumulous clouds, and flashes of warmth between breezes that presaged the stifling heat that would descend like a suffocating blanket in a couple of months. Howard took off the jacket his mother had made him bring and tied the arms around his waist. The boys stood on the corner outside a modern blue-glass building, and Howard made a mental list of activities and snacks in the shopping district: a popcorn ball from Topsy's, a lemonade from Putsch's coffee shop, a browse through the latest titles at Bennett Schneider's book store. They could even catch a movie at the Plaza Theater, if something good were playing and the show timing was right. And, as a last resort, he could even drag Mike through Jack Henry's and Woolf Brothers to see if there were anything worth buying with all his gift certificates, which he doubted.

Since the entire escapade had been devised as a means to consult Mike about his father's dilemma, Howard thought that perhaps he shouldn't be so eager to have a good time. But the allures of the Plaza were too many to ignore, and there was no reason not to mix business with pleasure.

When the traffic light changed to green, Howard started to walk across the street, but Mike stood in place.

"Let's go," said Howard, turning around once he realized Mike was not with him.

But Mike had evidently come up with an entirely different short list during their moment of shared silence. He had been inspecting the bus schedule posted on the metal bus sign support.

"Here comes the bus," said Mike, pointing.

Howard backtracked to the curb, uncomprehending.

"But we just got here!" he protested.

"You ever been to Wonderland?" Mike asked.

"What?" Howard was pretty familiar with the Country Club Plaza shops and couldn't recall ever having heard or seen that one.

"Wonderland. The Penny Arcade."

"No. Where's that?"

"Twelfth and Grand. Downtown."

"Downtown!"

"You heard me, man. And here's the downtown bus." The Metro bus was pulling over to the curb, brakes squealing. Howard smelled fumes, the exhaust from the rear wafting toward him in the warm breeze. His thoughts were a confused jumble of cautions and prohibitions, all in his mother's intonations. Despite these, the pneumatic doors opened, right in front of them, with a welcoming and enticing hiss.

"Got any change?" Mike asked, about to make his first upward step into the vehicle.

Howard was at a crossroads, preparing to embark on perhaps the most audacious action of his twelve and three-quarters years. He might as well have been enlisting in the Armed Forces, signing on the dotted line at the goading of some burly recruiter with a buzz cut and a glint in his eye.

"I've always got change," Howard said, heart pounding, committed and past the point of no return. He sidled past his friend up the steps, reaching into his pocket. He had no idea where the adrenaline surge had come from, but the rush was relatively short, as the realization that he was in a bus going downtown suddenly took his breath away, less exhilaration than asphyxiation.

Howard had no inkling what a bus trip cost, so he looked expectantly at the driver, a rotund black man seemingly on the verge of bursting out of his uniform. His police-style hat was tilted back from his forehead, pushed there the first time sweat had been wiped away with the back of his arm three hours earlier.

"Quarter," he said, swiping his arm along his forehead, the fabric on his sleeve a shade darker and shinier than the rest of the jacket material.

Howard deposited the fares casually through the slot, as if it were something he did every day, using money which, under normal circumstances, would have been held in reserve for a blue metal box.

The bus promptly lurched forward, and Howard—not anticipating movement until he had found his seat—lost his balance and lunged at the closest support pole to keep himself from tumbling. Mike, not caught unprepared, moved beyond him to the rear of the bus with the sure footedness of a Grand Canyon mule. Howard followed, bracing every step with a hand gripping the top of each passing seat.

They plopped down onto the brown vinyl covered seat, and Howard assessed his surroundings. The bus was about a third full of middle-aged black women. Some looked like shoppers who had come to the Plaza from downtown, but most appeared to be domestics, heading back home from the suburbs after half a day's weekend work. Many were preoccupied with newspapers or knitting; a couple looked up and gave him a friendly glance.

Howard pointedly gave a polite smile, but Mike was simply grinning, purposelessly, sitting straight back in his seat with his hands in his lap.

"Ah," he finally said, stretching his arms behind his head, "this is the life of Riley."

"Yeah," agreed Howard, his expression betraying uncertainty.

"You've never been on a bus before, have you?" Mike said.

"A school bus," said Howard, adding, "not that often, though, since my Mom usually drives me to school. Although now I can ride my bike if I want."

Mike didn't respond, since the answer had been obvious, his question rhetorical, and any interest in pursuing the point totally lacking.

"School buses are a lot smaller," said Howard, now considering himself somewhat of an expert on the subject, "and the drivers usually wait until you're seated before they take off like that. It may be a law."

Mike shut his eyes, continuing to smile, and yawned contentedly, as if he had just left a banquet table, fully sated.

"Ah," he said, "this is the life."

"Yeah," said Howard, anticipating an encounter with the unknown in the vaguest possible sense. He lacked an adequate store of imagery to help him envision what could lie ahead. Fearful without knowing why, he was waiting to be told by someone exactly what he should be dreading. After all, they were heading straight into the maw of downtown Kansas City, and the possibilities were as endless as difficult to fathom.

***

From the moment he entered Wonderland—the "World's Finest Arcade" according to the large sign in front—sights, sounds, and smells overwhelmed him. The rather seedy entertainment center, packed to the gills and cloaked in cigarette smoke, was jammed with games of skill and chance in a seemingly random hodge-podge, with more pinball machines than one could imagine crammed into a space of its size, creating a maze of passageways and pass-throughs. The electronic racket, incesssant ringing and clattering, was deafening.

Most of the patrons were black or latin, although a number of scruffy-looking whites were represented. They were the most intimidating characters overall, with slicked hair and long burns, sunglasses, and rolled-up shirtsleeves exposing home-made tattoos. These males fell under the generic description of "hoods," and Howard had never seen them this close, let alone shared the same social setting. He and Mike were among the younger kids in the place, but the age span was fairly broad and Howard was surprised to see what seemed to be second and third graders: clearly little hood tadpoles awaiting a more mature form.

"I spent the day in a downtown game arcade with a bunch of hoods," Howard might sum up to his mother if she were heavily sedated with animal tranquilizers. Realistically, the only person to whom he could relate his adventures would be Stinky, and Stinky wouldn't believe him.

"Get out of town," Stinky would say.

A handful of girls roamed the place, mostly tomboyish participants, and others who were relegated to providing encouragement or simply fawning. They were most notable for having adult-size breasts, and some even showed real cleavage, as if they had been volunteers in some type of hormone experiment. Until then, all the girls that Howard had had any contact with appeared to be in the control group. Unable to come up with a single word to describe these females, Howard ultimately settled on "the kind of girls that hang around with hoods" in case Stinky asked.

All the players were too occupied with their games to pay Howard any mind. They brushed by him or nudged him out of the way without acknowledgment—and of course without apology—eyeing their next game conquest and checking out the lines. Howard maybe didn't stick out as much as he had thought; nevertheless, he untucked his polo shirt and avoided making eye contact. He shuddered at the realization that any number of scenarios had the potential for mob violence. A power outage, for instance, could provoke any latent anti-Semitism in the room. Remembering with great relief that he didn't actually look Jewish, Howard's fear momentarily dissipated to a tolerable level, but couldn't be quashed completely. Religious prejudices aside, as a rich white kid he'd still be one of the first to die if violence broke out.

"Do you think we should go now?" Howard did not feel like pushing his luck.

Mike was astonished. "No pinball?"

"We have things to discuss," said Howard, doing his best to turn his wan expression into one of enticement.

"You're just afraid of me beating you, you spaz," said Mike.

Howard placated Mike by nodding. Not hardly, he was thinking. Just afraid.

***

They settled on the fountain counter of a Woolworth's, where Howard spooned into the comfort of a hot fudge sundae and Mike sipped a root beer float. Howard finally had the chance to pull out his memo pad and read from his notes. He had forgotten about his need to swallow for quite a while.

Mike listened without interrupting, then said, "No question. You have no choice. You have to help your Dad."

"How exactly can I do that?" asked Howard.

"With me, of course," said Mike.

Mike had finished using the straw and was getting at the ice cream at the bottom with a spoon. Howard waited

80

patiently, occupying himself with his own sundae. Clearly, Mike was thinking things through and shouldn't be rushed.

"Okay," Mike finally said. "First we need to assemble a team. Who can we absolutely trust?" He wiped his mouth with a crumpled paper napkin as he considered. "Someone fearless. Someone dedicated. Someone willing to risk his life for the mission."

Howard hesitated.

"Stinky," he said. "I think Stinky would help. We can count on Stinky."

"Okay. Stinky. That makes you, me, and Stinky. Who else?"

The boys pondered silently. They went back to their desserts and finished them off. Mike slid his empty float glass forward on the counter. He took a sip of water.

"There are some advantages to a small team," Mike said.

***

The boys left Woolworth's and strolled down Broadway in the direction of a bus stop they had passed earlier.

"Wait a minute," said Mike. He pointed down a quiet side street with a discount men's clothing store several doors down, indicated by a sandwich sign on the sidewalk that announced: "WALTER'S CLOTHING SALE. PRICES SLASHED."

"We need some gear," said Mike.

The store was a black business enterprise, with an enormous stock of men's wear running the gamut from surplus Army/Navy items to garishly-colored tuxedos. The racks and displays were jammed together in a manner that reminded Howard of Wonderland, except the place was deserted and eerily quiet. The proprietor, a wiry black man with a pencil moustache and wavy slicked backed hair, was idly reading a newspaper behind his elevated counter and barely took notice of the boys' entrance. Lighting in the place was patchy; the fluorescent bulbs were several thousand watts lacking for adequate illumination, especially since a number of them had burnt out. A few of them flickered annoyingly, and portions of the store were almost in complete shadow. Howard would later describe it to Stinky as "not exactly Jack Henry's."

Only one other customer was shopping as far as Howard could tell, a black youth of about sixteen, overdressed in a baggy suit, two-toned shoes, and a fedora. This was out-on-the-town wear, a modified zoot suit, which seemed out of place in mid-day, even in Walter's Clothing. When Howard glanced at him, the boy eyed him suspiciously, so he immediately broke eye contact and pretended to be enamored with the nearest available sweater, a gold angora that looked like it had been manufactured from remnants of shag carpeting. When he checked again, the boy was still looking at him, and this time Howard looked away with the subtlety of a pig on ice. The crowd in the arcade had provided him anonymity; but here, in this dusky and nearly empty store, Howard could not hide the fact that he was out of place, a suburban white kid in a downtown Negro men's store. He didn't belong, and he was antsy to leave.

"Wow, what a place," said Mike, surveying the clothes-lined racks and tables piled with stacks of shirts. The first draw for him was predictably the Army/Navy surplus, but after a quick inventory, he made a beeline to a grouping of tables with clothing articles heaped in mounds. As if the appeal of the disorganization weren't enough, these stations were labeled "Clearance."

Howard aimlessly walked up and down the aisles, not sure exactly what type of gear he should be looking for. The items held little interest for him; even Jack Henry's was a more interesting browse—the upscale Plaza store at least had interesting men's accessories and a variety of colognes in spray bottles that could be sampled. Howard heard a tinkling from the bell on the entrance door and looked up to see that the sole other customer—who had been giving him the hairy eyeball—had left. Howard breathed a sigh of relief.

Mike was now in the back of the store, plowing through a pile of clothing. For brief moments he seemed to disappear, as if he were a pearl diver.

Mike emerged from the pile triumphantly, holding a black short-sleeved T-shirt.

"My size," he yelled out. "You'll need one too!" With that, Mike dove back into the pile.

The search became prolonged and tedious, with Howard joining in at the table and then venturing to other clearance piles. At one point, nearly giving up, Mike asked the proprietor if he had a second identical shirt in stock and was told to "check the piles."

"Here's one my size," Howard said during the search, holding up his find.

"That's not black. It's dark green."

"It's pretty close."

"How can it be standard issue if it isn't the same color?" Mike asked.

"Maybe we can find another green one and dark green can be standard issue instead," suggested Howard.

"Standard issue is black," Mike said firmly.

Eventually the hunt for the second identical black T-shirt was successful. Howard's enthusiasm for the purchase was tempered—he was simply glad the pursuit was over—but Mike seemed incredibly excited by the acquisition of the particular gear, explaining: "We may have to do work at night." Howard, ready to go home, intentionally did not bring up the topic of matching wear for Stinky. He wasn't about to go looking for a third black shirt.

The boys paid for their purchases, unaware that the baggy-suited boy was loitering near the shop entrance, watching their every move through the window. When he saw they were heading for the door to pay, he leaned back against the outside brick wall, took a toothpick from his pocket, wiped off the lint, and began chewing on it, like he just happened to be hanging out in front of Walter's, picking his teeth.

Howard saw him first, as the shop door closed behind them. He heard the faint tingle of the bells from the inside, which might have been mistaken as the signal for his heart to pick up speed.

"How you gentlemen doin' today?" asked the youth.

"We're fine," said Mike, walking around Howard, who had frozen in his tracks.

"See ya around," said Mike, with obviously fake casualness.

The intruder had moved from his perch against the wall and blocked Mike's way.

"Now jus' wait a minute here," he said, a shade less friendly.

"We're kinda in a hurry," said Mike. "We got a bus to catch."

"How about if you two kind gentlemen lend me some money before you catch your bus?"

Howard unconsciously began fingering the change in his pocket. He had to pee.

"We only have enough for bus fare home," Mike said.

"My money's for the *pishka*, so things like this won't happen," Howard might have said, but thought better of it. Mike was handling the situation.

"Fare's only a quarter. You mean to tell me you gentlemen jus' have a quarter?"

"We're about to miss our bus."

"You kin catch the next one. Whatcha got in that there bag?" he asked, removing the toothpick and using it as a pointer.

"Shirts. Just shirts," Mike answered. He was getting squirmy, and nervously looked back at Howard, though he knew the situation was his to manage.

"Les see 'em."

Mike was hesitant to comply with the request. Howard was still too frightened to say or do anything and could only look at the youth's face intently. The kid was about four years older than they were, but trying to act like a thirty-year-old professional. And apparently he had finished with the pseudo-friendly bantering and was ready to get down to business. Placing the toothpick back into his mouth, he stuck his right hand in his suit jacket pocket and poked a finger behind the fabric, as if brandishing a weapon. The contour of the protrusion was less than convincing.

"You wanna see my knife?" he asked, indicating the bulge from his pocket.

The boys had no choice but to take the bulge seriously, as improbable as it appeared. Howard said nothing, but thought to himself, "That's his finger. It looks like a boner."

Mike was getting shaky. "Here. Here," he said, handing over the bag containing both shirts. "That's okay. Take them." And rather immaterially he added, "But they're not your size."

"Not my size?" pondered the mugger, cued by Mike's trivial afterthought. He raised his eyebrows with astute realization.

"Then I'll jus' hafta get my money back, seein' as I got my receipt in this here bag. You gentlemen have a good day, now."

With that, the robber fished out the receipt from the bag and re-entered the store. Howard heard the bells ring. Would the proprietor refund the money without asking any questions? Howard couldn't believe the cheekiness of the robber, or the dishonesty of Walter, if that's who it was.

"Quick! Run!" shouted Mike.

"Wait a sec," said Howard, grabbing him by the shirt.

"Howie—you wanna get slashed?" He noticed the sign. "Like these prices? Let's get the hell out of here before he comes back!"

"You think he really has a knife?"

"I don't know and I don't care! Come on!"

"Looked more like a boner than a knife."

"Are you nuts? It's just a couple of T-shirts! Let's go!"

"No, wait a sec," demanded Howard. He looked through the window and saw the boy getting cash for his exchange. Soon he emerged from the store, counting the money in his hands. When he looked up and saw the two boys still waiting there, he was taken aback.

"Whatchu want? Whatchu still doing here?" he snarled.

Howard moved over and stood directly in front of him. He was two feet away, and had to raise his head up to look his assailant in the eye.

Howard's lip quivered at the beginning, but by the time he was finished speaking, he sounded more than assertive.

"I'm gonna tell your Momma, Junior Lee!"

***

Later, the two boys sat on the bus, again at the rear. The bus was nearly empty for the return route—few domestics were heading into the suburbs to work on a late Saturday afternoon—but again they were the only white riders. Both wore identical black T-shirts, their old shirts stowed away in a bag that Mike held in his lap. Howard still had his jacket around his waist by the arms, the jacket he had never worn because of the mild spring day.

Mike stretched his arms back over his head and grinned. Then he put his hands back in his lap and rested them on the bag. The bag crackled. Mike nudged Howard with his elbow.

"I think we can really count on Junior Lee," he said.

Chapter Seven

The Broadway bus took the boys only as far south as the Plaza, requiring them to take a different bus to complete the journey home. Mike consulted the posted bus schedule, while Howard rested on a bench at the stop. It was after four, and the breeze was beginning to chill.

"We've still got a few minutes for the Ward Parkway," said Mike, tracing the schedule with his pointed finger. "Time to make contact."

"What?" Howard was tired and spaced out.

Mike indicated a phone booth on the corner.

"Call her on the phone. Gimme your pad."

Howard, oblivious to the rationale for the command, stood up obediently, pulled the memo pad out of his back pocket, and handed it over. Still failing to track, he found himself trailing behind Mike to the phone booth.

"Who? What are you talking about?"

Mike, ignoring him, first thumbed through the pad, then rapidly began flipping the pages of the phone book, repeatedly licking his fingers for traction.

"Here it is! The lady behind all this!" he exclaimed after much rustling and an occasional page tear. "H. Stringer. On Benton. On the Missouri side."

Howard peered over his shoulder at the listing.

"How do you know that's 'Hannah'?"

"It's the only one," explained Mike. "And it's the initial 'H.' Women always use their initials in the phone book so they won't get crank calls."

"Like nobody can figure that one out," said Howard, who up until just that moment had not been aware of the convention.

"Woman can be dumb like that. They just don't think it through."

Mike took the eraserless half pencil that Howard had conveniently fit through the metal spirals of the pad—monogrammed "Meadowbrook Golf Club"—and wrote the number down on a blank page.

Then he reached out to Howard, palm up.

"Dime."

For the first time in recent memory, Howard was actually beginning to run low on change, which, by his way of thinking, meant that he had less than a dollar's worth. Nonetheless, he fished out the thinnest of the remaining coins in his pocket by feel.

Mike put the coin through the slot, consulted the notation in the memo pad, and carefully dialed the number while Howard peered around nervously.

"Relax," said Mike. "This call can't be traced."

Howard forced a swallow. "What are you going to say?"

"Shh! Allo?"

Mike spoke in a very bizarre accent—mostly French sounding, but also a bit Chinese, with an overlay of Eastern European. While altogether an odd dialect, Mike was able to maintain a remarkable consistency, so much so that Howard wondered if Mike had spent time practicing.

"Is thees Madame Hannah Stringer?" he continued. "It ees? Thees ees Johanne Peters, from ze billing department of Menorah 'Ospeetal. You were a patient in Feboorie, no? Yes?"

Mike nodded excitedly to Howard, who moved in closer to the phone receiver. On the other end of the line, Hannah Stringer was having trouble understanding the caller, so she put down her tumbler of bourbon and turned down the television. She had been dozing, though fortunately her grip had not loosened on the glass. She breathed in the stale, musty air from the cluttered and poorly ventilated room and gathered her bearings. Disturbed from restless sleep in such a manner, she was nauseated and couldn't determine if she were drunk or sober.

"What is this about?" she belched.

"I am so sorree to bother you," Mike continued. "Did you get ze bill yet?"

"What bill?" Hannah adjusted her bra.

"Ah, yes, thees is why I call you today. We are veree sorree for your sichuation and to tell you that you will not have to pay ze bill becuz. . . ." Here Mike paused, but only momentarily, awaiting inspiration. ". . . becuz with good luck ze bill rings up on ze register with a red star on ze pepper, which means everysing will be free."

"What bill?" asked Hannah, reaching down for her tumbler and taking a swig. She needed more ice.

"Ze 'ospeetal bill."

"I didn't get no bill," said Hannah, partially piecing together the intent of the call, or at least the subject of it. "That was ages ago, and Dr. Huntley said he was taking care of all that."

"Ach—you moost know Dr. Huntley well, no? Yes?"

"I'll say. Been taking care of me for years, through good times and bad. A good man, that Dr. Huntley, and willing to help a girl out."

Howard was so close to Mike that they could have been conjoined twins, attached at the side of the head.

Upon registering the last exchange, they looked at each other, wide-eyed.

"Veree good," Mike said into the phone, not wanting to press his luck. "Maybee we talk later, yes? No? Goodbye."

He placed with receiver in the cradle with forced calmness. Somewhat later, realizing that the conversation had ended, Hannah hung up as well.

The boys stood in silence, until Howard finally uttered "Whoa."

"Yeah," said Mike.

"Huntley was supposed to be an expert witness. But Hannah Stringer was his patient. He knew her from before," said Howard.

"Yep. Looks like your Dad was set up all right, Howie."

"I thought so! Wait 'till I tell him!"

"Not so fast," said Mike. "You can't do that."

"Why not?"

"No hard evidence," said Mike. "If Stringer and Huntley are tipped off, they'll cover their tracks. Your Dad already was suspicious, right? And what good was it?"

Howard pondered, then saw a bus pulling up to where he had been sitting on the bench. "Is that our bus?"

"Run for it!" yelled Mike, tearing off.

***

91

The return bus ride was uneventful, as was the two-block walk from Ward Parkway to Howard's house. Howard had easily wrangled a dinner invitation for Mike; Jeanette was so relieved at her son's safe return that she would have agreed to virtually anything. Before dinner there was time to reassess the situation and plot out the mission. Howard took Mike up to his bedroom, then left to make a brief foray into his father's study. While he was gone, Mike surveyed the room, amazed by its overall cleanliness—it was like a hotel room and hardly looked lived-in. No clothes were visible, and all of the books were neatly ordered on bookshelves, except for a stack of thesauruses on Howard's desk. Mike was looking at the identical volumes, perplexed, when Howard returned.

"We're going to eat early instead of waiting for my Dad," Howard said, holding up the booklet he had retrieved from the downstairs study, his index finger sandwiched between pages as a marker. "This will help. It's the Jackson County Medical Directory." He flipped open the book. "And here's Huntley. . . ." He held up the page for Mike to see.

"Chadwick Huntley, MD," Mike read. "What a mug. He lives on Wenonga Drive. That's Mission Hills."

"Real close," Howard said. "I ride my bike down that street all the time."

"We'll plan for surveillance," said Mike.

"Gotcha," said Howard, barely able to contain his growing excitement.

"So," said Mike, still distracted by the stack of books, "what's with all the thesauruses?"

"Bar Mitzvah gifts," said Howard. "Want a couple?"

"No thanks."

"And what are these?" Mike was shifting a collection of identical-appearing envelopes on the desk, sliding them around in a loose version of three-card Monty.

"Gift certificates."

Mike read the outside of one of the envelopes.

"Jack Henry?"

"There's also a bunch of Wolff Brothers in there."

"Shit—these are worthless."

"You can get wool slacks," said Howard. "Want some?"

"No thanks. Any from. . . the Toon Shop?"

"Not yet."

"You know how many forty-fives you could buy with all this dough?"

Howard didn't respond, and Mike shook his head in disgust and befuddlement.

"Anyway," he went on, "back to the stake out. Do you have binoculars?"

"My Mom has a pair," said Howard. "I think they're opera glasses, actually. They're pretty small—they'll fit in a purse—and mother of pearl."

"Mother of pearl? Maybe we need something more powerful. What does your Dad use for hunting?"

Howard was taken aback by a question he had never before been asked.

"He doesn't hunt," Howard eventually replied.

"Okay, then," said Mike, not masking his disappointment, "bring your Mom's. Small will work, and if it doesn't, well. . . you can just move in closer."

"Right," said Howard.

"And we're definitely going to need back-up, the whole team."

"I'll call Stinky."

"And have him bring his binoculars."

Howard paused. "Uh . . . he might not have any."

"His dad doesn't hunt, either?" This struck Mike as coincidental.

Howard took a deep breath. Mike seemed confused and awaited an explanation. Howard would be as clear and succinct as possible.

"Jews don't hunt, Mike," he said.

Mike looked at him blankly.

***

At school on Monday, Howard wanted to waste no time in getting Stinky up to speed. He had decided against phoning over the weekend. Jeanette, of course, was the greatest security risk for eavesdropping, although Howard could have called when she was out shopping. But he had no such control over Stinky's mom, who also had a propensity for listening in. But since Stinky was grounded, it was unlikely that he was allowed to use the phone anyway.

Howard found an opportunity for a locker-side conversation with Stinky between second and third periods. He avoided the specifics, only saying that they needed him the following Saturday afternoon for an extremely urgent mission. There would be more details when the three-man team got together at lunch.

"I'm still grounded," said Stinky, twirling the knob on his combination lock. He yanked up on the handle, which didn't release. He twiddled the lock on the dial and started over.

"Tell your mom you're coming over to my house to practice your *Haftorah*."

"That's lying. Hold on a second." Stinky concentrated on the third rotation of the lock, eased the notches into place, and yanked on the handle again. The lock clanked with the upward force, but held firm. "Shit," he said, starting over.

"It's not lying," continued Howard. "It's deceit. Part of the mission. Your mom can't know what's going on, okay?"

"Hell," said Stinky, "I don't even know what's going on."

"You're missing the point. It's not lying, because you're not telling her for her own safety. You're actually protecting her. It's necessary deceit."

Stinky shot him a dubious glance.

"I do it all the time with my mom," Howard added. "Otherwise, she'd be a mental case."

Stinky succeeded in opening his locker.

"It still feels like lying," he said, rummaging at the bottom of his locker for his American History book.

Howard tried a different tack.

"You heard of James Bond? Double-oh seven?" Howard had recently been acquainted with the British secret agent and his exploits through Mike, who had already seen the new movie, "Dr. No," several times.

"Sure, the English spy in the movie. I really want to see it," said Stinky, "but my mom won't let me because of the dirty parts. I hear the babes are really hot."

Howard nodded enthusiastically.

"He gets laid all the time."

"Cool."

"Anyway," maneuvered Howard, "Ever think about James Bond's mom?"

"Not really," said Stinky. "Come to think of it, I didn't ever really think about him having a mom."

"Well, of course he has a mom. And do you think she knows what he's up to?"

"I hadn't really thought about it."

"She probably thinks he's a civil engineer or something."

"Makes sense, I guess. Otherwise she'd worry."

"It's basically the same thing, right? He's not really lying to his mom, he's just protecting her with deceit."

"I guess so," said Stinky, not entirely convinced. "Maybe I'd feel better about it if James Bond was Jewish."

"I think he may be half Jewish," said Howard.

"You mean he changed his name?" asked Stinky, considering the plausibleness.

Howard nodded with authority. "Probably at the same time they gave him the numbers."

"And he dates all those hot *shiksas*," said Stinky, excited by the thought.

"I bet he doesn't tell his mother about that!"

Stinky tried to slam his locker shut, but the door rattled and bounced back at him. With his foot he manipulated some crumpled papers protruding from the floor of the locker, and carefully pushed the door until it clicked in place.

"No way," Stinky said, twirling the combination lock with abandon.

***

At lunchtime, Howard, Mike, and Stinky found a table for themselves near the back corner of the cafeteria, an ideal location for a private meeting. Finished eating, they slid their orange plastic trays across the table and huddled over a street map that Mike had carefully unfolded. Mike began tracing a route with a red pen while Howard and Stinky alternated between looking at the map and surveying the cafeteria suspiciously.

"What the hell are they up to?" Chris Beaman asked Ryan O'Hearn, a few tables away. He cut into his Swedish meatball with his fork, suddenly annoyed for no apparent reason.

"They're looking at a map," said Ryan, finishing his milk. He resumed checking out the girls in the room, which was a more purposeful distraction. Neither boy was especially bright, but Ryan was the less intellectually curious of the two. Aside from showing off his athletic skills, Ryan's sole mission in life basically boiled down to fingering a girl. He had yet to actually do this, but felt he was making headway, testosterone springing eternal.

"I think Sally Olson's wearing falsies," he said. "She definitely looks bigger today."

"They're being secretive."

"I think Sally Olson is horny."

Distracted by thoughts of Sally Olson, Ryan flicked the stands of straight blonde hair back from his forehead, the trademark move of junior high school boys and perfected to an art form by Ryan O'Hearn. Ryan's continual hair-flick bordered on the tic-like, and occasionally, in the presence of girls he was trying to impress, verged on symptoms of a neurological disorder.

"They look like they're up to something," said Chris. "They keep looking around."

Indeed they did, especially Stinky, who was visibly jittery and perspiring heavily. Howard seemed jumpy as well, but Stinky, sweeping his gaze continually across the room, was the essence of clandestine screaming for attention. Spilling his milk all over the map was the clincher. Chris watched as the boys frantically mopped up the wetness with their available napkins. Then they dabbed at the milk that had dripped on their laps. Lunch was over. Mike stood up, folded the soggy map, and placed it inside his notebook.

"By the way, it isn't enough to watch from the street," he said. "We have to make actual contact."

Howard and Stinky looked at each other and raised their eyebrows. Mike was serious, and he was certain to come up with an actual plan for contact that they were obliged to carry out. Howard swallowed hard. Stinky began chewing on his thumbnail.

"I'll come up with a plan by seventh period tomorrow," Mike continued. "See you later, men."

***

The next day in gym class, the three were not paying attention as the flag football sides were being chosen by Captain Chris and Captain Ryan. Oblivious to the penetrating cold May breeze, they huddled in their shorts and white T-shirts apart from the rest of the class. Choices for the sides were progressing in the predictable order.

"I've got it worked out," whispered Mike.

"How?" asked Howard.

"Need to know."

"'Need to know' what?" asked Stinky.

"On a 'need to know' basis is standard protocol, Stinky," explained Howard.

"You'll find out when the time comes. It's safer that way," Mike said.

"Oh. Okay—"

"Listen up," Mike interrupted. "Stinky, dig up some Hershey bars and bring them with you to the checkpoint. Can you manage that?"

"Sure thing. With or without almonds?" Stinky asked, pleased with the responsibility with which he had been entrusted, not to mention a task that was well within his comfort zone.

"Your call," said Mike.

"Hunsacker!" Chris yelled. "Old yeller shorts! Hey, Hunsacker, we're stuck with you again!"

"Yeah, yeah," Mike replied, pulling his shirt off, but without the usual struggling and trashing about.

Before jogging off toward Chris and the other team members, Mike had final instructions for Stinky.

"Howie and I will meet you at the rendezvous," he said, "And don't forget to wear the proper clothes!"

Howard and Stinky waited for their calls.

"Oh, Blo—ock," aped Ryan.

Howard gave Stinky a final concerned look.

"No problemo, I'll be there," Stinky said somewhat defensively. "And I got the outfit all figured out."

Without waiting for any 'fat Jew' remarks, Stinky slipped off his shirt, seemingly for the first time without self-consciousness. This was kid's stuff, after all. The teams were already heading to their respective end of the field for the kick-off. Stinky ran to catch up.

***

Later, when Howard and Stinky were already on their way to the synagogue for Bar Mitzvah class, Mike was occupied in the back of the deserted art classroom, his hair still wet from the end of seventh period shower. Scissors, construction paper, and magic markers were laid out in front of him, as well as Mr. Stevens' professional art drafting pen, which he had purloined from the teacher's unlocked desk drawer. The pen made beautiful thin lines, but was always kept out of students' hands.

He put the finishing touches on the second of the two identical name badges, then looked up at the wall clock. Well within schedule, according to plan. Holding out one of the badges at arm's length, he admired his work. A brilliant fake, no question about it. But Howard and Stinky would have to wait until the next morning to see his handiwork.

"Yessiree," Mike muttered to himself, grinning. His counterfeit ID badges were just the ticket for making contact.

Chapter Eight

At the intersection of State Line Road and Wenonga Road, Mike and Howard sat on their bikes, waiting. Yet another glorious spring day, with a cloudless sky, the perfect weather for spy work. Both boys wore their black T-shirts from Walter's Clothing. Jeanette's mother-of-pearl opera glasses were slung over Howard's neck on a heavy piece of twine, a rigging he had devised himself upon consulting an old cub scout handbook for an appropriate knot. Mike's own binoculars, a large pair designed for outdoor sporting use, were suspended from his neck by sturdy factory strapping. His bicycle, a beat-up three-speed with standard handlebars, had a double-sided metal basket secured to the rear fender, with his familiar burlap bag in one side and a small brown paper grocery bag in the other.

"Let me take these for now," Mike said, lifting the opera glasses off Howard's neck. "We don't want to arouse suspicion." He turned them over in his hands, appraising them, then shook his head and muttered "Really weird," before carefully placing them in the grocery bag.

"Nice binoculars," he said to Howard, conscious of the previous slight and not wanting to diminish morale before an important mission. "Now," he went on, "we go up Wenonga and the house should be down the street a ways, even number, on the left side of the block. We go right past it, straight to the destination point. Stay with me. Got it?"

Howard nodded. With Mike leading the way, they began leisurely biking down the street, checking the address numbers along the way. Mike indicated the house with a tilt of the head as he passed it, then sped up. Howard felt a sinking feeling, but pedaled harder to keep up. He had ridden by Chadwick Huntley's Colonial style brick house before and never known it. Not two weeks before, in fact, he had taken note of it, because of the girl who lived there and had come outside to fetch the paper.

The prearranged destination point, a landscaped green space with a fountain and decorative wall, was even closer than Mike had anticipated. Four houses away, the Huntley house was clearly visible. The boys got off their bikes and leaned them against the wall.

"Ideal look-out. Perfect," said Mike.

Howard was less enthused.

"Uh, Mike," he began, "I don't quite know how to say this, but I think I know someone who lives in that house."

"Crapola!" blurted Mike. "That screws up everything!" He began the questioning in earnest. "How well do they know you? Do they know your name?"

"No," Howard replied a bit hesitantly, then "Definitely not."

"Who is it?"

"Some girl about our age. And I think she has an older sister."

"She go to Indian Hills?"

"Don't think so. No. I'd know it if she did."

"Probably goes to a private school, judging by the house," said Mike.

"Barstow or Sunset Hill," said Howard.

"Right. She a babe?"

"Pretty much."

"Damn, there's always a babe balling these things up."

"I think it will be okay," Howard said.

Mike, however, wasn't quite through with the debriefing.

"Tits?" he asked.

"Yeah," said Howard.

"We'll just have to risk it," said Mike. He looked at his watch.

"Where's Stinky, anyhow?"

The boys sat in the grass, relaxing and enjoying the sunshine, ostensibly a couple of junior highers taking a break from a bike ride. That was their cover, anyway. Stinky arrived after a few minutes, clumsily making way on his bike, having problems steering with one hand as he cradled a box of Hershey bars under his left arm. He had obviously taken his own break earlier and gotten into the box, since he had chocolate smeared on one side of his face.

Mike stood up to greet him and took the box from under his arm.

"A whole box, almost," he said. "Great."

"I mixed plain with almonds," said Stinky. "We always keep a couple of boxes of each kind in our pantry."

Mike shook his head approvingly.

"And nice threads."

Stinky beamed. He wore a black LaCoste polo shirt, black Sans-a-belt dress slacks, and his tassled black dress penny loafers with the usual thin-ribbed calf socks, also black.

"This is actually the only black shirt I own," said Stinky.

"One of those alligator shirts," said Mike. "Cool."

"I know I'm a little formal, but my Mom said that if I was going over to Dr. Block's house I had to make a good impression."

"You look real good in black," Howard said encouragingly. "It makes you look slimmer."

Stinky beamed while Mike worked the top off the Hershey box. A lime green covered pamphlet was on top. Stinky reached quickly and removed it, revealing the chocolate bars, minus one, underneath.

"That's my *Haftorah* book," he explained to Mike. "It was the only way I could get out of the house. Because I'm still grounded. I could only come because I promised to practice my *Haftorah* with Howard. If I didn't bring it, I'd be lying to my Mom."

"Right." Mike didn't exactly know what a *Haftorah* book was, but deemed it irrelevant to the mission. "Well. Whatever," he said.

Mike retrieved both his burlap bag and the grocery bag from his bicycle basket, and led the other two boys to a conferencing spot against the stone wall. While they sat together on the ground, partially hidden from view by the fountain, Mike explained the plan. He removed the two forged name tags from the grocery bag with a flourish, put one on himself, and gave the other to Howard. Each name tag read: "Junior American Cancer Society, Official Fund Raiser." Howard and Stinky were suitably impressed, although Stinky couldn't hide his disappointment at not having a tag of his own.

"Only two of us are going in, Howard and me," Mike said. "Stinky, you're going to stay here and be the look-out person. Got it?"

Stinky looked relieved.

"I can get in a little *Haftorah* practice," he said, quickly adding, "just pretending to practice while I wait here, so not as to arouse suspicion."

"Good cover," said Mike. "You're just like any person who happens to be doing the Toro Toro thing on a nice Saturday afternoon. People must do that all the time. But you still need binoculars to keep an eye on us." He pulled out Howard's pair from the sack, and lifted his own pair off his neck. Which pair do you want?"

"The big black ones go with my outfit," he said, looking over at Howard for validation. Clearly he preferred the opera glasses. "But the little ones are more. . . discreet. Those look like mother of pearl."

"They are," said Howard.

"I thought so." He paused. "You know, the alligator on my shirt is white, so they kinda coordinate. . . ."

"It's a nice contrast with all the black," said Howard.

"I really like the mother of pearl. What do you think, Mike?"

Mike had not been expecting the conversation to turn in this manner. "I'll just leave both of them with you," he said. "You can switch off. Whatever."

"Cool. Thanks," said Stinky, nodding appreciatively. He looked over at Howard, who was also nodding and gave him the thumbs up. "You sure you don't mind, Mike?" asked Stinky.

"Fine," Mike said curtly, then, catching himself, added, "You'll have a back-up pair. Details like this can sometimes be very important."

A few minutes later, Stinky was sitting in front of the fountain, both pairs of vision enhancers around his neck, pretending to read his *Haftorah* pamphlet. Mike, who was leaving nothing to chance, had positioned him in that exact spot. Laying the pamphlet on the grass beside him, Stinky casually selected the mother of pearl opera glasses and looked up at the trees around him as if he were a bird-watcher. Most everything was a green blur, but he didn't bother focusing until he had lowered his gaze to the door stoop of the Huntley house. Or in the rough vicinity.

Howard and Mike, standing stiffly on the threshold, flashed in and out of his vision. Stinky tried to hold his hands steady, but the slightest movement sent his buddies careening from view, although he did manage to momentarily spot the Hershey bar box in Howard's hand. Swirling his head around methodically, Stinky tried to get his visual bearings. Eventually he gave up, assuming the large pair would be even more unwieldy. With his naked eye, Stinky watched Mike's arm reaching out for the doorbell. Contact was imminent. He quickly picked up his pamphlet and held it in front of his face so he could look right over the top. Now he could see the backs of both boys, the box of chocolate hidden from view. Not knowing how long the stakeout might last, Stinky regretted not having had the foresight to grab another one of the bars. With almonds.

Mike and Howard had their faces frozen in a smile when the door opened, revealing the younger of the Huntley daughters. She recognized Howard immediately, though pretended she didn't. Howard was holding the Hershey bars in front of his chest, like a ring bearer. He was more than tongue-tied, he was stricken. The girl clearly had her interest piqued, but was more capable of keeping a lid on her emotions as she pursued her own initiatives. She wore Bermuda shorts and a white blouse, translucent enough for Howard to make out the outlines of her bra.

"Yes?" she asked, since neither boy appeared equipped to begin speaking. "I've got it, Juanita," she said loudly over her shoulder, evidently to a maid who was out of view somewhere in the expansive house.

"Hello, Ma'am," began Mike, as he had rehearsed the night before at home. "We're volunteers for the Junior American Cancer Society. . . " here he indicated his badge with a slight drop of his head, "and we're raising money to help cure this deadly and crippling disease by selling these here Hershey bars."

He nudged Howard, who silently displayed the product to better advantage by extending his arms forward a few inches.

Mike continued. "For only ten cents per bar. A small price to pay to cure such a deadly and crippling disease."

The girl hesitated. The issue was not whether or not to buy, but rather deciding on the best course of action in approaching a boy she found interesting, the quiet one with the chocolates. Of course, she had already decided to outwardly concentrate most of her attentions on the speaker, precisely for that reason.

The spokesman, meanwhile, misinterpreting her silence, felt compelled to continue the sales pitch.

"Perhaps your mother or father would be interested in curing this deadly and crippling disease—"

"My father's working today and my mom's at the club with her bridge group," she interrupted.

"I see," said Mike. "In that case, maybe we can come back some other—"

"And my parents give to a lot of charities. My father's a doctor, so—"

This time it was Mike who interrupted, as the conversational pattern seemed not to allow anyone to complete a sentence.

"—then he must know first hand how deadly and crippling—"

"—so I'm sure he gives at the office."

"Uh, what kind of doctor is he?" Mike asked, segueing into a more purposeful direction of conversation.

"He's a psychiatrist," said the girl.

Mike acted surprised. "Very interesting," he said, "like Freud."

"You're both wearing black," the girl observed.

"Right," said Mike. "The black is to symbolize, you know, death. . . umm, you know, mourning. We're in symbolic mourning, like Johnny Cash. For all those crippled people who die and. . . but if our volunteers sell enough Hershey bars, we won't need to wear black anymore. We can even wear white, or any other color, for that matter. Stripes, plaid, paisley, madras. . . ."

"And you won't need to sell Hershey bars anymore, anyway," said the girl.

"Exactly," said Mike. "But you'll still be able to buy them in stores, though . . . the Hershey bars, I mean."

"Well," she said, "I suppose I could buy a couple of bars for myself."

"Great. They'll be good for you. I mean, it doesn't look like you have a problem with zits or anything."

She half-smiled, uncertain how to respond to the backhanded compliment.

"I'll be right back with the money," she said.

She scurried away, but not without first pointedly flashing a smile at Howard, whose own frozen smile had devolved into an expressionless slack-jawed look. After traversing the corridor, she headed up a staircase, presumably to her bedroom. Mike peered into the hall through the door and took in as much as he could, which wasn't very much.

"Gee," Howard finally said, "that last comment, about the zits. . . ."

Mike was peeved at himself, too, but directed his irritation at Howard.

"Well, feel free to jump in at any time and help out. She probably thinks you're some kind of a mute."

"She's really cute," said Howard.

"So is Honey Ryder in 'Dr. No.' And you have no idea how much trouble she ended up being."

The boys soon heard footsteps coming down the stairs, and resettled into their stiff, business-like demeanor. When she faced them again from inside the doorway, it was as if they had not moved a muscle in the interim.

She handed Mike three dimes.

"Three bars, please," she said.

Howard again held his arms out into a petrified, fully extended position.

"With or without almonds" Howard said, clearing his throat in mid sentence.

"I'll take two with almonds, and the third one plain," she said, sifting through the box. She found the combination quickly. Howard's eyes met hers during the maneuvering, but when she spoke again, she still addressed Mike.

"So, are you guys from around here? Where do you go to school?"

Mike, appropriately guarded, answered her with his own question. "You don't go to Indian Hills, do you?"

"No," she said, "I'm at Barstow."

Howard and Mike exchanged glances without moving their heads toward one another. Obviously.

"Do you know many people at Indian Hills?" he continued his line of questioning.

"Not really," she said.

That was a good answer, the correct answer. "We go to Indian Hills, then." Mike said, feeling reasonably safe. "Well, we'd better be going. . . ."

"Wait a sec," the girl said. "There's a Young Life meeting here next Saturday night. Would you like to come? It's a really friendly group. And you might have something in common with some of the people. Some of them do volunteer church work."

"Thanks, anyway," said Mike, "but my family's going fishing in the Ozarks next weekend. The. . . uh. . . Cancer Society is giving me time off. They have to—Child Labor Laws, you know. I'm not allowed to work every weekend. So I'm going fishing at the Lake of the Ozarks."

"I'll come," said Howard, out of nowhere, startled by the sound of his own voice, not to mention its content.

"I was just going to suggest that," said Mike, smiling broadly.

"Great," said he girl, addressing Howard directly for the first time. "I'll see you on Saturday night, then. About seven."

"Great," said Howard.

"See ya," said Mike, as both boys turned and started to leave.

"Wait!" said the girl. "I don't even know your names! I'm Melissa Huntley."

"The name's Bond," said Mike, "Jimmy Bond."

"Nice meeting you, Jimmy."

110

Howard started with "And I'm—" pausing just long enough for Mike to jump in.

"And this is my friend Mike. Mike Hunsacker," Mike said.

"Nice meeting you too, Mike," said Melissa. "I'll see you on Saturday, then."

Mike and Howard walked back toward the base camp, looking back over their shoulders to make sure the door was closed and they weren't being watched. They saw Stinky by the fountain, the green pamphlet held awkwardly in front of his face. They composed themselves enough to walk at a slow pace, though they wanted to burst into a run out of excitement and relief.

"I can't believe you gave her your name for me!" said Howard.

"You couldn't use your real name!"

"I know that, I'm not a moron! I would have thought of something!"

"It sort of gives things away if the question is 'What's your name?' and you have to ask for more time. So now you're Mike Hunsacker. Don't let the family down. And by the way," he added, "You call those tits?"

"There's something there," said Howard defensively. "And she's still growing."

They arrived at the fountain, where Stinky was anxiously awaiting a report.

"You guys took forever. I was getting worried. Did you learn anything?"

"You can put your book down now," said Howard.

"Better than that," answered Mike. "Howie's going undercover on Saturday night. Inside the house!"

"Wow!" said Stinky.

"And that's the other thing," Howard said. "Besides the name business. Why am I going alone? How come you chickened out on me?"

"I didn't chicken out!" Mike said. "My Dad and I really are going fishing! And my Mom and sisters are coming along to spend the weekend at Tan-Tara."

"Great," said Howard, "I'm having to go solo, without any backup."

"Relax," said Mike. "We have a week to make preparations. You'll be ready for anything. We'll cover all possible contingencies. Once you're inside—I'll bet anything Huntley has an office, and I bet he has files. There's always files."

"I'm going to steal his files?"

"If you have to," said Mike. "Any evidence you can get your hands on. That's the whole point, isn't it? Are you going to back out now?"

Howard hesitated. "No," he said. "Of course not," he added, more to convince himself than Mike.

Stinky jumped in. "What exactly's going on Saturday night? A party?"

"A Young Life meeting," said Mike.

"Howie's going to a Young Life meeting?" Stinky was incredulous.

"What's Young Life, anyway?" Howard asked.

"Just a youth group," said Mike.

"It's a CHRISTIAN youth group!" Stinky had put his hands on his head and was literally grabbing his own hair for emphasis. "It's youth for Jesus, Howie! They may even have you kneel! That's a sin!"

"No it isn't," said Howard.

"Yes it is," said Stinky. "My mom told me it's a sin to go into a Catholic church. Because they kneel. Jews don't kneel, Howie! Jews don't kneel!"

Stinky was really worked up, and Mike couldn't get why.

"I didn't know that," he said. "I knew Jews don't hunt."

"Well, they don't kneel! That's why it's worse for a Jew to marry a Catholic than a Presbyterian. It all has to do with the kneeling! That's the only difference—"

"I won't kneel," Howard said emphatically, suddenly needing to swallow.

"They may make you!" shouted Stinky, on the verge of hysterics. "What are you going to do? Say you can't kneel and blow your cover?"

"Mike?" Howard looked over at him, hoping he would have an answer.

"I don't even think they really kneel at Young Life meetings. I've never gone to one myself, personally. It's not only Catholic, though. They just sing and stuff and maybe do a little praying."

"That's a sin, too," shrieked Stinky, "I'm sure of it!"

"But YOU pray," Mike said to Stinky.

"It's not the same thing!" Stinky was now exasperated. "Howard! Explain it to him!"

"Wait," said Howard calmly, pushing his hands down as if he were playing a series of piano chords. "I'll be undercover, so it's deceit. I'm sure the Torah has an exception for that. Like drinking water on Yom Kippur so you can take a pill." The thought reminded him that he needed to swallow again, which he did with some difficulty.

"Sure," Stinky said sarcastically. "Sure," he said again, not only increasing the sarcasm, but spreading the word over two syllables.

"Stay at the back and lie low," said Mike. And just move your lips like you know the words to the songs. You can fake it."

"A SIN," said Stinky adamantly.

Howard had reached his limit, and no longer felt the need to restrain himself to spare Stinky's feelings. "Stinky," he said, "You ate pork rinds in *shul*. Talk about a sin!" He swallowed.

"That's breaking a dietary law, Howie. That's not nearly as big a deal as KNEELING! YOU eat pork all the time!"

"At home, but not at the SYNAGOGUE!" Howard was getting defensive, and swallowing was increasingly becoming a problem. In fact, he couldn't disguise the grimaces that came with each momentary panic.

"And it wasn't even in the main sanctuary," continued Stinky, nearly trembling with animation. "It was in the BASEMENT!"

Mike, having trouble tracking the argument, was becoming exasperated himself.

"You won't need to kneel, already!" he said, raising his voice for the first time.

"I won't need to kneel," said Howard softly, with faked assuredness.

Stinky, trumped, shook his head. "It's a sin," he muttered under his breath.

Chapter Nine

Preparation began in earnest the next day during a Sunday matinee of "Dr. No" at the Brookside Theater. Mike had ridden his bike over to the Block's house after church, and Jeanette had obligingly driven the boys to the theater. The movie request was a timely one, since additional office business was scheduled at the Block residence that very afternoon, and Jeanette preferred that Howard wasn't around. She didn't want her son upset by things he couldn't understand; or more accurately, she didn't want to have to worry about him being upset. Jeanette wanted to focus her worrying on Jack.

"You say you've already seen this one?" Jeanette asked Mike, glancing at the marquee as the boys were about to get out of the car.

"Five times," bragged Mike.

"And your mother thought it was alright for kids?"

"A couple of times we saw it as a family," lied Mike. "My mother loved it."

"It must be a good movie, then," said Jeanette.

"It's more than good," said Mike, glancing pointedly at Howard. "It's essential."

Jeanette, preoccupied, did not register Mike's obtuse comment.

The essential lesson of the movie was obvious and conveniently situated near the beginning of the film. Howard and Mike were seated in the first row, slouched in their seats with the screen towering over them like a diorama. Transfixed on the projected image, they were eating popcorn and drinking Cokes. Right before their eyes, Strandway's secretary was shot through the window and then the three Jamaicans broke into the office to steal the "Dr. No" and "Crab Island" dossiers. At this juncture, Mike knocked Howard's thigh with his own; the force was enough to jolt some of Howard's popcorn from the box.

On the screen, resting upon the desk, were the black files.

"See," whispered Mike, "there's always a file. Always."

Lesson complete, the boys could enjoy the rest of the movie without the further pressures of didacticism. The payoff for the lesson learned, of course, was when Ursula Andress, as Honey Rider, emerged from the ocean in her bikini.

"Now, *those* are tits," Mike whispered.

***

Even Mike Hunsacker was unaware of how prescient his observation about files had been. At that exact moment, Martin Oliver and two other suited associates from his law firm were sitting around the coffee table in the Block den. Martin had pulled a file from his briefcase. One of the associates was fiddling with a full-sized tape recorder that had been set up on the table. Jeanette had returned from her chauffeuring duties well in advance and was lurking, again under the guise of serving coffee.

Martin opened the file and looked at the top page intently, as if he could garner wisdom from the mere sight of the typewritten words, which he couldn't.

"Jack, it's still not too late to discuss settling."

"How many times do I have to tell you 'no'?" said Jack.

"You pay me to give you advice, Jack. I'm your lawyer."

"I'm telling you for the last time. I'm not settling. Now, goddamit, stop *haking me a chainik*. Let's get this over with."

Martin, expecting nothing different and knowing better than to push harder, nodded in resignation, then nodded to each of his associates, signaling the go-ahead.

Jeanette had crept over to the coffee table like a Green Beret on patrol behind enemy lines, and was holding out the pot.

"More cof—" she began, but Jack immediately held up his palm emphatically to silence her. Without even setting down the coffee pot, she walked backwards, retracing her steps as unobtrusively as she was able, and again took up her post beside the bar. One of Martin's Oliver's minions leaned over to turn on the tape recorder. The click of the contiguous "start" and "record" buttons was substantial, leaving no doubt that the designated electronic functioning was underway. The tape began winding.

"Today is May 18, 1963," Martin began, bending over to be nearer to the microphone. "We are here to take the deposition of Jack Block, MD, in the matter of. . . ."

Martin had closed the manila folder as soon as he began speaking but held the file in his lap. Most of the details he knew by heart, at least the pertinent ones, but the papers—his legal security blanket—would remain near at hand in case of need.

Martin Oliver was not alone in his compulsion to keep his file nearby. Lounging comfortably in his private study a few blocks away in the ritzier section of Mission Hills, Chadwick Huntley felt much the same way about another file—yes, there was always a file—Mike's insight holding true in this particular case beyond even his own wildest expectations. The latter file was a thick one, also manila backed, but battered and dog-eared and fraying on the overly stretched spine.

This file—in common medical parlance known as a chart—was more complicated than Martin's, being seem-ingly a disorganized affair nearly bursting with order sheets; progress notes from physicians, consultants, and social work-ers; laboratory and radiology results; EKG rhythm strips; and anything else relevant to a person's well-being or lack of such. Separate hospital admissions were bundled together with separating tabs, but the arrangement of the individual sections would appear random to all but those professionally acquainted with the system.

The files in the possession of both men were interlinked not by purpose or locale, but by content. Specifically, both files shared the names of Chadwick Huntley and Hannah Stringer, to a greater or lesser degree. The extensive medical one, which was normally kept in the Department of Medical Records at Menorah Hospital, had been borrowed—Chadwick would have bristled at the use of the term "pil-fered" even though he had neglected to sign it out—for an indefinite period of time. In short, Chadwick Huntley was in sole possession of the medical history of Hannah Stringer.

Chadwick flipped through the thick file with no partic-ular purpose in mind. Then, gripping the heft of the chart in his left hand, he paused to take a healthy drink from his tumbler of iced whiskey with his right, emitting a satisfying "ahhh" after the final gulp. Setting down his glass, he stood up beside his desk and slid over a foot-high pile of psychiatric medical journals from the corner. He planted Hannah's chart neatly in that corner spot, then buried it under the stack of journals. He patted the edges to line up the spines.

Sitting back down, he refilled his tumbler from the half-empty bottle of Johnny Walker Black that was conveniently at hand, his current "office" bottle, as distinguished from the kitchen and wet bar supplies. Chadwick swirled the ice around in the liquid and considered, staring at the tumbler in his hand.

He needed more ice.

***

The following Tuesday, Howard, Mike and Stinky again sat at their customary cafeteria lunch table, scheming. Surprisingly, the three of them now actually looked forward to Tuesdays and Thursday, because—despite the negative associations—gym class was the only period that all three of them shared. Thus, outside of lunch, free moments before and after flag football afforded them opportunities for further scheming, and scheming modifications. Long chains of conversation were divided into snippets, but proceeded down their intended course as if without interruption.

The subsequent phase of the operation had Howard undercover at Melissa Huntley's Young Life Meeting in only four days time. The goal of the mission was to gather information from the actual files. The use of a miniature spy camera was discussed and soon eliminated, as none had access to one, though Howard did offer the use of his Polaroid.

"I'm not sure the resolution is good enough," said Mike. "And, it would take forever. Even worse, each film pack has only twelve pictures, and there may be hundreds of pages of documents!"

Howard and Stinky were at an impasse, but Mike had long known the only viable solution and was merely bringing the others up to speed by logically eliminating the other possibilities.

"There's no alternative but to steal the files, smuggle them out," Mike said.

"This is getting risky," said Stinky.

"Not for you," said Howard irritably. "I'm the one going in!"

Mike looked at Stinky closely. "So we've eliminated the possibility of you going in with Howie. . . ."

"I'm still grounded," said Stinky. "Not to mention—I'm just not comfortable with that whole kneeling thing."

Mike, not convinced that Stinky actually represented an asset in an undercover operation, was not disappointed. But out of courtesy he felt obliged to extend the offer.

"Okay, then," he said. "Let's go over the supply list."

Howard readied his pen and memo pad.

"Let me do it," said Stinky, reaching for the pad. "I want to help."

Howard handed them over.

"Soft-soled shoes," said Mike.

"I'll wear my tennis shoes," said Howard.

Stinky hurriedly scribbled in the pad.

"Check," he said.

"They need to be black,"

"I'll take care of it."

"Black. Got it. Check," said Stinky.

"Small flashlight."

"Got plenty of those," said Howard.

"Those cool disposable ones that your Dad keeps in the fridge?" asked Stinky. "I wouldn't mind having one."

"Sure."

"Let me write that down," said Stinky, scribbling away. "And I'll add the reminder here for you to bring one for me."

"I'll bring you a couple," offered Howard, "We have bunches of them."

"Thanks, Howie."

Mike rolled his eyes, looked at the cafeteria wall clock, then cleared his throat, anxious to get back on task before lunch ended. He wanted a couple of those flashlights for himself, but this wasn't the time or place to ask. They needed to move down the list.

"Anything in your billfold with your name on it?"

"Sure. My name and address," said Howard. "Just in case I lose it."

"No ID," said Mike. "Leave your billfold at home."

"Gotcha," said Howard.

"Billfold at home," Stinky spoke as he wrote. "Check."

"Okay," said Mike, "we need something to carry any evidence."

"How about this?" Stinky held up his green book bag. He reached in to remove a schoolbook and a couple of spiral notebooks and handed it to Mike for examination.

"Perfect," Mike said, flipping it over in his hands, and checking its heft by lifting it up and down in his hand. "We'll put a book in it. A bible. Of course. A bible. Perfect."

"I've got a bible," said Howard.

"Bible. Check," said Stinky.

"The New Testament?" asked Mike.

"The Five Books of Moses," said Howard.

"That won't do at a Young Life Meeting. You'll need the both the Old and New Testaments. I'll lend you mine."

"The New Testament?" asked Stinky. "In my book bag?"

"Stinky. . . " Howard warned.

"I'm just not sure how I feel about that, I mean, the NEW Testament. . . "

Howard promptly grabbed the book bag from Mike and reached into the bottom of the bag, pulling out an empty pork rinds wrapper. He gave it to Stinky and looked at him, eyes narrowing.

"Think of it just as a prop, not a real bible, okay?"

Stinky, adequately chastised, nodded and began writing again in the pad.

"Prop bible. Check."

"That's just about it, I think," said Mike.

"Do you want me to read you back the list?" asked Stinky.

"I don't think that will be necessary," said Mike. "But, wait!"

Both Howard and Stinky were startled. Gaining his composure, Stinky readied himself to write.

"Kneepads," said Mike. "We'll need basketball kneepads, just in case you have to kneel, Howie, for a really, really long time. Stinky, do you have a pair?"

"CHRIST!" said Stinky.

Howard and Mike laughed.

"He's just joking, Stinky," said Howard. "He's just joking."

"Christ," Stinky repeated, but softly.

***

Later, waiting outside for flag football sides to be chosen, they continued their conferencing. The weather had turned cool again and was threatening rain, but Mr. Saunders had refused all entreaties for an indoor activity. Even Chris and Ryan had been pushing for dodge ball in the gym. Howard was not disappointed with the executive decision, as he would rather risk hypothermia than play dodge ball.

"Okay," said Mike, continuing from where they left off at lunch, "how are you going to get there?"

"I haven't thought about that," said Howard. "But I'm sure my Mom could drive me and then pick me up afterwards."

"Sure thing," said Stinky. "'Mom, will you drive me over to the house of Dad's mortal enemy for a Young Life Meeting?' She'll have a cow."

"He's right," said Mike. "Too risky."

"Well, then," Howard said, "Maybe I could ride my bike."

"Right," said Mike.

Stinky was shaking his head in disbelief, pushed beyond sarcasm.

"No way. Your Mom isn't going to let you ride your bike at night, Howie! Not in a million years!"

"Okay, I've got it," said Mike. "You'll ride your bike to my house before dark to spend the night."

"But you and your whole family will be in the Ozarks," Howard protested.

"Does your mom know that?" Mike asked.

Mike wasn't expecting an answer. Howard immediately knew the implications, and was creeped out at the thought of it. He would spend the night all by himself at the Hunsacker house?

"It's settled, then," said Mike, interpreting Howard's stunned silence as tacit agreement.

The three contemplated the plan silently, almost trance-like, until the spell was rudely broken by Chris Beamon beckoning Mike with the all-too-familiar "Old Yeller shorts!"

Lost in thought, Mike didn't respond the first time.

"Hey you!" Chris repeated, "Old Yeller shorts! We're stuck with you!"

Mike turned to his buddies.

"This is a real nuisance, and he's a pain in the ass." Then turning back to Chris, he yelled, "I'm not deaf! And the name's Hunsacker!" Under his breath, not to be heard by anyone but himself, he added "asshole."

During a pass play, Howard was assigned defense in the backfield, and Mike and Stinky shared positions on the offensive line. On the snap, a defender pushed straight between Mike and Stinky and rushed quarterback Chris on his throw. Howard found the ball looping in the air toward him, and surprising himself, caught it and ran. Stinky and Mike both collapsed to the ground in front of their teammates, tripping three of them and enabling Howard to score a touchdown.

Howard, along with Stinky and Mike, celebrated in the end zone, to the bafflement and irritation of both team captains.

Chapter Ten

Mike had reminded Howard that in missions such as theirs, secret agents always needed to be prepared for the unexpected. Still, Howard was completely befuddled when informed by his mother on Thursday morning that instead of going to school, he had a 10 o'clock appointment with the radiologist Dr. Weiner. After numerous protestations, increasing in intensity and desperation, Howard's ultimate entreaty, accompanied by tears, was that "he couldn't possibly miss gym class," a ridiculous notion to Jeanette. Surely Howard wouldn't want to get behind in Math or Social Studies—and she would drive by the school to pick up any assignments and make-up work—but gym? With that *goyishe kopf* Saunders with the big scar on his forehead? When she actually laughed, Howard knew that the argument was lost, the turn of events catastrophic. He, along with Mike and Stinky, had planned to use gym class to review final preparations for "Operation No Kneeling"—every mission had a Code Name, according to Mike—which was a mere two days away.

Howard quickly regained his perspective when Jeannette, trying to soothe his agitation, justified the need for the appointment.

"Your father and I just want to make sure everything is okay so you can spend the night with Mike Hunsacker on Saturday night. You wouldn't want him to catch anything, would you, Howard?"

Howard was successfully soothed. Things could have been much worse—at least Saturday's plans could proceed as scheduled, the ultimate disaster had been averted.

"And you should be grateful that when your father spoke with him this morning, Dr. Weiner had a cancellation," she added.

Howard realized that he had not been as adept at hiding his persisting swallowing difficulties from his parents as he had thought. His mother's more recent attentive gazing at him, which he mistook as a rising tide of her adoration, was thus explained. Still, his father—and he was the only one in the family with the medical degree, after all—had expressed no particular concerns, so undoubtedly Jeanette had been the driving force behind diagnostic testing. This was, in fact, the case, as Jack had decided that the risk of exposing his son to the ionizing radiation of a barium swallow was well worth the benefit of getting Jeanette off his back, and had been completely forthright with Henry Weiner on that point when they spoke over breakfast in the hospital cafeteria.

The wait in Dr. Weiner's small reception room was brief, and Howard soon found himself sitting on a stool, shirtless, in a darkened fluoroscopy suite in front of the unwieldy ra-diographic machine that looked less medical and more like something found in a manufacturing plant. He had been po-sitioned to Dr. Weiner's satisfaction, the cold metal surface pressed against his chest and a paper cup filled with a thick white liquid in his hand. Dr. Weiner, a large man wearing a green lead apron and large red goggles, was on the other side, a maniacal science fiction character at the controls.

"Now, take a mouthful and hold it until I tell you to swallow. Just hold it in your mouth and don't swallow 'till I tell you to swallow."

Howard lifted the cup from his left hand to his mouth as best he could, head turned sideward, sandwiched by the rectangular apparatus pressed ever more firmly against his cheek and chest by the radiologist. He cautiously sucked in some of the thick chalky paste.

"More, more. Be a *chazer*," cajoled Dr. Weiner.

The barium mixture was dripping down his chin but Howard couldn't use his other hand to wipe since it was pinned at his side. He kept filling his mouth sip by sip until his cheeks puffed out.

Click, followed by humming. The green fluoroscopic beam seemed to spring from his chest, an alien beacon signal weakly slicing the darkness.

"Okay, now. . . SWALLOW!"

At the moment, easier said than done.

"Go ahead. . . you can swallow now!" Harold Weiner was determined not to give Jack's son any more radiation exposure than was absolutely necessary. Why zap the kid because Jeanette Block was an over-anxious mother?

Howard had heard him the first time and was still working on it. He had tilted his neck back and tightened. Then he had jutted his neck forward, pursing his lips together and squinting. But nothing would go down. And until things would go down, he couldn't take a breath.

Hungry for air, Howard panicked.

His neck and face were hot and tingly, and he was drenched with sweat. He had to run, get out of there, but he was trapped! He couldn't breathe!

The panic lasted a second or two at most, but felt like an eternity. Finally the release came and the barium rushed down his throat as if a trap door had suddenly opened. The external humming yielded to a door slam, a jarring mechanical shifting of film plates, and the green tinge faded into the darkness.

"Excellent, Howard." Dr. Weiner stood up from his stool to make eye contact with the boy as best he could in the darkness. The radiologist smiled, looking bug-like in his red goggles, a Jewish fighter pilot on a night mission. He released a latch, partially easing the pressure on Howard's chest.

"Now you're going to turn your head to the other side, I'll look some more, and then we'll be done. Everything looks fine, Howard, perfectly normal."

"But I . . . I don't have. . . the stuff's all gone, I drank it all." He could barely get the words out, since he was panting. And he was suddenly very nauseated.

Dr. Weiner laughed. "Oh, there's more where that came from! Let me fill 'er up!" He took Howard's cup and walked over to a side counter. There was a pitcherful of the crap, and Weiner was not stingy with it.

"You know, your father and I used to play together in Westport when I was just about your age. I remember getting candy from your grandfather's store. Your father's the best doctor in the world, you know that? There's nobody like your father. You gonna be one like him when you grow up, right? "

"Sure," said Howard, stock answer, this time complicated by the chalk sediment thickening his tongue, although his breathing had just about returned to normal.

Dr. Weiner, weighted down by his lead apron, waddled back to Howard with the full cup. He positioned Howard's head to the other side, placed the cup in the boy's right hand, then again squeezed his chest against the cold metal. Positioning complete, he shifted his stool and squirmed into working position.

"And not too long until the big day, huh? When's the big day?"

"June 22nd."

"Bet you're excited, huh?"

"Sure." Since Howard was known as a top student and an obedient, well-behaved boy, his muted responses were usually interpreted as shyness, when in fact they reflected ambivalence.

"Your father's really proud. But I don't have to tell you that! By the way, how's your *Haftorah* coming? Got it memorized yet?" The radiologist pressed harder.

"Not completely," Howard grunted, feeling like his ribs were about to crack. He hadn't thought of the language lab and Cantor Birenboim for at least a few hours, and didn't want to be reminded. Besides, he was distracted by more urgent thoughts. The saliva had been building up and Howard needed to swallow. A small test constriction was unsuccessful. It wasn't going to be easier with the mortar mix in his mouth. Howard's face flushed as he futilely worked his tongue.

"Okay, take a mouthful, a BIG mouthful."

Howard started sipping, but forgot to first take a deep breath. Already, he needed air.

Click, followed by humming. Howard Block again emitted an aura of green. Perhaps the alien forces were wondering why the young earthling couldn't swallow.

"Swallow, Bar Mitzvah boy, " said Dr. Weiner. "SWALLOW!"

***

A short time later, after Howard had put his shirt back on and rinsed out his mouth, Henry Weiner led the boy out to the reception room, where Jeanette was anxiously waiting.

"He's absolutely fine," Dr. Weiner told her, patting Howard on the shoulder in a patronizing way, as if his own medical skills had been responsible for such a good digestive showing. He was still wearing his lead apron, which lent credence.

"Oh, I'm so relieved, Henry," gushed Jeanette, "you have no idea how grateful I am—"

Weiner waved her off with a wave of one of his large arms. "My pleasure," he said.

Jeanette's smile transformed into a look of neutrality and then slid into a one of concern. Her thinking had proceeded to the next logical step.

"But if everything's alright," she began, "why is he—"

Weiner waved her silent again. He had other patients, a full schedule, and didn't want to fall behind. He had not actually had a cancellation—only feigned one—but had squeezed Howard in as a favor, since he would do anything for Jack Block. Jeanette Block could be a supreme *nudnik*, even worse than his own wife Rose, and the radiologist had prepared his exit strategy. Admittedly, the explanation was not of his own devising but had been suggested to him by Jack at breakfast.

"When you're done," Jack had advised him, "tell her it's nothing and has been going around."

130

And so Dr. Weiner did, and so it worked.

"Thank God," said Jeanette.

***

"Can't anyone take a crap in peace, anymore?" said Jack, straining out some gas. Howard had already jumped up on the counter in their customary meeting place. Jack had tired of the dinner conversation, which had been monopolized by Jeanette's play-by-play of the earlier appointment with Henry Weiner—she tended to blather more when she was relieved of her anxiety than when she was burdened by it, for some reason—and he had made a concerted effort to get away. Even the most patient of men had his limits. Although his usual custom was to read in his study before later bathroom obligations, Jeanette felt no compunctions about interrupting him there, and so he had headed to the bathroom right after dinner. More accurately, he had cut dinner short, passing on dessert and confessing that he had somewhat of an unsettled stomach, which was a lie. He intended to stay in the bathroom as long as he could, until his cheeks became numb from the prolonged weighted contact with the toilet seat. He would squeeze out every last bit of flatulence, if he had to, but he was staying put for the foreseeable future.

"Did you think I needed the barium swallow?" asked Howard.

"Well, I didn't think it would hurt," his father answered, "and your mother was concerned."

"And you're not?"

"I think you're having trouble swallowing, and I think it will pass. How's your *Haftorah* coming?"

"Okay, I guess."

"Stinky still grounded?"

"For sure."

"I wonder if those fried pork rinds were worth it."

"They're pretty good," said Howard, chuckling.

"I know," said Jack.

Howard paused and took a swallow. Jack looked at him closely.

"What?" he prompted.

"Is it a sin to kneel?" Howard asked.

"A sin? Is this something you learned in *heder*? Bettinger again?"

"No, no," said Howard. "I just heard somewhere that Jews don't kneel." He forced another swallow, unsuccessfully attempting to slip it past his father's notice.

Jack considered the question before speaking.

"Well," he said, "we don't kneel in our services, you know that. It's just not the custom. Different faiths have different customs."

"Good," said Howard, relief in his voice. "I mean, that's what I was hoping you'd say."

Nonetheless, he found he needed to force the next swallow. Whatever good the barium exam had done in theory, the procedure hadn't been therapeutic. If anything, Howard felt like things were getting progressively worse, what with all the attention paid to it, the legitimacy of a medical test confirming its existence as something real.

"You know," said Jack, "I've been giving your dysphasia some thought, and I've come up with a theory of my own."

"My swallowing?" asked Howard, as if the subject had come up out of nowhere. Fixated now, and knowing that he was under intense scrutiny, he let the saliva accumulate in his mouth.

Jack looked away, almost as if he knew that Howard wouldn't manage the next swallow if being watched. Howard swallowed.

"You know," Jack said, "your mother and I decided to belong to B'nai Jeshurun because of the family. It's almost orthodox by Kansas City standards, but to—let's say—a New Yorker, it would be considered conservative at best. But what you call it is beside the point. It's where your grandparents and most of the relatives go. But we don't practice a religious life style in our home. You know that."

Jack scrutinized his son before continuing.

"I think that maybe your eating pork at home and what Bettinger tells you at *heder* is giving you a conflict. And that conflict is confusing you, and it is manifesting itself in certain ways that are, you know, physical. So, let me give you some advice. Listen to your heart and feel righteousness in your own personal way. A custom is something less important. Whether you kneel or not. Whether you eat pork or not. Think about it, Howard. Maybe you'll find it easier to swallow. Will you think about that?"

Howard was stunned. He had emerged from a dungeon onto a vast open beach in the sunshine. Jack waited for a response, and when he was sure that none was forthcoming, he went on.

"You don't need to say anything to your mother; you know how much she worries. This is just between us *mensches*."

Howard still couldn't speak but managed a nod.

"I have a feeling your swallowing will get better now," Jack said.

"I do too," said Howard.

"So," continued Jack, "is everything else okay?"

"I'm fine, Dad."

"Good. Don't take all this *mishigas* too seriously."

The consultation was over. The best diagnostician in the entire world reached for some toilet paper.

Chapter Eleven

Howard stood in the doorway, Stinky's green book bag slung over his shoulder. Inside were Mike Hunsacker's copy of the King James Bible, the memo pad and pencil, three disposable penlights, and his toothbrush. He had decided to wear his specially modified shoes rather than drag around the extra pair in his bag. They were his formerly white low top Red Ball Jets which he had blackened out completely with a Magic Marker the night before. Replacing the white shoe-laces with a pair of black dress shoelaces that he found in his father's bureau drawer had saved him the need of inking the laces. He had hoped his mother wouldn't notice the shoes, and so far she hadn't, which he supposed was the reason Mike had insisted on him wearing black shoes to begin with. Mike really knew his espionage.

"I need to leave already, Mom," he said impatiently, "before it gets dark." He wondered if it would ever be possible for him just to say good-bye and walk out the door—an uncomplicated exit that happened all the time in the houses of normal people. He imagined it frequently, the sound of his voice saying "Good-bye," followed immediately by the sound of the closing door. This was something he could never recall having experienced, since there was always a scene and last minute checks, like the way his mother would go back into the kitchen several times to make sure the stove was off before she left the house herself.

"Don't forget to call tonight," said Jeanette.

"We're all going to the movies. Everybody. The entire Hunsacker family. And we won't get back 'till late. So I'll call you in the morning."

"But I have their phone number, right?"

"I left it on the kitchen counter. But no one will be home until late," he added with emphasis, "so there will be no point in calling, since no one will be home to answer it. No one."

"How late?" asked Jeanette.

"Pretty late," said Howard. "Really late."

"Just in case of an emergency, let me check and make sure the number's there." Jeanette scurried into the kitchen to confirm the piece of paper with the phone number had not disappeared, perhaps blown off the counter by a draft and stuck under the refrigerator. There it was, the small sheet from one of Jack's pharmaceutical company give-away note pads advertising *Diuril*. She checked that the number was legible and contained the appropriate number of digits before placing it back down on the counter. She set a nearby salt shaker on top so it couldn't be blown away. Then she got the blue box, and carried it back with her to the entryway.

Howard had already pulled a handful of change from his pocket.

"How much do you need?" he asked.

"Thirteen cents," Jeanette said.

He handed her the correct change and she placed the coins through the slot. "Oh!" blurted Jeanette, mid-deposit. "A snack!"

"I don't need—"

"I'll get something for you. . . " Before scurrying back to the kitchen, she absent-mindedly thrust the blue box into his hands. "Hold this—" and she was gone.

"It's not safe for me to ride my bike when it gets dark," Howard shouted to the kitchen. "You wouldn't want me riding my bike in the. . . ."

Already he could hear the haphazard opening and closing of kitchen cabinets—each shutting with its unique timbre, like a set of drums—so he didn't waste his breath finishing the sentence. He looked at the blue box in his hands and felt its weight. Considering, he took a deep breath and reached into his pockets for the remainder of his change. A dollar and thirty-seven cents. Methodically, he placed each coin through the slot until none were left. He told himself that he wasn't superstitious and giving to charity was unlikely to protect him during the night ahead of him. But what would be the point of wearing soft-soled shoes if the jingling of coins in his pocket could be heard a mile away? Somehow, though, the absence of money in his pocket made him feel naked and vulnerable. Not even a dime for a phone call.

He waited by the front door, shifting his weight from foot to foot, and checked his watch.

Jeanette returned to the entryway, holding a small box of Sun Maid raisins. The box was still dripping.

Howard took the box with his thumb and index finger, the way he might hold a bug.

"Thanks, Mom," he said, leaning forward to kiss her on the cheek. Prompted by her furrowed brow and that characteristic look of worry, he added the obligatory, "Don't worry, I'll be careful."

She smiled with resignation, nodding her head, as if she were sending him back to a dangerous overseas military mission.

"What in the world did you do to your shoes?" she asked, just then noticing his inked-over Red Ball Jets.

"It's a fad," explained Howard. "All the kids are doing it."

This was his prepared answer, and although he knew where it would lead, he could come up with nothing better.

"Well," said Jeanette, cued into one of her own prepared speeches, "if all the kids were to go out and rob a bank—"

"The kids at *heder*," he quickly qualified, wondering why this flash of insight had not occurred to him earlier. "You know, like on the High Holidays, when they wear the tennis shoes since they can't wear leather. . . you know how stupid the white tennis shoes look with suits. . . so some of the kids thought that this would be a good solution." Howard stopped to catch his breath.

"In that case," said Jeanette, "I suppose it's okay. Maybe the Jews will be trendsetters for a change."

This time it was she who leaned forward to kiss him on the cheek.

"Don't worry, I'll be careful," he repeated, using exactly the same intonation as before, just the way Cantor Birenboim repeated the short phrases of his *Haftorah* on the tapes in the Bar Mitzvah language lab.

"Howard, be careful," said Jeanette.

***

The Schwinn was resting on its kickstand in the driveway at the side of the house. Howard tossed the soggy box of raisins into the outside garbage can before mounting and heading off, the green book bag slung over his left shoulder by the strap. With plenty of time to kill, he contemplated stopping by the Hunsacker house to check out the evening's accommodations ahead of time. He decided against this, considering that some nosey neighbor might see him entering with the key Mike had left under the door mat and get suspicious, possibly even call the police. Instead, Howard took a meandering ride through Old Mission Hills, trying to calm himself into the proper state of mind for the daunting task ahead.

This wasn't to say he avoided Wenonga Road and the Huntley residence, which he rode by multiple times, checking out the gradual but steady accumulation of cars in the driveway and along the street, but Mike had cautioned him about showing up too soon. The earlier he arrived, the longer he would have to fake being Christian and the greater the chances of him revealing his total ignorance of all things gentile, at least as far as church and religious matters went. His background research had been confined to reading and rereading the "Christianity" section from his World Book Encyclopedia, which prepared him to finesse things only so far. Awkward questions could be avoided if he entered late, mingled with the existing crowd, and steered clear of one-on-one conversations.

"Keep a low profile and blend in with the crowd," Mike had coached him.

He held out until 7:15 p.m.; the rate and intensity of arrivals had slowed down considerably, although there were still some stragglers being dropped off in front of the house by their parents. Dusk was creeping into night, and the moon hid behind a cotton wad of clouds. The Huntley house appeared to be lit in every room, and sounds from within indicated that it was bustling with youthful activity. Passing the brick colonial one final time, he dismounted at the familiar nearby green space, hid his bike behind the tall hedge, and stealthily made his way across the street in the shadows. He paused a house away and watched as a car dropped off another late arrival, a pre-teen girl in a party dress. Howard then hustled to the walkway himself, walking a few paces behind the girl, as if he, too, had been dropped off by a parent.

Melissa was holding the door open for the girl in front of him, who passed through with a cursory greeting. But Melissa noticeably brightened for Howard. She had been starting to worry that he might not show up.

"Mike! I'm so glad you could make it!" She said, backing up so he could enter, then closing the door behind him. "Go downstairs and introduce yourself around, but first . . . "

The older girl that Howard had seen walking with Melissa along Ward Parkway, whom he had assumed to be her older sister, was chatting with a group of other, similarly-aged girls congregating in the entry. Melissa tapped her on the shoulder to get her attention.

"Mike," she said, "I want you to meet my sister Anne."

"Nice to meet you," said Anne, somewhat annoyed at being disengaged from her conversation. For her kid sister's sake, she feigned as much interest as she possibly could about meeting a male at least three years younger than herself.

Howard stood mutely—he still had yet to say a word—and could remain so for a bit longer since an athletic-looking sixteen-year-old boy bounded out of nowhere with the clear intent of hustling Anne away.

"Come on, Anne," he implored, his hand firmly tugging her upper arm.

"And this is her friend Tripp Anderson—" said Melissa.

Tripp barely acknowledged the introduction, which also meant that Howard still wasn't required to speak. Freckled and with a crew cut, Tripp's starched white Oxford shirt and loose blue jeans bespoke of his being one of the cool kids at the high school.

"Come on, Anne," Tripp pestered. Anne obviously didn't object to such manhandling, clearly within the bounds of flirtation. Only a boyfriend could act that way without a rebuff or at least a dirty look, and that she proceeded to giggle foolishly was ample confirmation to Howard that the two were a pair. The couple disappeared into the crowd of kids that was moving herd-like from the entryway into more spacious realms of the house. The group, of course, was not allowed to occupy the house proper but would gradually make its way through the den and kitchen and down the stairs into the capacious recreation room.

Melissa misinterpreted Howard's silence as indignation at her sister and her boyfriend's rudeness. She felt awkward, convinced that the boy standing silently in front of her was judging her unfavorably, so she became chatty to compensate.

"I told my parents all about you and they'd really like to meet you. But they're not home right now. Can you blame them?" she asked rhetorically.

Howard shrugged non-committally. Melissa Huntley, the daughter of his father's arch-nemesis, was just about the most beautiful girl he had ever seen. He needed to warm up his voice—in the bathroom, perhaps—because he was afraid if he spoke it would squeak. He had a tightness in his chest, and was overwhelmed by an awareness of its cause. Not a virus, not bacterial, not allergic, but the result of an infatuation that would have to play itself out. He would not mention these symptoms to his mother. She would make him take decongestants.

"Well," said Melissa, shrugging her shoulders in response to Howard's throat clearing, "Anne's no help. I suppose I better get everybody downstairs so we can get started." With that, she resumed her role as hostess. Howard trailed behind for a short ways, checking out as much of the layout of the house that he could under the guise of admiring glances, and made his way down to the lower level.

The recreation room was crowded and bustling with generalized youthful commotion. The Block's basement had a cement floor, and while Howard had friends with basements converted to rec rooms, he had never seen one as nice as this. The flooring was actual ceramic tile, not linoleum, with oriental-style area rugs scattered about, and the ceiling was high and smooth, not a dropped one with acoustic tiles. The furniture was new and matching instead of the usual hodge-podge of old worn-out stuff. Most strikingly, there was not an inch of visible concrete, no stored junk anywhere, not even a washing machine and dryer tucked away in a corner. For all intents and purposes, this could have been an upstairs room. Not a bad place to sit out a tornado, Howard thought.

A stocky college-aged group leader named Jeremiah, who was already showing signs of early baldness, was helping to get the kids settled down. All the spots on the sofas and upholstered chairs were taken, as well as folding chairs that had been set up throughout the room. In the remaining available spaces kids were on the carpet, sitting cross-legged or stretched out, leaning on elbows. A tablecloth-covered refreshment table for later was set up against the back wall, with plates of cookies and brownies and bottles of Coke and Dr. Pepper.

Jeremiah started distributing bundles of stapled mimeographed sheets that were then passed hand-to-hand by the group members themselves, and Howard managed to snare one. Luckily, he now had the equivalent of a newspaper to hide behind, if needed. The group leader then called the animated group to order, repeating his supplications for silence with gradual success, making his way to the front of the room. When he uttered what was unmistakably his final plea for quiet—with a level of irritation that indicated limits to Christian patience—Howard hurried to an inconspicuous corner at the back of the room, near the refreshment table. Jeremiah was preparing to lead the group in an opening prayer and Howard needed to be in position.

And it was then, on the way to his chosen corner, that Howard spotted Chris Beamon. If Chris's presence had been an unpleasant shock that qualified as an unforeseen circumstance, the fact that Ryan O'Hearn was sitting next to him was not surprising. Howard quickly averted his face, covering it with the sheaf of papers, and stepped backwards to where a pillar had been fortuitously placed for structural purposes. The group, heads bowed, began to pray. Howard—hidden from his classmates' view—prayed along with them. He wasn't registering the content of the group prayer, but nonetheless joined them in earnest, praying on his part that neither Chris nor Ryan would spot him.

Howard flattened himself against the pillar, alternating between watching Chris and Ryan and keeping tabs on Melissa, who, like a diligent student, was attentively involved, no joking around. During the second prayer recitation, Howard tried to summon courage for his next move, but was overwhelmed by the weirdness of the whole situation. Here was a diverse group—not unlike kids he went to school with every

143

day—revealing an entire secret world that he knew nothing about. Never before, except in the abstract, had he really understood the divide between Christian and Jew. He had always felt different, and now he knew why. And wouldn't these kids, if thrust into Cantor Birenboim's Bar Mitzvah lab, find things equally bizarre?

Then the singing began. Everyone seemed to know the first song without looking at the cheat sheet, but Howard had never heard it before, or any of those that followed. He tried to pick up the tunes, in the meantime simply moved his lips, figuring that if he looked too closely at the words on the page he could give himself away.

***

Some time later the group was still singing in hearty chorus, this time a number called "They Hung Him On A Cross," but Howard was still unresolved about how to proceed with the mission.

"They hung Him on a cross. . . " Jeremiah warbled. "For me, one day when I was lost (so lost) . . ."

"They hung Him on a cross (oh yeah) . . . "

"They hung Him on a cross for me . . . "

After seven subsequent verses in this pattern, including "They whipped him up a hill," "They speared him in the side," "Then, he hung his head and He died," Howard had pretty much mastered the ditty, especially since the "so lost" and "oh yeah" parts were a consistent response. Compared to the memory work required for his *Haftorah* study, and the senseless foreign syllables that Cantor Birenboim bellowed on the recordings, this number was a piece of cake.

144

Howard stayed on pitch, and found himself singing loudly and confidently.

"He rose on Easter morn. . . " Jeremiah crooned, "for me one day when I was lost (so lost) . . . "

"He rose on Easter morn (oh, yeah) . . . " sang Howard, "He rose on Easter morn for me!"

With all of this singing, Howard was sure that his voice must have warmed up sufficiently to say something to Melissa. That, of course, was subordinate to the mission.

"Okay, people, that was terrific," said Jeremiah. "But tell me. . . How did Jesus bring joy into your life today? Let's go around the room. Who wants to start?"

The cue for Howard to make a move could not have been clearer. Circumstances dictated timing, and there was no turning back. Fortunately, Chris and Ryan were not between him and the stairwell. After slipping the song sheets into the book bag and casting one final longing glance in Melissa's direction, Howard inched his way around the pillar to the stairwell and made his escape.

He was looking for the bathroom, that would be his explanation if he ran into anyone along the way. He figured there was a toilet somewhere on the basement level, but he would play dumb and act surprised if caught. Fortunately, no one met him in the stairwell, and the brightly-lit kitchen at the top of the stairs was empty. As far as he could tell, all inhabitants of the house were in the rec room, and the main floor of the house was deserted. Howard passed through the kitchen and the semi-lit den toward the main entryway, where he remembered an intersecting corridor. With any luck, Huntley's study was on the main floor and the hallway would lead to it.

Each step forward along the carpeted corridor brought an increased gradation of darkness. The carpet was so thick and

pliant, and his movements so silent, that Howard realized—
not without remorse—that ruining his Red Ball Jets had
been an unnecessary precaution. The first door on his left was
open and revealed a guest bathroom. Proceeding down the
hallway, only two doors remained: one straight ahead at the
very end of the corridor, and another again on his left. The
end room had to be the master bedroom, and the other. . . .

Howard quietly opened the door to the room, entered a
space of total blackness, and eased the door closed behind
him. He pressed his back against the door as if to barricade
it and took some deep breaths to calm his nerves. The room
smelled of tobacco; he was in Chadwick Huntley's study, alright. Huntley didn't smoke Cherry Blend—Howard could
tell from the heavier aroma, smokier rather than sweet.
Probably one of the more expensive custom blends from a
pipe shop, Howard figured.

The familiarity of the tobacco smell aside, Howard
couldn't calm himself down. He felt tingly, even nauseated,
and could hear the whooshing of his pulse in his head just
deep to his ears, but he had to press on. By now his eyes
had further adjusted to the dark, and he could make out the
forms of a desk positioned away from the back wall, floor-
to-ceiling bookshelves, a small sofa, an armchair, and a file
cabinet. Howard reached into his book bag for one of the
penlights.

With his back still against the door, he jerkily illuminated
small circles of the room, sweeping the focus haphazardly
before becoming more systematic with his lighting. First he
surveyed the wall of medical books, from left to right, up and
down, like a continuous waveform parading across the back
wall. Then the wooden file cabinet, no more than five paces
away. He darted over to the cabinet and pulled on each of the

four vertical doors sequentially, but all were locked. Maybe the key was in the desk drawer, he hoped.

He made his way around the desk and pulled the swivel desk chair back enough to open the narrow pencil drawer. Light upon the drawer's contents revealed a neat arrangement of pencils, pens, paper clips, index cards, and the like, but no keys. He crouched to check the deeper side drawers when his light, passing the level of the desktop, flashed across a stack of medical journals on one corner. What caught Howard's eye was a certain asymmetry. The journals were all neatly stacked and of roughly similar thickness, like the monthly journals his father subscribed to, except for one at the bottom of the pile.

Howard quickly stood up and went to the side of the desk. The odd journal at the bottom wasn't a journal at all. It was thick and manila covered, with pages stuck in it unevenly. A series of numbers and blocks letters were written on the spine in black magic marker, along with a name. THE name. Howard couldn't believe it! He had actually found Hannah Stringer's missing hospital file! A file, Mike had assured him, there's always a file, and he had found it!

Howard's hands were trembling as he slid the chart out from the stack, careful not to topple the whole pile. He placed the pen light in his mouth to free up both hands and frantically riffled through the pages. He wasn't sure what he was looking for or where he would find it, but the mere presence of the chart in Chadwick Huntley's possession proved what he and Mike had suspected all along. Again, he forced himself to slow down and approach the mass of information systematically. There were dividing sections, each with a tab indicating a different date. These were chronological and presumably represented different admissions to the hospital. If on one of those earlier admissions—

Howard froze at the click of the door latch. He had heard nothing in the hallway; no advance warning that someone had come upstairs, let alone was entering the study. The inexplicability of it all disoriented him, which had the up-side of his jaw involuntarily going lax and the penlight not only immediately shutting off but falling from his lips onto the carpet. Fortunately, his loss of bearings was short-lived. Terrified, he dropped to the floor behind the desk, pulling his knees into his chest and curling into a ball like an irritat-ed caterpillar. Reflexively, he had snapped the chart shut and abandoned it, leaving it closed on the edge of the desk next to the stack of journals. He had no time to replace it prop-erly. If Chadwick Huntley were to enter the room, he would know immediately that something was amiss.

Had the door opened in a normal fashion, followed by a hand swiping the wall for the light switch, Howard would have been caught standing there, stupefied and slack-jawed, a pen light falling from his mouth. But the door had opened slowly, cautiously, and not more than halfway. More puz-zling, no hand reached to the wall for the light switch—the room remained in darkness. Fortunately Howard had pushed the desk chair back earlier, so his head and upper body were close to the recess for the chair. By pressing the side of his face against the carpet, Howard had a six-inch gap under the desk front for ground level visibility.

But Howard heard the whispers before he could see any-thing, just before the second click of the latch as the door closed. Now he understood the absence of any forewarning sounds; the intruders, like him, had entered the room by stealth. And there were two of them, the whispering came in tandem, the shadowy forms of legs approaching the desk. Howard stiffened, bracing himself. But the shadows moved away, to the right of the desk, followed by soft squeaking, the sounds of a compressing cushion and fabric sliding against leather. The visitors were sitting on the sofa, whispering, adjusting their positions, getting comfortable.

A distinct female giggle put an end to all of Howard's speculations. Anne Huntley had ditched the Young Life meeting and snuck into her father's study to make out with Tripp Anderson.

Smooching and smacking sounds commenced, interspersed with Anne's irritating giggle.

Howard relaxed his shoulders into the rug and closed his eyes against the darkness, straining to think.

Shit-a-brick, he thought to himself.

***

Meanwhile, almost directly beneath him, Ryan O'Hearn was concluding a rambling explanation loosely tied to the general topics of Jesus and joy.

"And I know Jesus has made me the athlete that I am," he was saying. "And that really gives me joy every day, even when I'm not playing a game or anything. And—and I guess that's all."

He blushed and self-consciously sidled away from his position at the front of the room. Jeremiah, who had been leaning against the nearby sidewall listening respectfully, had been inching forward as he sensed that the remarks were nearing conclusion.

"Thank you so much, Ryan," he said. "That was very inspiring. Who's next? Marcus? Amy?"

Ryan negotiated his way back through the open spaces in the crowd, but instead of sitting back down on the floor next to Chris, continued meandering in the general direction of the refreshment table, or more specifically, the bathroom behind the closed door next to it.

"I really gotta pee," he had bent down to whisper to Chris in passing, by way of explanation.

Melissa, sitting cross-legged on the floor near the front of the room, watched Amy Pearson make her own way across the room to center stage. The form of Amy heading front-ward intersected with that of Ryan heading back, and Melissa found her eyes, for no particular reason, continuing to follow Ryan as he pressed further back into what, in any gathering of paying patrons, would be the cheap seats.

Away from the action was always Anne's preferred seating. Less diligent than Melissa in general, she couldn't have cared less about the youth group, other than the opportunity it gave her to be with Tripp. For her, a Young Life Meeting was a variation of a date, and the two would always select the co-ziest spot in the house for sitting the meeting out. And there, in semi-privacy, they would hold hands and huddle up next to one another like it was freezing in the place.

Melissa turned her attention away from Ryan and began a more purposeful scan of what had been a fuzzy backdrop of bodies and faces in the rest of the room. Anne was not among them, not even sitting against either side of the sofa. Melissa craned her neck around and searched the entire room. No Anne. No Tripp.

It didn't take a rocket scientist to figure this one out—the explanation was obvious. Anne and Tripp had snuck out of the meeting and gone somewhere to make out. Melissa felt the heat rising up her neck. Not that she was sexually protective of her sister, nor was she the least bit jealous. What riled her was the unfairness, getting dumped on. She looked at her watch. Perhaps a couple more speakers to come at best, then the refreshments. Melissa wasn't about to be the only one to make sure the ice chest was filled or that there were enough napkins and paper plates or that coasters were used if anybody set anything on the uncovered side tables, like her mother had reminded them several times before leaving. Who would get paper towels if somebody spilled a drink? Who would pick up the mashed pieces of a brownie that had been crushed on the floor? And who wouldn't be able to socialize herself; in particular, get to know Mike Hunsacker better? No way big sis was going to wriggle out of her share of the hostess responsibilities. Siblings have an inherent, genetically-driven understanding of fairness. This wasn't fair, and Melissa wasn't going to stand for it. She headed upstairs.

Ryan was perturbed to discover that the rec room bathroom was occupied. With no intention of waiting, he also headed for the stairs. There had to be at least a couple of bathrooms on the main floor, and he really had to pee.

Howard, upstairs and still lying on his stomach on the plush carpeting behind Chadwick Huntley's desk, also had no intention of waiting any longer. With Anne and Tripp otherwise occupied—Anne's giggles and half-hearted protestations had finally subsided—Howard had wriggled forward a couple of feet, prompted by the unremitting sounds of smacking and saliva sharing. Soon he had advanced far enough to peer around the side of the desk, where he had a full view of the room and decided that he should make a break for it. The necking pair was now stretched out along the length of the sofa, and Howard could see that Tripp's hand was making cautious but persistent progress under and up Anne's blouse, now untucked from her skirt on one side. Despite the unavoidable click latching, Howard had convinced himself that he could make an undetected exit if he timed things carefully enough. Could there be a greater distraction for Tripp Anderson than Anne Huntley's bare left breast?

In retrospect, Howard might have reconsidered his options, but his anxiety had overcome the requisite patience and composure. Instead, he found himself crawling on the rug, until he was directly behind the back of the sofa.

Howard waited a few moments there, girding himself for the second and more treacherous half of the escape. Anne was making little grunting sounds, and Tripp seemed downright winded, as if he had just sprinted forty yards downfield for an overthrown pass. The sofa, while not actually advancing, seemed to be jerking itself toward the door in staccato bursts, threatening to skittle across the room ahead of Howard.

Howard made his move and began the crawl in earnest, an infantryman slithering along the battlefield, determined not to stop until taking the hill as ordered.

If Howard had been stunned by the earlier entrance of Anne and Tripp, the sensation he encountered when Melissa barged into the room and turned on the light was cataclysmic and paralyzing. This was the type of moment when susceptible individuals could lose bladder and bowel control, and Howard was conscious of an escaping renegade fart, fortuitously masked by the sound of the door banging against the doorstop. "I can't believe I cut one" he had time to think, before refocusing on his dire predicament.

Tripp and Anne had bolted up from the sofa with the same explosiveness of Howard's burst of gas, and Anne was frantically rearranging herself and tucking in her blouse. She was unpleasantly aware that Tripp's fingernail had grazed her nipple on the way out.

"You guys!" shouted an annoyed Melissa. But what was going on? What was Mike Hunsacker doing, lying on the floor?

"Mike!" she shouted, her tone conveying questioning as well as surprise.

Howard clumsily brought himself up to his knees, still holding the book bag in his left hand. He unconsciously pulled the strap over his left shoulder as if he had been caught naked and were covering his privates with a towel.

"I. . . I can explain," he quavered, in a manner suggesting that an explanation was the last thing in the world he would be able to provide.

Had he known how to begin, he might have, had he not been interrupted by Anne, who had turned her head from her position on the sofa, followed her sister's gaze, and realized that someone else—and not family—was in the room.

Predictably, she reacted strongly. After all, if a girl couldn't let a guy feel her up in the privacy of her own home with the parents gone for the evening, where could she be safe?

"What are YOU doing here?" she demanded. The obvious answer was that he was watching Tripp doing a doggie maneuver on her, and the whole notion was a painful personal intrusion. "What are you, some kind of PERVERT?" she screamed, emotions cut loose. Her choices were to either scream or cry with humiliation, and she wisely chose the former.

"I don't understand! What's going on here?" That was Melissa, who was nearer to the crying than the screaming. She had done nothing wrong, yet she was the one about to fall apart. Was that fair?

No one answered, since no one knew what to say and each was waiting for someone, anyone, to start talking first. This was not something that could go on forever, although four or five seconds in these circumstances was nearly enough to feel like forever. Melissa stood in the doorway. Howard remained on his knees. Anne forgot about tucking in her blouse. Tripp still had a boner and wasn't about to get up from the sofa unless he was significantly distracted. The silence-breaking salvation would not come from any of the involved parties. No, the savior would be Ryan O'Hearn, recently emerged from the bathroom down the corridor and taking a few steps out of his way to check out the commotion. He appeared in the doorway, as if by magic, and even gave Melissa a subtle body check to move her a bit to the side so he could have an unimpeded view.

Ryan assessed the situation quickly. He knew, of course, that he didn't have a clue as to what was going on, but it was good to be there anyway. It was almost as if Jesus had brought him exactly there, at that moment, so he could experience some joy. Whatever was happening, he knew that he had no dog in the hunt, and thus no compunctions about speaking his mind.

"What's the deal here?" he asked. Sensing that Howard, kneeling on the floor, was clearly the odd man out, he added his own color commentary. "Hey, if it isn't Block. What are you doing here, Block? I almost didn't recognize you without your fat Jew friend."

An auspicious opening, breaking the conversational ice and bringing yet another twist.

"Block? Mike?" Melissa asked.

"Who the hell are you, anyway?" Anne piped in, adding, "besides being a PERVERT!"

"That's Howard Block," Ryan answered, pleased to be in the know about one thing even if he still had absolutely no idea what was going on. Apparently no one else did either. Luckily he was there. Ryan O'Hearn had taken control of a completely unknown situation. He was feeling joyful. Thank you, Jesus.

Ryan triumphantly continued. "He's in my PE class at Indian Hills."

"Mike?" Melissa asked. "What's going on? Mike?" She took a step forward into the room. Ryan, encouraged, did the same. Howard worked his way, ungracefully, to his feet, still not answering.

Ryan, now comfortably in control of the conversation, answered for him.

"It's Howard, not Mike. His name is Howard," he said.

Perhaps because Howard could not possibly explain his position without revealing his mission, or possibly because Ryan had sent Howard back to a place that he didn't want to go, that place belonging to another Howard more fixed in the real world, he responded in a completely uncharacteristic manner.

Anger somehow overcame his fear and humiliation. And Ryan had triggered it.

"And I'm a Jew, too, you stupid asshole!" With that Howard stormed out of the room, pushing Ryan aside. Once in the hallway, he ran like hell to get out of the house.

The group, now of slightly different composition and dynamic, was again in an awkward position of silence. Each individual's mind was racing in a slightly different manner, but all were failing to engage, as if they were unsure how to release a mental clutch pedal. They waited several more seconds in silence. No one moved, and nothing happened in the ensuing total, heavy silence. Tripp suddenly realized he had lost his boner, which spoke much about the collective mental distractions.

Not surprisingly, Ryan was the one to speak first. The drag race occurring in his own mind had taken place on a much different track.

He shook his head. Before he had been curious, but now he was confused. Really confused.

"Jeez," he said. "I didn't know Block was a Jew. And I heard him. . . he knew all the songs!"

Melissa, speechless, ran out of the room after Howard.

Below, refreshments were being served.

Chapter Twelve

Howard was pulling his bicycle out from behind the hedge when Melissa caught up with him. She stopped in front of the fountain and hesitated, out of breath from running. The moonlight reflected off her hair in a soft glow. She looked like the Madonna, a painting of whom Howard had recently seen during his research of Christianity in his World Book Encyclopedia, only prettier. The moon had to really be full to glow like that, Howard thought, and looked skyward. The moon, in fact, was nearly full, but most of the reflection, he realized, came from the streetlight.

They stared at each other. Melissa was still beautiful, but her sadness had cast a pall over her being—she looked frail and vulnerable. Her demeanor gave the encounter all the makings of a break-up, without them ever having been together. Howard wasn't exactly at his best either, and his stomach hurt.

Melissa sat down on the edge of the fountain, what could be taken for either a conciliatory gesture or simple fatigue. Howard slapped the kickstand of his Schwinn, made sure the bike was steady, and sat nearby. Not exactly beside her, but a respectable two feet away.

"Mike. Whoever you are. What IS your name, anyway?"

"Howard Block."

"What's going on? I thought your name was—your friend Jimmy said—"

"Jimmy is Mike Hunsacker," said Howard. "He said his name was Jimmy Bond. You know, Jimmy, like short for James. James Bond."

Melissa looked at him blankly.

"Have you seen 'Dr. No'? The movie?" This was first date material, almost, talking about the picture shows. Right after favorite colors and astrological signs. Casual conversation would be short lived, however.

Melissa shook her head.

"The movie? 'Dr. No'?" Howard was disbelieving. She must not have heard him right.

"No," she verbalized this time. "I haven't seen it."

"Never mind," said Howard, abandoning all hope for diversionary small talk.

"Well, then," said Melissa, getting the conversation back on track. "I guess you're both liars, you and Mike. Were you trying to make fun of me? Was that it?"

This notion was inconceivable to Howard. His gut reaction was to blurt out "Why would I do that?" but he held back. The romantic response would have been "That is the last thing I would ever do to you," but Howard only thought of that one later that evening, as he lay awake in bed trying to sleep. At the time, he came out with the simplest explanation, which happened to be the truth.

"We thought you might recognize my name," he said.

Melissa gave him a puzzled look that was similar to her response to the "Dr. No" query. She didn't have an inkling.

"Our dads know each other," Howard explained.

"So what? Who's your Dad?"

"Jack Block. Dr. Jack Block."

"Maybe I've heard of him," said Melissa, with a shrug. "I think I may have."

"I'll bet. The name Hannah Stringer ring a bell?"

"No. Is she in the movie?"

Howard rolled his eyes. The summation wasn't going very well. Perhaps he should have had a draft prepared as a contingency. But not even Mike could have imagined this scenario!

"I'm not talking about the dumb movie," Howard said irritably. "I'm talking about real life. Forget the movie. Let's not talk about the movie anymore, alright? Hannah Stringer is a real person. The name doesn't ring a bell?"

"No. No it doesn't. It still doesn't."

"I'll bet." Howard spit out the words, which he realized he was overusing as much as the expression "ring a bell." He signed deeply in frustration, unable to move forward, as if stuck in a repeating conversation loop. He had dreams like that before. But this was real life, not a dream. And not a damn movie!

He took another deep breath and began again, hoping for enough momentum to get his mental back wheels out of the mud.

"Your father's setting my dad up for a big malpractice suit. And it's all a big fraud!"

"I don't know what you're talking about!" Melissa insisted.

Howard was convinced. Melissa wasn't dumb, and she wasn't playing dumb. She just didn't know anything. No further confirmation was necessary—no master spy could pull anything more out of her with a lie detector test, or truth serum, or torture. Howard believed her. Which came as a relief, sort of.

"Okay," he said, "I believe you. So let me explain. She—Hannah Stringer—supposedly went crazy after my dad treated her, but she was crazy all along, and your father knew it. And he's lying about it and pretending he never took care of her before."

Predictably, this was not something Melissa was inclined to take at face value. Her father had his faults, and sometimes she hated him, but she was still his daughter, after all. So her gut reaction was to defend him, unquestioning and unequivocally.

"You're wrong!" she shouted, the first time her voice had risen above the level of earnest discourse. "It's all a mistake! My father wouldn't do such a thing!"

"I can prove it!" Howard's voice had risen to the occasion as well. "Your father has her file—chart! On the desk in his study! Get me the file and I'll prove it to you!"

"You're crazy!" yelled Melissa.

"Oh, yeah? Then what's he doing with Hannah Stringer's hospital chart? Answer me that! A hospital chart never leaves the hospital. . . unless somebody steals it!"

"You're a liar, Howard Block!" The discussion had reached its inevitable impasse and was rapidly coming to its end. "Get away from me and never come back!"

And with that, Melissa ran off toward her house, leaving Howard sitting on the edge of the fountain, heavily shadowed from natural and artificial light.

***

Melissa stopped halfway down the stairs to the rec room and surveyed the scene. The tableaux was noisy and frenetic. The business and religious portion of the Young Life Meeting was over, and the socializing part—for some the *raison d être* for the gathering—had begun. Tripp and Anne were together by the refreshment table, limiting their socializing to themselves, oblivious to others sharing their space. Feeding Anne a brownie, in groom to bride wedding cake fashion, Tripp was overzealous and made a mess on the floor. The giggling Anne, brownie bits escaping through her lips, covered her mouth and laughed even harder. Tripp, trying to sip his Coke amidst the gaiety, began choking himself. To the outsider, the previous invasion of their privacy appeared a forgotten memory. But the sexual milestone of feeling up Anne Huntley for the very first time would be etched in Tripp's memory forever, destined to survive all future encounters, all future relationships, and even dementia.

Ryan was also at the refreshment table with Chris. Melissa didn't know either boy all that well, only through Young Life meetings, since they were among the public school kids in the group from Indian Hills. Ryan had overfilled his cup with 7-Up, and was carefully bringing it mouthward. Just before sipping, though, he flipped his hair back, and small carbonated breakers sloshed over the top. Executing a bunny hop backwards to avoid getting wet, he couldn't prevent most of the cup from empting on the floor. All of this seemed very amusing to the boys. The floor was going to be a mess, but Melissa didn't care and wasn't about to clean it up.

She remained on the stairs, debating whether or not to enter the fray, when Ryan looked at her inquiringly, almost beseechingly, squinting one eye and raising the eyebrow of the other. Clearly he wanted the lowdown—he was sort of involved, after all—and would seek her out as his highest social priority. Melissa, revealing nothing by her expression, quickly turned and ran back up the stairs.

Ryan had already run the encounter by Chris, who couldn't make sense of it either. Now Ryan didn't understand what had prompted Melissa's retreat. For sure, nothing he had done. Shaking it off with a shrug, he reached across the table for another cookie and noticed that some girl was just entering the bathroom. That explained Melissa's abrupt departure. Of course, she had to pee, that explained why she rushed off.

She'd return soon enough, though, and then he'd find out what the deal was with Howard Block. No wonder he ran around with that Jew Stinky. He was a Jew himself. And was Old Yeller Shorts a Jew too? Ryan needed to calibrate his perception of the world. If there were three Jews in a single gym class, then Jews were everywhere, more than he'd ever imagined. Ryan shook his head in confused consternation, then bit into the chocolate chip cookie and smiled. Chewy, just the way he liked them. Whatever the case, he could really unload some shit on all three of them come next gym class. And in the meantime, maybe he'd ask Melissa Huntley out on a date.

Ryan didn't get the opportunity that evening, since Melissa never returned to the rec room until all the guests had left, including Tripp. Only then did she tidy up a bit, leaving most of the clean-up for Juanita, who would be back on Monday. Not surprisingly, Anne did nothing to help, which really wasn't fair. Until the place cleared out, though, Melissa had remained in her room with the door closed and locked, avoiding any contact with the kids.

Before sequestering herself, though, she took a brief detour to her father's study to turn off the lights. He would be livid if he found out that any of the guests had violated his private space. Were it in her nature, she could tattle on her sister and really watch the sparks fly, but all she wanted was to cover the tracks. At the doorway, she reached for the light switch on the wall, then hesitated and surveyed the room. Nothing seemed out of place. But she couldn't help but notice a hospital medical chart sitting askew atop a stack of her father's psychiatric journals.

A sensation of dread overcoming her, she walked over to the desk. As she already suspected but wished otherwise, the name on the chart was "Hannah Stringer." Melissa picked the folder up and flipped once through the pages. With a houseful of kids and already one interrupted encounter in that very room, this was not the time to be snooping among her father's things. She'd return later, after everyone was asleep, take her time, and prove to herself that the whole thing was a big mistake. Despite exhaustion, she knew a sleepless night was inevitable. She also knew that she was going to cry, she could feel it coming, and was beyond the point of holding it back.

Melissa set the chart down on top of the stack of journals, exactly the way she had found it. Or, almost exactly. As she slightly changed the angle, adjusted the relationship of the chart to the journals below it, she decided not to say anything to anyone. Until the bad dream was over she would cover for Howard Block. Anne would as well, for the more compelling reason of self-protection.

That decided, Melissa went up to her room to get the cry out.

***

Howard rode his bike cautiously at first. He had never ridden at night before, nor used the single headlight that was mounted at the center of the handlebars, a custom add-on that the previous owner had affixed. The two double A batteries had been dead, of course, but Howard had the foresight to test the light and then replace the batteries before leaving his house earlier. That seemed like a long time ago. Actually, Mike had reminded him about the headlight batteries, but he was the one who had thought to bring along extra ones in the book bag, part of the supply kit, in case the replacements were faulty. Even Mike agreed that was a sensible precaution.

The effect of the small single beam on the road ahead was eerie and disorienting, despite the streetlights. Howard was temporarily blinded by the high beams of a couple of oncoming cars, but fortunately the side streets were fairly empty, especially along the pre-planned route which he had specifically chosen to avoid any real traffic.

Howard was dejected and nervous, but most of all angry with himself. The running dialogue of mental castigation along the way was relentless. How could he have been so stupid! Why hadn't he taken the chart? He had more than enough opportunities for sure. For starters, he should have held onto the file when he hit the deck instead of leaving it on the desk. Admittedly there had been extenuating circumstances, he had been surprised. Still, how could he have had such a lapse? It was all about the files! And getting them had been the whole point of the entire mission! How could he have been such a klutz?

But it was worse. Once hidden behind the desk, he easily could have reached up for the chart and placed it in the book bag, undetected. What had he been thinking, lying there all that time and doing nothing, when the chart was just in reach above him? After all the training and preparation, he had completely blown it! And had he been caught, it wouldn't even have mattered, since he would have had the file in his book bag when he left! And he would have it now!

In between these tirades, he was reminded that Melissa Huntley totally hated his guts. He tried to block this thought from his mind, but it kept popping up. Howard much preferred beating himself to a psychological bloody pulp for not taking the files than contemplating the major screw-up with Melissa.

Howard stopped his bike at the top of Mike's street, where the house first came into sight. To his unpleasant surprise, the Hunsacker house was completely dark. Not a single light! Jeanette Block always left a lamp on in different rooms—rotating the rooms so they weren't predictably the same ones—not just for a trip out of town, but even when the family went out for dinner. She would also leave one of the radios on, with the volume way up. These light and sound techniques, designed to trick burglars into choosing a different house to rob, were evidently not practiced by the Hunsacker family. Maybe their neighborhood wasn't as likely to get robbed, thought Howard, or maybe they just figured that burglars weren't as stupid as Jeanette Block imagined them to be.

The darkness, from the view of an agent on a mission, had its advantages, but Howard still had the nagging worry of discovery by neighbors. He imagined the nightmare scenario of the police being called, coming to the house with flashing lights, searching the house to find him huddled and quaking under a bed, taking him to the station house in Prairie Village, and calling his parents to pick him up. The horrible parent scenario was not one that even James Bond would ever have to face. He had, of course, taken precautions. In addition to his blacked out sneakers, black socks, and black slacks, Howard had worn a light yellow Oxford shirt to the

Young Life Meeting (all black for the meeting, Mike had thought, would stand out and seem weird at a religious gathering). But now Howard untucked and unbuttoned the shirt and crammed it into his book bag. Underneath was his standard issue black T-shirt from Walter's Clothing. A gust of cool night air made him shiver, but he wouldn't be outside much longer. Howard pedaled down the street to the Hunsacker house.

With no back alley or direct access to the fenced-in back yard, Howard had no choice but to come through the front. Now he knew better than to park his Schwinn in the driveway, kickstand down. From the opposite side of the street, at slow velocity, Howard made an abrupt left turn, angling across the front portion of the driveway into the grass, where he slid with his bike to the ground behind the large juniper bush. He forcefully shoved the Schwinn as far under the bush as he could, careful to avoid Yuri's gravesite, before racing to the side entryway. The key was under the mat, where Mike said it would be. Howard assumed that Mike had only recently placed it there, but actually the key was always kept there in case one of the kids locked themselves out. Had Mike mentioned that, Howard might have informed him that Jews, in addition to not hunting or kneeling, didn't ever leave their house keys under the doormat.

The dark house was spooky, and Howard would have been more scared had he not experienced the considerably scarier events that had transpired that evening. Halfway up the second flight of stars, Howard could smell the animals. Once he stepped into Mike's bedroom, he retrieved a penlight from Stinky's bag and pressed it on, keeping the beam angled towards the floor. This was safe, he knew, because Mike had assured him all the drapes would be drawn, and any light gaps had been sealed with strips of electrical tape. In the shadows above the downwardly directed light beam, Howard could make out the lizard, snake, and fish tanks, the hamster cage, the bird cage, and, of course, the mouse cage, home of a recent replacement for Yuri I. The new white mouse was officially Yuri II, but went by Yuri. According to Mike, he was less of a fitness buff than his predecessor—in fact, he was lazy—but this character flaw didn't seem overly important since he would remain earthbound. Howard shined the light into the cage, frightening Yuri into a corner. The menagerie had been given enough food to last the weekend, but before Howard left in the morning he would sprinkle some fish food into the tank and make sure all the water bottles were filled.

The unzipped sleeping bag was lying on top of Mike's unmade bed, which had otherwise been cleared of all the piles of clothes and other obstructions. Howard went to the bathroom to pee and take a sip of water from under the faucet, but didn't bother to brush his teeth or take off any clothes, other than his shoes. He didn't like being alone in the strange house. He reminded himself that he had stupidly replaced the key under the mat at the side door, just where any burglar could find it. Any burglar who would assume the house was empty because all the lights had been off since before dark.

Howard got up to lock the bedroom door and returned to bed to lie stiffly on his back and stare toward a ceiling that he knew was above him but couldn't see. He would be up all night, thinking about what a schmuck he was, how he had failed the team, how he had failed his father, how Melissa Huntley hated his guts. He had screwed everything up. And then he would think about how scared he was, alone in a dark and creepy house that sometimes seemed to creak for no apparent reason, with an entrance key on the doorstop readily available to anyone in the neighborhood with criminal intent. Despite all these negative thoughts, Howard never once thought about swallowing. That particular problem, he couldn't exactly remember when, had disappeared as quickly and mysteriously as it had come.

Perhaps all the spent adrenaline was responsible, but Howard did fall asleep, sooner than he might have ever imagined, lulled into a peaceful slumber by the hypnotic sound of the wheel revolving in the hamster cage. Ferdinand the hamster, unlike Yuri II, really liked to get in his exercise.

***

Around midnight, a somewhat erratically driven 1962 Lincoln Continental pulled into the driveway on Wenonga Road, and the double garage doors opened by remote control. Melissa, lying awake in her pajamas in her bedroom, heard her parents' arrival. She had intended to greet them, since Anne was already asleep, but stood hesitantly at the top of the stairs. She could barely make out the sound of the car doors slamming in tandem in the garage and then heard the familiar sound of the kitchen door entrance, the only door in the house that stuck, squeaking because of the ill-fitting weather stripping. Elaine and Chad Huntley were considerately speaking in undertones so not to awaken the girls. Their shoes tapped across the kitchen and den floors, but all sounds of further progress disappeared as soon as they hit the carpeted corridor. Melissa knew that her mother would soon begin her pre-bedtime make-up removal, facial scrub, and cold cream ritual, while her father would head into his study for a nightcap, which he probably didn't need. Her mother's facial cleansing obsessiveness could be considered vanity, but her father's behavioral pattern was most definitely alcoholism.

Melissa hadn't made it to the bottom of the stairs when the shouting started.

"Who's been in here?" Chadwick bellowed.

Melissa froze but could make out her mother, in a state of semi-undress, scuttling down the hallway from the bedroom to the study.

"Someone's been messing with my things!" Chadwick continued. "Who's moved my things?"

"Chad, dear," came Elaine's soothing voice, "it's nothing to be upset about—"

"The hell it isn't!" screamed her husband. "I can't leave this goddam house for fifteen minutes!"

"What is it, Chad?" asked Elaine, maintaining her controlled and refined tone. She had learned many years earlier that a placating tone worked better than trying to out shout her husband, especially when he was in his cups.

"Somebody moved this chart!" he yelled, picking up Hannah Stringer's file and thumbing through it, as if to reassure himself that the record was complete and unadulterated.

Melissa crept down the remaining couple of stairs and partially down the corridor. Only the filing cabinet was visible from where she stood, but she didn't want to risk moving any closer. If her mother came out first, she would be okay. Elaine would not give her away, but merely shoosh her back upstairs with flicks of the back of her hand. Her father's response, however, was more unpredictable, and he could easily direct his rage her way. Melissa needed to be there, but she didn't want to be caught.

"Maybe Juanita moved things around when she was cleaning—"

"I don't want anyone in my goddam study! Do you understand? Do you hear me? Nobody comes in here! No one!"

"Chad, honey," said Elaine, "I'll take care of it. Don't you worry. . . ."

Luckily for Elaine, Chadwick was focusing less on her than on the chart in his hand. He tossed off his rantings almost as an afterthought, a hissing of steam released from a pressure cooker. The chart, more than Elaine's voice, was what seemed to calm him down. All was well, everything was present and accounted for. He had worked himself up for nothing. Chadwick strode over to the file cabinet, shoving his wife aside and slightly losing his balance in the process.

Melissa could see him standing in front of the file cabinet, fumbling in his pocket for his keychain, then fumbling for the correct key, and finally fumbling to get the key in the lock. He opened the top drawer and placed the chart in it. Melissa heard the file door slamming behind her as she ran toward the stairs.

"Everything's alright, right, Chad honey?" said Elaine.

"Don't 'Chad honey' me, godammit! Shut up and get out of here!"

***

The situation defused, Elaine headed back to her bedroom, then to the master bath, where she would sit on her vanity and apply face cleanser. During the time she scrubbed, Chad managed to go to the kitchen to fill up the ice bucket, had returned to the study, and was pouring himself a Scotch from the bottle in his desk. He leaned back in his chair and tried to relax.

Chadwick managed to force himself out of the chair to turn out the overhead light before returning. Had the light been on, he might have noticed the pocket light on the carpet beside the desk. Juanita would find it on Monday and put it in the top drawer of his desk.

In the bathroom, Elaine rubbed the cream on her face in small circles. In the study, Chadwick, eyes closed, soothed himself with the clinking of the ice in the tumbler he slowly twirled. Upstairs, Melissa pulled up her bed sheet and turned off the nightstand lamp. She started crying again. This was not the night for parental greeting.

In a less affluent part of town, Ferdinand the hamster raced on his wheel with reckless abandon, disturbing no one.

Chapter Thirteen

Howard, experiencing what he imagined a hang-over might feel like, found himself sullen and unable to concentrate on Sunday. Up at dawn, he had filled the menagerie water bottles and biked home by 6:30 a.m., even before his father had awakened. It was June 2nd, and his Bar Mitzvah was less than three weeks away. Running through his *Haftorah* or going over his speech would have been time well spent, but Howard couldn't bear the thought of either task. Compared to the mission, a Bar Mitzvah seemed of little consequence, and Howard couldn't muster much enthusiasm. He was surprised by his ambivalence, by how little he actually thought about this ceremonial milestone, and the fact that he wasn't even worried about it.

As the hours passed, Howard stayed up in his room, mainly fidgeting and pacing. Since the last week of school was approaching—and not even a full week, since it ended on Thursday—there was no homework. Academics had petered down to nothing. The yearbook would be coming out, so there would be designated book signing times in extended home room periods, movies to watch in the multi-purpose room, and a couple all-school programs in the gym.

When he was able to settle himself down, Howard lay on his bed and read back issues of "Mad Magazine." Aware that his lassitude could be construed as illness by his mother and in no mood to undergo health-related questioning, Howard moved downstairs to the den to watch TV while Jack read medical journals in his favorite armchair and Jeanette puttered around cleaning, or rather rearranging, the house. He dialed Mike's home phone repeatedly, not sure when the Hunsacker family was returning from the Ozarks, but no one answered.

Time dragged, and Howard's mood didn't improve.

"Anything wrong, Howard?" Jeanette asked during every commercial break. Jack would briefly look up over his journal, then return to his reading, puffing away on his pipe.

"Just thinking about my Bar Mitzvah," he replied each time, which appeared to satisfy her until something possessed her to inquire again.

After dinner and midway during the Ed Sullivan Show, Howard snuck upstairs to use the phone on his father's nightstand and finally reached Mike. The Hunsackers had just walked through the door and Mike was a bit out of breath when he first spoke.

"Mike!" Howard sighed with relief.

"Is this a secure line?" asked Mike.

"They're downstairs watching Ed Sullivan."

"That seems safe enough."

Howard launched into the story of the previous night's debacle, trying to describe events sequentially, but getting muddled and having to start over and repeat himself. Mike got the gist of things, though. Basically, mission failure. Howard was near tears when he ran out of further relevant things to say. So he started beating up on himself, this time aloud. Mike interrupted him.

"Did you fill up the water bottles?"

"Yeah—"

"Thanks."

"Is that all you have to say?" Howard knew that Mike was thinking hard and didn't have any bright ideas. Apparently this was the case, since Mike didn't answer him.

"I really screwed up," said Howard, filling up the sound void.

"These things never go smoothly," said Mike. "There's always a Plan B."

"It's hopeless," moaned Howard.

"Forget Huntley and the file."

"But—"

"There's always a Plan B, Howie. Just like there's always a file. A basic rule of espionage. Trust me. I know this business."

"So what's Plan B?"

"Let's go back to the source. The real thing, not a bunch of papers. The source. Hannah Stringer."

"But you said we needed hard evidence!"

Mike prepared to drop the bombshell that had just come to him in a flash of inspiration. Out of the blankness—bang! Of course, he needed time to work out the details. But everything would revolve around his father's brand new Wollensak tape recorder.

"I'll fill you in at school."

"Tell me now."

"Need to know."

"Mike. . . please—"

"Alright," said Mike, relenting. "How about a taped confession? Is that hard evidence enough?"

***

On the following Wednesday evening before dinner, Mike Hunsacker sat in front of his cluttered desk, having cleared just enough space on it to make room for the telephone and his father's new Wollensak reel-to-reel tape recorder. At the ready was a paper-sized sheet of thin cardboard, a pair of scissors, a tube of model airplane glue, and electrical tape. Mike crookedly rolled the piece of cardboard into a funnel, and once he had cut away the excess and shaped it into the configuration of a megaphone, glued the cardboard to itself, holding it in shape with long strips of electrical tape until the glue could dry. A stack of forty-fives was loaded on his record player across the room, and he was listening to "The Duke of Earl" by Gene Chandler. He checked his watch: 6:53 p.m., almost, in about ten seconds. Hopefully, Howard's watch said the same thing, give or take a few seconds, since they had synchronized them at the end of the school day.

School had been a bust, but with assemblies and free time for yearbook signing, he, Howard, and Stinky had had plenty of free time for conferencing without having to rely solely on lunch periods or gym class. Gym class had been odd, since that idiot Saunders, who couldn't care less anyway, had let them do whatever they wanted, inside or out. Stinky, Howard, and Mike—once it was revealed that Chris, Ryan, and the rest of the flag football crowd had chosen to run the cross country course—had decided to remain inside and play "HORSE." They discussed plans and plotted in between basketball shots. Before heading out to the field, though, Ryan O'Hearn had been particularly aggressive and obnoxious toward them, which had been expected. He had greeted Howard with a "snooping Jew" remark, and made some opaque reference to Jesus and joy. Neither Mike nor Stinky understood the allusion, of course. But what had really confused Mike was when Ryan had called him "Old Yeller Jew." What was that about, anyway? Ryan had to know that Mike Hunsacker wasn't Jewish—how could he make a mistake like that? Or was it just a metaphor of some kind?

Mike lifted the phone receiver off the cradle. He had told his parents that he was expecting an important call about school business from Howard and had cautioned his sisters that he would let the snake out in their room if he caught them using the phone. Normally there wasn't a phone upstairs, so Mike had retrieved the old one from the bottom of his mother's closet, where it had been languishing ever since being replaced by a new Princess phone for the bedroom. Mike had spliced together some extra phone cord from his father's workshop so the connection reached from the nearest outlet, an unused one just inside the door of his parent's bedroom on the floor below. He had run the wiring out of their room, up the flight of stairs, and then through the gap under his door, which he had locked. Then he had stuffed underwear in the rest of the gap, and covered that with two rolled up bath towels, so as to soundproof the room as much as possible. These were unnecessary precautions, of course, since little of the goings on in the room could be heard when the family was in the den two stories below, and no one else could tolerate the smell in his room, anyway. Security and privacy were a sure thing. The same couldn't be said of the Block household, where Howard's mom needed constant monitoring.

The next forty-five dropped into place on the turntable, and the needle carriage eased down into place. "Peppermint

Twist" was more upbeat than the Gene Chandler number, and a song Mike never tired of even though he had been regularly playing it for well over a year. Mike tapped his foot and swiveled his torso in time to the music as he again lifted the receiver from the cradle and this time set a heavy metal rod, which he had also fabricated from scraps in his father's workshop, in its place. He checked to make sure the line was not open, confirming that there was no dial tone. Check. He shuffled his hips from side to side in his chair in time to Joey Dee singing *"Yeah the name of the dance is the Peppermint Twist. . . ."*

"Bop shoo op, a bop bop shoo-op," Mike sang along with the Starliters, cutting off long strips of electrical tape and hanging them in a line from the front of his desk. He had to stop swiveling for the next step, which was to secure the small end of the cardboard funnel around the top speaker portion of the telephone receiver with the electrical tape. Still, intent on his task, he sang along softly:

"It goes round and round, up and down. . . Round and round, up and down. . . . "

He wrapped the tape round and round as he sang "round and round." And again round and round with the tape, until the makeshift megaphone held in place without support.

"And a one two three kick, one two three jump. . . . "

Mike jumped up from his chair, a couple beats later than the lyrics had directed, and checked his watch: 6:55 p.m. There was time to listen to the rest of the song, which he was glad about. The song seemed particularly relevant, almost an anthem—though admittedly it had little in common with James Bond's theme—and it lifted his already heady mood. So he danced across the room, fists clenched and arms working like pistons, hips rocking side to side, twisting while making forward progress toward the record player. Once there he swiveled and gyrated in place, occasionally giving a little kick with his right foot as if he were nudging a soccer ball toward an unprotected goal.

As the song neared its end, Mike reached out with his right arm and, just as the song ended, lifted the needle off the record, incorporating this gesture into his final dance move. He directed the needle arm back into its cradle before the automatic release of the next forty-five, but let the turntable keep spinning. He didn't know what was up next—maybe "Palisades Park" or the more recent "Da Doo Ron Ron"— but he wanted to hear "Peppermint Twist" again. Not yet, though, as he had to finalize his preparations. He went back to his desk.

The modified phone receiver rested near the edge of the desk. Using another strip of electrical tape, Mike taped the microphone of the Wollensak by its cord to the outer rim of cardboard, so that the microphone itself dangled in the center of the wide portion of the megaphone, then switched it to the "On" position. Next he powered up the Wollensak and looked at his watch. Just about zero hour. He paced with anticipation, continually looking at his watch. Then he took the pillow from his bed and tossed it onto the floor beside the desk chair, directly in line with the phone receiver setup.

From his cage, pushed to a far corner of the desk, Yuri II appeared fascinated with what was going on. Mike opened the door and reached into the cage, extended his palm, and watched as Yuri crawled onto it without hesitation. He gently stroked Yuri's back with the index finger of his free hand and was doing so when the phone rang. Mike pushed the "play" and "record" buttons of the tape recorder and watched the reels rotate a couple of times to make sure the recording tape had been properly fed. The phone rang again. Mike lifted the metal rod off the phone cradle and set Yuri on the desk for him to explore. Howard's voice was muted, but Mike could still hear him.

"Mike?"

Mike fell to his knees in front of the desk, landing on the pillow he had purposefully placed there. His chin was at the level of the surface of the desk, and by jutting his neck slightly forward, he could nearly touch the transmitting end of the phone receiver with his lips.

"I'm here. Keep talking," he said. He reached over to the tape recorder and depressed the small button that reset the tape play indicators to zero.

"What do you want me to say," Howard asked. "Like testing one-two-three?" Receiving no reply, Howard said "Testing one-two-three. Testing one-two-three."

Mike still said nothing, but kept an eye on the revolving reels of the recorder.

"More?" he heard Howard ask.

"Okay," Howard continued, not waiting for an answer. "I got it. Here goes. 'We interrupt this program to test the Conelrad Emergency Broadcast System.'" He made a long beeping sound and paused before continuing. "'This is only a test. Had this been a real emergency, you would have been asked to tune in to a designated emergency station in your area.' Mike?"

"And instructed to put your head between your legs and kiss your ass goodbye," Mike said, breaking his silence. That was an old joke, heard so often that it was second nature, if not obligatory, to at least think it whenever the actual Conelrad testing came over on the radio. "Hold on."

Mike stood up and leaned over to stop the recorder, removed the cardboard from the headset, and placed the telephone mouthpiece near the speaker of the tape recorder. He rewound the spool to where the indicator showed three zeros and pressed the "play" button. Mike needed to crank up the volume, but after he did, Howard could hear his own words played back at him, a bit echoey and with some background static, but clear enough. When the playback recording had finished, including his own final quip, Mike stopped the recorder.

"We're ready," he said into the phone.

"It really works," said Howard.

"I knew it would. It's my Dad's new Wollensak. I asked him if I could borrow it so I could tape some music. It sounds great."

"When?"

"Saturday morning, ten o'clock sharp."

"I'll ride my bike over to your house. But don't we need to set Hannah up? Make sure she's home? This may be our only chance."

"You've got a point," said Mike. "I'll call her beforehand—tonight, in fact—after I come up with something. You know, something like, 'expect a very important call Saturday morning at ten.'"

"Say something about the money," suggested Howard.

"Good idea."

"I trust you," said Howard.

"Tomorrow at school. I'll give you all the details."

"Right. See ya then."

Mike listened to "Peppermint Twist" one final time before going downstairs to see what was up with dinner. He danced as before, except this time he had a partner, Yuri, balanced in his palm. For the "Bob shoo-op parts," Mike brought his palm close to his face and crooned directly to Yuri, who responded by noticeably stiffening. In preparation for the second verse, Mike shuffled his way over to the tape recorder, gently set Yuri down on the pick-up reel, and hit the "play" button.

"It goes round and round, up and down" sang Joey Dee, and round and round went Yuri, on the tape spool, stance widespread like a drunk, hesitant to make a move without aid. Yuri wasn't going anywhere until the big hand decided to move him.

Mike broke into a grin as he watched Yuri continue to slowly revolve on the reel while he improvised a cool up and down move for himself.

"Round and round. . . this song is so. . . perfect!" Mike said gleefully. "And you—" he addressed Yuri, "you're a lazy bum but you can still do the Peppermint Twist!"

"And a one two three kick, one two three jump!" On the first "three" Mike gave a kick that would have propelled a football through the uprights from forty yards out. And again, on three, he jumped in jubilation over the score. Success! The mission was back on track!

***

The next morning, Mike groggily manhandled his alarm clock so it would shut up. With his eyes half-closed, he rummaged through the pile of clothes on his bed for something suitable to wear, sniffing his way though at least three shirts before finding one that seemed reasonably fresh. The jeans were not a problem, since you could almost wear them forever, and the longer you did, the better they got. He was stutter-stepping over to his bureau for a clean pair of underwear and socks when something on the desk caught his eye. The tape on the recorder was not wound right.

Now startled into complete wakefulness, Mike rushed over for a closer look. The tape was broken, but it had not snapped on its own, it had been gnawed through. Both ends hung loosely, their edges ragged, while the short piece that had previously connected them remained between the heads. Mouse droppings rested upon the shiny silver housing of the new Wollensak.

"Yuri! Shit!'

Yuri was in his cage, oblivious. The hatch left undone, he had explored as much as he wanted and returned to the familiarity and comfort of his cage on his own.

"Crap!" said Mike. The tape itself was not an issue—worse, Yuri appeared to have chewed on the tape heads of the recorder itself. Mike turned the machine on and frantically coaxed out the remaining bit of tape that was lodged between the heads. He removed the take-up reel, and holding on to the free end of tape, released the spool, which fell to the ground like a yo-yo. Hand over hand, Mike unwound the remaining tape as if he were pulling in a fishing line, while the spool skidded and bounced on the floor.

Tossing aside the tape and picking up the now empty spool, he replaced it on its sprocket and re-threaded the tape from the other reel, first jimmying the thin film back and forth and downward in a tooth-flossing maneuver through the heads, then securely winding it twice around the take-up reel. Holding his breath, he pushed down the "play" and "record" buttons. The take up reel turned, slowed, then strained. Then the tape snapped. The tape heads were shot. His dad's brand new Wollensak tape recorder was busted.

"Shit shit shit shit," said Mike.

He reminded himself what he had told Howard earlier. "These things never go smoothly. There's always a Plan B."

"Shit," Mike said again. "Shit shit shit."

If he didn't hurry he was going to miss his bus and be late for school.

***

The three boys were having an impromptu emergency conference outside Howard's locker before first period. Mike had searched out Howard and Stinky happened to be with him.

Mike was distraught and more disheveled-looking than usual. This put Stinky and Howard ill at ease, since Mike never seemed mentally ruffled. This had to be serious.

"I can't believe it!" Mike kept repeating, after he had managed to spill the gory details. "And it's my Dad's new tape recorder! He's going to kill me!"

"Calm down," said Stinky, assuming an unaccustomed and unfamiliar role. "It will be alright. We'll figure something out."

"You can get it fixed," said Howard.

"Right. It can be fixed, I'm sure. And I'll have to pay for it. But there's no time to get it fixed by tomorrow morning!"

"There's always a Plan B," said Howard, unconvinced.

"That WAS the damn Plan B!" Mike blurted. He had realized this earlier, attempting to console himself. There would have to be a Plan C, and who the hell ever said anything about a damn Plan C?

"Why tomorrow morning?" Stinky asked.

"It's already been set up, Stinky. Mike called Hannah Stringer last night and arranged the call for 10 a.m. on Saturday."

"So call her back and make it another time. . . after you get the tape recorder fixed," countered Stinky.

"She'll get suspicious," said Mike, rubbing his hand through his hair and really mussing it up. "She's probably already suspicious. We're lucky she hasn't talked to Huntley already. That'll blow everything! EVERYTHING!"

"You're right," said Howard. "We have to move, and we have to move NOW."

"Agreed," said Mike.

"Agreed," mimed Stinky.

Howard had taken charge, or, at least, the two other boys were looking at him as if he had, anticipating that he would say something first.

"Okay," he said, "Let's think about this. What do we need?"

"A really good tape recorder, with a microphone," Mike answered with forced calmness. "Do you have one?"

He was asking Howard, not expecting much from Stinky, but Stinky was the first to answer.

"No," he said. "Sorry."

"My Dad's office has one," said Howard. "They listen to Audio Digest tapes. Medical lectures that are recorded. I'm not sure how I could get a hold of it in time for Saturday, though, if at all."

"We need the whole set-up," Mike continued. "Recorders, amplifiers, microphones, a complete sound set-up. Professional quality. Dammit! Where can we find something like that this late in the game?"

Howard and Stinky looked at each other, knowing they were thinking the same thing. Howard raised his eyebrows at Stinky meaningfully.

"No way," said Stinky.

"Stinky . . . "

"It's the *Shabbos*," said Stinky.

"I know," said Howard. "That means nobody will be there."

"Nobody will be there, Howie, because it's the *Shabbos*. The *Shabbos*."

Mike was not following the conversation. They had skipped ahead somehow on their own and completely lost him.

"Wait," he said. "What's the *Shabbos*?"

Howard ignored the question, instead continuing to parley with Stinky.

"You don't have to if you don't want to, Stinky," he said.

"It's got to be a sin," said Stinky. "On the *Shabbos*."

"It's in the basement, Stinky."

"The basement of the *shul*," Stinky qualified. "And on *Shabbos*."

"Nobody's forcing you, Stinky. You can resign from the mission."

Stinky said nothing for a moment. Mike, still lost, didn't interrupt. If there was a viable Plan C, he'd learn about it soon enough.

Stinky took a deep breath and sighed.

"Aw, what the hell," he said.

Chapter Fourteen

"I can't tell you boys how thrilled I am that you wanted to go to services this morning!" Jeanette Block effused. "Such a surprise! And you look so nice, Irwin!" Waiting for the traffic light to turn green, she looked back over her shoulder and flashed him a maternal smile.

Stinky appreciated her noticing and the compliment. Indeed, he did look sharp, wearing a navy blue double-breasted blazer with gold buttons, gray dress slacks, a crisp white shirt with collar stays, and a striped Countess Mara tie. His mother, more than pleased that he would be attending Saturday morning services with Dr. Block's son—such a nice, smart boy, and such a good influence on her Irwin—had helped coordinate the outfit and gone so far as to appropriate one of her husband Sidney's best ties.

Stinky sat in the back seat of the Bel-Air with Mike, who had managed to put together a semblance of appropriate attire, starting with a tweed sport coat, too short in the sleeves, and beige khaki pants that wanted ironing. His white shirt was clean in the places that showed, and he had appropriated one of his father's best ties as well. Plus, Mike brought the combination together with his amber-tinted wrap-around aviator sunglasses, perfect for drawing the eye's attention away from the wrinkled pants. Howard's outfit was somewhere in between, being the simple dark brown suit from his cousin Barbara's wedding the previous February. His Bar Mitzvah suit had been hanging in plastic in his closet for three weeks and would not make its public premiere until the big day.

"And it was such a nice idea to bring a. . . friend," Jeanette continued as the light changed and she gradually depressed the accelerator, conscious of not wanting the Hunsacker boy to feel left out. Her pause had resulted from a rapid self-censorship of the initial words coming to mind; namely, "gentile" and "*shaygetz.*"

"We thought it would be something different," said Howard.

"I've become quite a student of the Jewish faith, Mrs. Block," said Mike. "I've learned a lot lately."

"That's wonderful," said Jeanette absently, turning into the B'nai Jeshurun parking lot. She maneuvered her car around those already parked there, pulling up in front of the back entrance stairs. She placed the car in "Park," and just in case, firmly pushed down the emergency brake. God forbid the car should get a mind to take off just as the boys were getting out.

"Irwin, are you sure your mother doesn't mind picking you boys up?" she asked, as all three car doors were being opened.

"We don't need—" Stinky began.

"Thank you very much, Mrs. Block," Mike interrupted, "but we've made arrangements."

"Not the bus, I hope," she said, her features instantaneously transfixed into profound worry.

187

"Don't worry, Mom," said Howard, taking her hand in his and slipping her seventeen cents in the process, "we'll call you if we can't get a ride home. No bus. I promise."

Relieved, Jeanette nodded appreciatively. It was her inclination, in these moments of relief, to allow herself a change of subject, generally to something not disposed to creating anxiety.

"I see you've brought your father's *tallis* to wear," she said, drawing attention to the blue velvet bag with a gold Star of David embroidered on the front.

"I didn't think he'd mind."

"Of course not, don't be silly. He'll be very pleased to know."

Neither Howard nor Stinky had their own personal *tallis,* or prayer shawl yet, so they generally used one of the dingy loaners that the synagogue provided, along with communal *yarmulkes*. The first real *tallis*—crisper and whiter than the shabby rejects available for borrowing, and adorned with embroidery of either gold or silver threading—was typically a gift from one of the grandfathers, and like the suit, would be showcased on the day of the Bar Mitzvah.

Jack Block kept his *tallis* in its bag in the bottom drawer of his bureau, where it remain undisturbed except for the High Holy Days. The prayer shawl itself was in fact in the drawer still, hidden under one of his father's alpaca cardigan sweaters. The bag itself, though, was being employed to smuggle supplies into the synagogue on the Sabbath. It now contained Howard's memo pad and pen, three disposable penlights, a box containing a brand new blank reel of Scotch magnetic tape, a spare empty reel, and a roll of electrical tape.

"Your father will be proud of you," Jeanette said.

"I hope so," said Howard, glancing heavenward as he got out of the car. For his own benefit, he couldn't stop himself from adding, completely heartfelt, "And I'll be careful." He slammed the passenger door shut.

"You're pretty safe in the synagogue," said Jeanette. Issuing her customary warning had not even occurred to her. She released the emergency brake, put the Chevy in gear, and slowly pulled away.

The boys waved good-bye, all smiles, as she drove to the parking lot exit and turned into the street. Once she was out of view, their expressions became serious.

"Let's walk around and go in through the front," said Howard.

"Okay, and maybe we can go over the plans one more time," said Stinky. He had been calm up until then but now had started to perspire.

The back door of the synagogue suddenly opened with a metal grating sound. Ernie Russell, the janitor, had propelled the door open with a push of his rear end and was dragging out a large aluminum garbage can. Ernie, a sinewy black man in his early sixties, was a fixture at B'nai Jeshurun, the lead janitor and a synagogue employee for at least three decades. He wore a gray striped single-piece work suit but had a *yarmulke* on his head. Howard had never seen Ernie without a yarmulke on his head, or recall a time when Ernie wore anything other than smile on his face.

Ernie twisted the garbage can around, planning to shimmy it down the short flight of stairs in front of him en route to the large green dumpster adjacent to the stairwell, but paused from his garbage transport to acknowledge the new arrivals. He and the can were blocking the stairs.

"You boys comin' up this way?" he asked, smiling as if he had said something amusing.

"We're walking around front," said Howard.

"Well, you boys have a good *Shabbos,*" said Ernie, his previous expression fixed.

"Good *Shabbos*, Ernie," Howard and Stinky said at the same time.

Mike perked up. That word again.

The three boys started to walk across the parking lot.

"I've been meaning to ask. . . ." said Mike.

***

As the boys were going to synagogue ostensibly for Saturday morning services, Melissa Huntley was sitting at the breakfast table with her mother. Her moodiness over the past week, ever since the night of the Young Life Meeting, had not escaped Elaine Huntley's notice. Maybe boy troubles, she thought.

Chad had laid into the girls fairly harshly the morning after the meeting, but Elaine doubted that to be the cause of her daughter's sullenness. The girls were used to their father's volatility and knew he meant nothing by it. He was on edge.

Chadwick had accused the girls of violating his privacy, or if not them personally, failing to keep an eye on their guests. He wouldn't stand for anyone disturbing his things in his private study. Private. He threatened never to allow them to host another Young Life meeting at their house. Anne played dumb, almost angelically, and expressed outrage that her father would even think such a thing. She had absolutely no idea what he was railing on about. She had been in the basement the entire evening, playing hostess. Melissa backed her up faithfully, best actress in a supporting role. Who was interested in his dumb things, anyway? The girls had shrugged and shook their heads in bewilderment. It must have been Juanita, or else he was imagining things. How could he be so sure, anyway? This, a not so subtle reference to his drinking, could have relit the fuse or snuffed it out. Chadwick had relented.

The breakfast room was bright and cheerfully decorated with a floral wallpaper and painted traditional furniture. Facing east, the room was suffused with morning sunlight.

Melissa sat pensively at the empty place setting. The glare of sunlight through the large mullioned windows was a bother. With both elbows on the table, she supported her head with the upturned palms of both hands, as if her head would flop down otherwise. Juanita was busying herself with breakfast preparations in the kitchen.

Elaine, wearing sheepskin–lined house slippers and her robe over her nightgown, was reading the "Kansas City Times."

"Anne not up yet?" she asked.

"I guess not," said Melissa, her downtrodden posture unaltered.

"What do you want to eat?"

"Juanita already asked. I'm not very hungry."

"You can't go without breakfast."

"Cereal, then," Melissa conceded. "Just cereal." She forced herself to sit upright in her chair and sighed.

"You can start with toast and juice," said Juanita, who had come over with two large glasses of fresh squeezed and set them on the table before making a return trip to the kitchen counter to retrieve the toast.

Elaine folded the front section of the paper and placed it on the table, not much interested in the news of the day. She didn't want to provoke her younger daughter first thing in the morning, on what looked to be a beautiful day. Nothing could ruin a beautiful day more than a moody adolescent. But couldn't they have a pleasant conversation to get Melissa's mind off her boy problems? Because boy problems, Elaine had concluded, had to be the explanation for Melissa's ill temper. Anne certainly hadn't been fazed by the shouting match with Chad. Her elder daughter had been downright chipper all week and sleeping like a baby.

"Your father's birthday is a week from tomorrow. You and your sister need to be buy him a nice gift. I'll give you some money. Or you can charge it."

"We're underage—they won't sell us Johnny Walker Black," said Melissa.

Elaine ignored the remark. Maybe it wasn't boy troubles after all.

"A nice silk tie from Jack Henry's. That's always safe. Something to go with his new gray pin-striped suit."

"Okay," said Melissa glumly, buttering her toast in slow motion. "Anne and I are going to the Plaza next Saturday anyway."

Melissa had changed course, given the choice between being disagreeable or agreeable, and choosing the latter. She had a motive, a need to know how much her mother knew, and didn't want the breakfast with her mother to turn sour.

"Mom," she began, "do you know anything about a legal court case Dad's involved in?"

"Not that I am aware of, honey. You know I don't concern myself with the business of his practice. Patient business is sensitive for a psychiatrist. The less I know, the better."

"How about Hannah Stringer? Ever heard of her?"

"That crazy loon!" exclaimed Elaine. "What's that old nutcase up to now? She didn't call here, did she? How do you know about her, anyway?"

"I—I just happened to see her name on a pile of things in Dad's study."

"Now, Melissa, you know better than to disturb your father's things. And what were you doing in his study?" She looked at her daughter sharply, squinting one eye. "Is this about Saturday night? Were you in his study and not telling the truth?"

Melissa was surprised at her own composure, and at the ease with which a child could lie to a parent.

"No, no, nothing to do with that," she said convincingly. Her explanation came seamlessly. "I went in there looking to see what kind of tobacco he liked. . . just a couple of days ago. . . since I was thinking of buying him some for his birthday. I just opened his desk drawer to see what kind of tobacco he needs."

This was believable enough to Elaine, especially given the earlier Johnny Walker Black reference. Chad, she knew, kept his tobacco tins in the bottom right desk drawer, along with his preferred brand of Scotch. "Tobacco would be fine, but I still think that a nice silk tie. . . . "

"Okay."

"And please, Melissa, stay out of your father's study. You know how upset he gets. It's all a question of confidentiality. You mustn't take it personally. A psychiatrist has to be extra careful."

"Then how do *you* know about Hannah Stringer?" Melissa asked, trying to make her tone sound curious rather than brazen.

"Well, Melissa, sometimes I hear things. I'm his wife, after all. But I never know about the specifics of any of his patients. That wouldn't be right."

"I'm sorry," said Melissa. "It won't happen again."

***

After her father's tirade the previous Sunday, the sisters—unyielding in their assertions of innocence—had retreated to the privacy of Anne's bedroom, where they had listened to records. During a third playing of Shelley Fabares singing "Johnny Angel," a somewhat contrite Anne had profusely thanked her younger sister for covering for her. Melissa, after all, had not committed any transgressions, only discovered her own.

"I owe you big time," Anne had said.

"No point in you getting grounded," Melissa had said. "You're the one with the driver's license. What good does it do me if you can't drive me anywhere?"

Melissa could afford to be gracious, knowing that under any other circumstances she would have ratted out her sister in a second. She had not been covering for Anne, she had been covering for Howard Block, a boy she hardly knew.

And though she didn't want to, she believed him. Believed him enough to risk sneaking into her parents' bedroom at 3 a.m. that Sunday morning to borrow the keys from the top of her father's bureau. Elaine was a sound sleeper, usually aided by samples of one sort or another prescription drug that Chadwick brought home for her. Chadwick himself had been snoring loudly and was in a deep, Scotch-induced slumber that had progressed beyond fitful awakening.

Melissa had then gone into the study and quietly opened the file cabinet, retrieved Hannah Stringer's chart, and read as much of it as she could comprehend. Replacing it when she had finished, she noticed what was directly behind it in the file drawer, a carbon copy of a deposition that her father had given regarding a lawsuit involving Hannah Stringer against one Dr. Jack Block. The deposition was more straightforward and easier to understand.

Howard Block had been telling the truth. And so had her mom. Hannah Stringer was indeed a real nutcase. What to make of her own father was more complicated.

***

Services were about to start, and the main sanctuary was reasonably full for *Shabbat* services, despite the fact that no Bar Mitzvah was scheduled for that day. Howard and Mike sat at the back, next to an outside aisle. Both wore loaner *yarmulkes* and *tallises*. From their chosen seats—and some planning had gone into this—they could make a fairly inconspicuous exit once services started. Howard thought that at least two of them needed to establish a legitimate reason for their presence at the synagogue, and equally important, they needed complete assurance that the principal synagogue players would be otherwise detained by religious obligations. Once services started, there would be a good forty-five minute window of safety. Stinky, in *yarmulke* only, had been assigned look-out and was waiting in the vestibule, having returned from scouting out the old basement sanctuary and language lab. As anticipated, the room was unlit and unoccupied.

A middle-aged couple and their pre-teen daughter approached their row and were waiting to sidle past them.

"Excuse us," said Mr. Cohen, who Howard recognized, he and his wife being patients of his father.

Howard, sitting on the aisle clutching the *tallis* bag, stood up, followed by Mike. Mr. Cohen waited politely, motioning his daughter Lael and his wife Ruth to precede him past the boys to the open seats beside them. Howard also knew Lael from Sunday School but she was a year behind him. She flashed him a bracey smile in passing.

Yitzhak Cohen took his seat besides Mike.

"You look like a nice young man," he said. "Very nice sunglasses. I haven't seen you here before."

"I'm an exchange student," Mike replied, hoping to cut off any pleasantries before they could lead anywhere problematic. He spoke in a vaguely European accent, perhaps Dutch, according to his thinking, and certainly obscure enough. Who the hell knew what somebody from Amsterdam sounded like, anyway? "Jewish Field Service," he qualified. He already had come up with his cover, if asked. His father was a contractor in the Netherlands—dike construction.

"Very impressive," said Mr. Cohen, easing back into his seat. He turned to his wife and smiled. She would want a full report on the exchange later. Howard had often heard his mother refer to Ruth Cohen as a "business person." "Everything is her business," Jeanette would say.

Cantor Birenboim, wearing a long black robe and traditional cantor's hat, emerged from the screen behind the pulpit and shook hands with Rabbi Margolis and Yakov Bettinger, who were sitting in the throne-like chairs on opposite sides of the altar. Services were about to begin, and the three greatest threats to the security of the mission were sufficiently out of the way.

"All clear," whispered Howard to Mike. "Let's go."

As if they had simultaneously been struck by a sudden urge to pee, both boys left their seats and headed purposefully up the aisle to the exit.

Ruth Cohen immediately leaned over to her husband.

"I've never seen him before. He must be Lael's age. Who are his parents?"

"What would I know from his parents?" Mr. Cohen replied. "He's a Jewish exchange student. Enough that he's friends with Dr. Block's son, isn't it?

***

Stinky was pacing in the empty vestibule when Mike and Howard emerged from the sanctuary. Howard had given him one of the penlights when they had split up, and he was flashing it on and off nervously.

"There you are! I thought services would never start!" he said.

"Is it all clear?" Howard asked.

"Yeah."

"He didn't lock the door, did he?"

"No, you know he never does. Who'd be crazy enough to go in there without permission?" Stinky answered his own question. "Us, that's who. Let's get this over with before I change my mind."

"Which way?" Mike asked. Being team leader was difficult without knowing the lay of the land, and he had not prepped himself for a mission in a synagogue. There was much about Jews that remained a mystery to him.

"Down here—" Stinky led the way, hustling across the vestibule and down a short flight of stairs that was the connection to the old section of the synagogue.

"Wait a sec," Howard said to Mike. He lifted the prayer shawl over his head, folded it in half neatly and then folded over again. Before placing it in one of the wooden bins that contained the loaner *tallises*, he brought it to his lips and lightly kissed it.

Mike removed his own shawl and looked at Howard questioningly.

"Do I kiss it? On our first date?" Mike smiled at his own joke.

"That's okay," said Howard. "You don't have to."

Mike folded his shawl, not quite as carefully as Howard had, and set it in the bin.

"What about my beanie?" he asked.

"That you keep on," said Howard. He unzipped the *tallis* bag and took out the two remaining penlights, one of which he handed to Mike.

"Let's get this done," he said.

Chapter Fifteen

"Wow," said Mike. "This is great. You guys weren't kidding."

"We told you," said Howard.

All three boys were huddled in the dark on the floor of Cantor Birenboim's language lab office, well below the observation window. Mike had made an initial assessment of the equipment by shining his penlight around.

"Whoa, and it's complicated," he said. He lifted himself up high enough to set his beam on the main console. "But first, the main power switch." A small red bulb lit up after he flicked the switch, and the console responded with a soft humming. "I just have to make sure we're recording to the correct unit. We'll use Recorder Number One." Already he was monkeying with some of the dials on the console. Satisfied, he straightened up just long enough to switch on the first of the tape players.

"Tape," he said to Howard, who was crouching beside him in the darkness.

From the *tallis* bag Howard pulled out the box with the blank magnetic tape and handed it over. Mike removed the tape from the its container and again stood full up in the darkness while Howard directed his penlight so Mike could see to install the tape. Threading completed, Mike depressed the "Play and "Record" buttons together and paused the recorder after a couple of revolutions. The winding spools froze, like two soldiers snapping to attention.

"Those Wollensacks are just like my Dad's, except there are EIGHT of them!" said Mike, barely able to contain the excitement in his voice. "We can use my Dad's microphone."

"You brought his microphone?" Stinky asked.

Howard and Stinky couldn't see Mike's smile very well, but they knew the grin was there. The mission commander reached down the front of his trousers and worked loose a hidden strip of electrical tape from the inside of his upper thigh, freeing up the loop of cord that was taped there. Then he reached under his left cuff and pulled out the microphone that had been hanging under his pant leg.

Howard and Stinky responded with appropriate admiration. Very cool, and neither had known about it. Of course, there had been no need to know until that very moment.

"That's not all," said a beaming Mike. He tucked himself onto his knees, lifted up his sport coat, and untucked the back of his shirt. Reaching under, he removed a creased piece of cardboard that had been hidden under his shirt all along as well. It was five sided, a rectangle with a long portion of one corner cut-off, a shape not unlike the boundaries of the state of Alabama.

"What's tha—"

Mike cut off Stinky with a shush.

"Electrical tape," he prompted Howard, the curt request of a surgeon to scrub nurse.

While Howard was again fishing around in the *tallis* bag, Mike reached up to the Cantor's desktop and brought the telephone down to the floor beside him. The fact that the cord was long enough to reach was testament to the practicality and foresight of Cantor Birenboim, who was not one to be caught with a short cable of any kind. Mike proceeded to rig the phone headset in the same manner that he had done for the test run in his bedroom. He had brought the short metal rod from his pocket to keep the switch hook depressed—and silence the dial tone—while he did his work.

Howard stayed focused on Mike's manipulations, but Stinky's attention began to wander. He shined his penlight around the confines of the office and happened upon a row of labeled boxes of tapes occupying a lower shelf. Focusing his flashlight, he turned his head sideways to read the labels, handwritten in Hebrew in dark marking pen.

"Lookee here, Howie," he said, pulling one of the boxes from the shelf. "This is your *Haftorah* tape. Lookee here. It says '*Matoth. Dibre Yirmayahu.*' That's your reading isn't it?"

Howard glanced over and nodded, not especially interested. Stinky had opened the box and was examining the reel of tape inside. "I wonder if I can find mine," he said, setting the box on the counter and turning his attention back to the other boxes of tapes on of the shelf.

"Stinky. . . " Mike said with strained politeness, but castigating nonetheless. He was intent on working and did not appreciate the distraction.

"Stinky," he repeated, tearing off a piece of electrical tape. "We need you as a look-out. Why don't you go to the other end of the room and stand guard? Stay out of sight and flash Howie with your light if anybody's coming."

"Right away," said Stinky. Back in the mission mindset, he slithered out the door, quite stealthily as far as he was concerned, and scurried across the room in the darkness.

201

Mike had finished rigging the funnel to the handset and was securing the microphone in place with the electrical tape.

"This is a great set-up," said Mike. "I've got it rigged so it will record internally without playing through the external speakers. That way we can really turn up the recording volume without blasting ourselves out and waking the dead."

Howard nodded eagerly. "Are you ready now?" he asked. "I got the number in my pad."

"I memorized it," said Mike. "We're all set. Ready to initiate operation, okay?" Not waiting for an answer, he stood up just long enough to hit the "Pause" button on the recorder and confirm that the "record" indicator light was on and the spools turning. He sat back down on the floor and picked up his modified handset. He spoke into the open end of the cardboard sound amplification device, as close as he could get to the suspended microphone.

"This is Mike Hunsacker, with Howard Block as my official witness. Today's date is June 8, 1963, and I am dialing Miss Hannah Stringer at Delmar 3. . . ."

He lifted the metal rod from the carriage, waited for the dial tone, and began dialing as he continued to record the event.

She answered after the third ring.

"Aloo? Is thees Madame Hannah Stringer?" Mike wiggled his butt on the floor to get more comfortable.

"It ees?" he continued. "Thees ees Johanne Peters. I call you before, no? Yes? We have very good news about ze monee, but first I must ask you zome questions. Ees okay, no? Yes?"

Howard sat beside him, electrified, heart pounding.

Above them both, the reels on Cantor Birenboim's Recorder Number One smoothly spun around and around.

Stinky's sentry spot was behind racks of folding chairs at the opposite end of the basement. From his position he could see the language lab carrels and the front entrance directly across the room, and to his left, he had clear view of the back entrance, a single windowed door at the far end of an adjacent dining area. The door led to the synagogue kitchen and bathrooms, as well as a stairwell going up to the school classrooms. All was dark behind the frosted glass window, Stinky was relieved to see. In their concern with the Holy Trinity of the Cantor, the Rabbi, and Bettinger, Stinky realized, the boys had forgotten about Ernie. Hopefully he was preoccupied with cleaning the classrooms upstairs, or just hanging out somewhere, but there was no telling.

Stinky had to make sure. He crept across the dining area and went through the back door. Ernie was nowhere within sight or sound. The kitchen was deserted and all the lights were off in the hallway and stairwell. Stinky observed the empty garbage can just inside the kitchen entrance; Ernie had emptied and replaced it. The supply closet next to the bathrooms was closed and locked. Stinky confirmed there was no light coming from under the door of the Ladies' room, and personally cleared the Men's room, which was also dark and empty. Everything in the old part of the *shul* seemed secure. Stinky had taken the initiative, for once, and was quite proud of himself.

Now back to his station, Stinky looked toward the Cantor's office. He could make out no signs of light or movement, not even a soft glow from one of the flashlights. Hard to believe, but it looked like they were actually going to be able to pull the mission off. Then he had a bad feeling. Was it possible that Mike and Howard had finished taping and had already left? No, not possible, he reassured himself, since he hadn't been gone all that long. Besides, they would never leave a member of the team behind.

Stinky turned his head to recheck the dining room. Again darkness behind the back door window. Then suddenly there was light! Someone had turned on the light in the back hallway!

Stinky gasped. He dropped to his hands and knees beside the rack and fumbled with the flashlight. At first he shined it into his own eyes, but then managed to signal in the appropriate direction. He flashed the beam on and off, on and off, frantically pressing and releasing the metal tab that made battery contact. He wished he knew Morse code—just knowing the signal for S.O.S. would have been enough—but he could do no more than flash the light randomly, repeating "S.O.S! S.O.S!" aloud to himself.

Howard had not been especially diligent about watching for a potential warning signal from Stinky. In fact, he had forgot about him completely, mesmerized by the one-sided conversation that he was witnessing.

As Stinky began his flashing, Mike was just getting into the meat of the interview.

"I zee. And what does Dr. Huntlee tell you to say?"

Howard was spellbound.

Stinky was now in a panic, furiously squeezing and unsqueezing the penlight. He was farting too, emitted nearly synchronously with his flashings like a sound and light show. Nothing seemed to make a difference; there was no response to his signal. All communications were dead.

Stinky wasn't sure what to do. Should he run across the room and warn them? Was there time? Or should he stay and wait it out? Maybe he was jumping the gun, he thought. Just because someone was in the hallway didn't mean. . . .

And then, abruptly, the dining room door was pushed open. The entrance would have been more dramatic had the lights burst on suddenly as well, but being fluorescent, they lagged, sputtering like a stammering Porky Pig before finally achieving full illumination. This did not prevent Stinky from nearly jumping out of his skin, however.

Ernie again made his entrance backwards, pushing the door open with his backside, this time pulling a wheeled mop bucket. The bucket was filled nearly to the brim with hot water and diluted Mr. Clean; the stick of the mop protruded from the bucket like a flagpole. Taking care not to slosh the water, Ernie negotiated the door carefully, adjusting the mop handle with one hand so that it wouldn't catch on the doorframe.

By the time Ernie had pulled the bucket through and swiveled it frontward, Irwin Devinki was walking across the dining room toward him, nonchalantly adjusting his *yarmulke*.

"Irwin, what are you doing—"

"I've been looking all over for you, Ernie. . . " said Stinky, his voice a bit unsteady.

***

Stinky tore across the old basement sanctuary in the darkness with uncharacteristic celerity, finishing his sprint with a slide onto the floor just by Birenboim's office door. He tapped on the door softly but with clear urgency. Howard shimmied across the floor inside on his bottom and reached up to twist the door handle. He opened the door only enough to peer out and give Stinky a "shush" gesture. Behind Howard, an irritated Mike placed his hand over the handset mouthpiece to muffle any sounds, while Hannah was evidently continuing to talk on the other end of the line.

"You gotta wrap it up!" Stinky spewed in a harsh whisper. "Ernie's about to come in here to do the floors! I stalled him for now but he's gonna be in here any minute!"

Howard kept the door only slightly ajar, and turned to Mike.

"You got enough?" he whispered. He pantomimed an unmistakable non-verbal signal for "We gotta get outta here," with an impromptu hand gesture suggesting a hitchhiker having a seizure.

"Got plenty!" replied Mike, pressing his finger down on one of the levers in the phone carriage to cut off the connection with Hannah. "Let's clean up and split!"

After setting the tape player to rewind, Mike recruited Howard to help him in the dismantling of the phone apparatus. Commands were brief and abrupt. They worked furiously. Eyes adapted to the dark by then, they couldn't be bothered with their flashlights, needing all their hands for the clean-up ahead of them.

"What can I do?" asked Stinky, who had crawled through the doors into the darkness and, still on all fours, was now trying to keep out of the way of the flinging arms.

"Get that tape off the deck as soon as it's rewound! Here's the box!" With a quick flap of his arm, Mike slid the open tape box across the floor in Stinky's direction.

Stinky struggled to stand up, bumping his shoulder against the edge of the counter, and started to remove the tape from the spool before stopping the recorder.

"Ouch!" he blurted. "I almost lost a finger!"

"Shush!" Mike and Howard said in unison.

206

Stinky managed to stop the tape recorder and turn the power off. But he was having trouble getting the tape spool off the machine.

"I can't get it—The tape won't come off—"

"You have to twist and pull at the same time," instructed Mike brusquely, replacing the Cantor's phone back on the counter.

Stinky did as he was told, twisting and pulling harder. The tape came off with unexpected force and threw him backwards. He tripped on his own foot and fell over, dropping the tape in the process.

"QUIET, Stinky!" Howard said louder than he should have.

Flustered, Stinky righted himself onto all fours, and patting the ground in the dark like a blind man, first found the tape and then the empty box. He carefully placed the tape in the box by feel and closed it.

"Put the microphone in the bag," Mike ordered Howard, quickly winding the cord into the semblance of a loop and slapping it into his hand like a relay baton. Howard crammed the mic into the bag.

"Here's the tape, Howie—" Stinky said, holding the box out and waving it until it bumped into Howard. Without responding, Howard grabbed it and tucked it into the *tallis* bag.

"What about the cardboard?" Howard asked Mike.

"We'll toss it on the way out. . . "

"Don't leave the flashlights. . . " said Howard, who had already put his in the bag.

"In my pocket," said Mike.

"Yours, Stinky?"

"I think it's on the floor here. . . got it."

207

While feeling for the penlight, Stinky's hands encountered another reel of tape. He realized he had knocked over the *Haftorah* tape that he had set on the counter earlier.

"Let's go!" Mike said.

"Hold it. . ." said Stinky, feeling around for the box, which had slid under the counter.

Mike and Howard had sprung from their crouches and were already out the door. Stinky struggled to get the tape in the box, then fit the box back into the correct slot on the shelf.

"Stinky!"

"Coming!" Stinky quickly adjusted the tape boxes so they were flush on the bottom shelf.

Then he, too, was out of the office, closing the door as quietly as he could. Emerging from the old sanctuary in the manner of football players walking back to the huddle after a hard hit, the three adjusted themselves with transient and migrating squirming.

No one saw them. To a casual observer—had there been one—the three boys just looked as if they had been praying really, really hard.

Walking across the vestibule toward the new sanctuary and the main synagogue entrance, Stinky adjusted his underwear, Howard zipped up his *tallis* bag, and Mike dropped a folded up piece of cardboard, with adhering strips of electrical tape, into a trash receptacle.

Then he casually reached into the front pocket of his sports coat for his sunglasses.

***

Ernie Russell stood over the toilet, plunger in hand, satisfied. For good measure, he flushed again and watched the emergence of the gush, the counter-clockwise whirlpool, and heard the satisfied gurgle, as if the toilet bowl were belching after a swig of good brew.

After replacing the plunger in the storage closet, he ambled back to the dining room, where he had left his mop and bucket. Between the old sanctuary and the dining room, there was a helluva lot of floor. His custom was to start in the Cantor Birenboim's office, work his way back from the carrels, and finish up with the dining room. Otherwise, he'd have to track back and forth over the wet floor to refill his bucket with clean water.

Ernie, dragging the bucket behind, headed across the dining room to the three light switches, just behind the racks of chairs. He flicked them all on with an upward sweep of his open hand and waited. The rows of fluorescent ceiling lights flickered haphazardly for a couple of seconds before the room was fully lit.

As anticipated, the capacious space was deserted. Ernie failed to notice that the double doors on the far side of the room were just then slowly closing.

***

The boys were ebullient.

"Man, once she got going, she wouldn't stop talking!" Mike was following Howard and Stinky as they exited the main sanctuary entrance, all having ditched their *yarmulkes* and what remained of services. Only Mr. Cohen, aware that the boys had never returned, would be struck by the oddity of their brief appearance. And Lael, intrigued by the boy she didn't know—the one who apparently had a sensitivity to light—was clearly disappointed.

The boys walked around the building to the back, the way they had come, and started threading their way through the parked cars in the parking lot, looking for their ride.

"Incredible!" Howard shouted.

"When are you going to play it?" Stinky asked.

"Can't until Monday night. When my Dad brings the tape recorder home from the office."

"Keep it safe," said Mike.

"You bet I will," said Howard.

"Over there, in the corner!" Stinky yelled out, pointing across the lot.

They picked up the pace simultaneously, trotting on individual circuitous paths between the parked cars. Soon they reached their destination, a pink four-door 1958 Oldsmobile Super Eight-Eight.

"Great car!" Howard said to the driver, who was leaning back in the seat, resting his left elbow on the open window.

"Appreciate it. Get in." Junior Lee was wearing a fedora and dark sunglasses.

Howard walked around to take the shotgun position, while Mike and Stinky opened the rear back doors.

"Nice shades," said Mike, scooching onto the seat. "And thanks for the lift."

"No problem. And your shades are pretty cool, too," said Junior. "So, how did it go?"

"Great," Howard told him. "It went perfect."

"Good news, no blues," said Junior. "I ain't had my breakfast, though."

"How about burgers?" Howard offered. "Our treat."

Junior answered by revving the engine.

***

". . . and a cherry coke with that."

Howard was the last to order, leaning across the seat with his face just below that of Junior's. They were parked in the lot of Winstead's, and Marilyn was their waitress again.

"And—oh yeah—all of us want paper plates and paper cups, please, if you don't mind," he added. Junior Lee was doing them a favor, even if he owed them one, but Howard couldn't bear the thought of his being singled out and humiliated.

"I have to hand it to you, Stinky," Mike said. "I had my doubts about you, and you're not always the quietest person in the world, but stalling that Ernie guy was a stroke of genius. You are a master of deceit."

Stinky beamed. He leaned forward, and saw that both Howard and Junior were looking over their shoulders for his response to the accolades.

"I just told him, 'I think the toilet down the hall is stopped up. You better check on it, Ernie, before it overflows.' Just like that. Like it was real serious. And he turned right around—left his bucket and mop right there on the spot—and headed to the closet for his plunger. And as soon as I made sure he was heading for the bathroom, that's when I ran back to tell you."

Stinky had maintained considerable calm at the time but apparently the nerves had only been delayed and were now leaking out of him. Quivering, he himself couldn't believe he had pulled that off, and just the thought of it was enough to make him shake. He absently flicked the penlight in his hand on and off.

"You saved our butts, Stinky, AND the mission," Howard said, shaking his head in admiration. He had been even more surprised than Mike by Stinky's rising to the occasion. "How did you ever think of that? Making up that story the toilet was plugged up?"

"It WAS plugged up," said Stinky. "I—I didn't really think of it," he stammered. "I mean, I didn't make it up. The toilet really was stopped up."

"Really stopped up?" Howard asked.

"Yeah."

The other three boys were now staring at him, the car awash in total silence. They were confused, and waiting for the explanation.

"I had to take a dump, alright?" said a somewhat defensive Stinky. "Before. . . when you guys first sent me as lookout," he explained. "I was checking out the bathroom, and, you know, I suddenly really had to go. Like really bad. This spy business has kinda upset my stomach. . . and when ya gotta go—"

Howard, Mike and Junior exploded in laughter. Catching on after a short delay, Stinky joined them. A big shit had never seemed so hilarious.

"Sue me," chortled Stinky.

Chapter Sixteen

Early Monday evening, Howard nervously awaited his father's return from work. Jeanette was preparing dinner in the kitchen, and Howard had forced himself to sit down in front of the television—made easier by the fact that "Maverick" was on—when the hum of the electric garage door opener made him bolt down the stairs to the garage to meet his father at the door.

"You bring it?" Howard asked excitedly. Jack was wearing a pale blue sport coat, a recent gift from Jeanette for springtime wear. Jack didn't concern himself with clothes much, so it mattered little that he was not particularly fond of it. Unless someone made a comment, he even forgot he was wearing it.

"In the car. Back seat."

"I'll get it for you."

"What's all the secrecy about?"

"It's a surprise," said Howard, pushing past him to retrieve the recorder. "I need you to hear something later. After dinner. Just the two of us."

Jack stood in the doorway but turned to watch his son, who had already opened the passenger door of the red Ford

Galaxy and pulled the seat forward, half of his body sticking into the car.

"I'll meet you upstairs," said Jack.

"I'll go ahead and plug it in. In the study," said Howard, wriggling his way out, dragging the tape recorder in one hand.

Jack laughed, shaking his head. He suspected the tape had something to do with the upcoming Bar Mitzvah. A recorded run-through, perhaps? But that didn't explain all the excitement. . . .

"By the way," said Howard, slamming the door. "You've got to burn that jacket."

"Your mother gave it to me," said Jack, jogging up the stairs.

Howard knew that.

***

Howard thought dinner would never end. He ate quickly, to Jeanette's consternation, and had nearly cleaned his plate before Jeanette had finished serving and sat down herself.

"That was great, Mom," he said.

"You ate too fast."

"You almost done, Dad?"

"Your father has barely started. You want both of you to get indigestion?"

While Jack didn't dispose of his meal any faster than usual, Howard took notice that he turned down Jeanette's offerings for second helpings, clearly on Howard's behalf. This was uncharacteristic behavior, so much so that Jeanette worriedly inquired if he were not feeling well. Jack defended himself by claiming a late lunch, undoubtedly a fib. His father could have a bigger nosh later, if not the leftovers, then a big hunk of cheese washed down with a glass of buttermilk, so Howard didn't feel too guilty. He would get it for him, in fact. In any case, the surprise he had in store was worth going hungry for.

Finally alone together in his father's lower level study, Howard struggled to control his hands as he threaded the tape into the recorder.

"I know how to do it," he reassured his father, who was sitting back in his lounge chair, as instructed, holding onto an unlit pipe.

Fairly bursting, Howard set his index finger on the "Play" button, looking directly at his father with a smile as he dramatically pressed it down. He lifted his hand off the machine with a flourish, a limp wave of the wrist, like a pianist coming to a fermata after a challenging cadenza.

The tape had a long lead. The anticipation was building, with even Jack bending forward in his chair. Then there came the sound of a pitch pipe. Howard froze in disbelief. Even before the melodious voice of Cantor Birenboim broke into the chanting of the *Haftorah,* Howard's emotional collapse had begun.

His expression changed from joyous anticipation to utter devastation, with a soundtrack in Hebrew accompanying the transformation. Thrusting himself into Jack's arms, Howard sobbed uncontrollably. He was incapable of speech, gasping for breath when he tried to talk.

Jack held on to him, uncomprehending, patting him gently on his back.

"What's the problem, boy? You can tell me. It can't be all that bad. Just between you and me, us *mensches.* What's the matter, huh?"

And the Cantor sang on.

***

On Tuesday, Jack Block had his receptionist reschedule some of his afternoon cases, and he asked Ed Foreman to check on a couple of his more critical hospital patients after work for him. None of his associates, no one in the office, asked for an explanation, and Jack did not offer one. Many assumed that there had been a death or illness in the Block family. If asked any specifics, he would have lied, or, rather, employed the art of deceit for their own protection. Dr. Block had become the most recent recruit to the team and was about to embark on his first mission.

Shortly before 4 p.m., Howard and Stinky were preparing for their synagogue session to begin. Ever since Danny Becker's Bar Mitzvah and hence graduation from the language lab, the cacophony—while still somewhat of a choral racket—had been appreciably more dulcet. All had taken their seats in their carrel of choice except for Howard, who was anxiously pacing and looking at his watch. The Cantor was in his office, already beginning the methodical process of setting up the tapes on the different recorders. Looking through his window, he saw that Howard had not yet taken his seat.

"Which carrel do you want, Howard?" he asked, sticking his head out around the door.

"Um. . . Number Two, I guess."

"I'll set you up shortly."

Cantor Birenboim was just beginning to thread Howard's *Haftorah* tape on Reel Number Two when Jack Block entered through the main old sanctuary doors, carrying his satchel. He acknowledged Howard with an abbreviated nod and proceeded directly to the Cantor's office. Howard, as well as Stinky, breathed a sigh of relief, having worried that he might get tied up and be late. They were unaware that Jack had been early, and waiting in the lobby of the main sanctuary for fifteen minutes.

Jack rapped lightly on the office window.

"Excuse me, Cantor. . . ."

The Cantor brightened. Dr. Block, of course, was his physician.

"What a surprise, Doctor! And such a pleasure to see you here, sir!"

"The pleasure is mine, Cantor. I've come to ask you a favor."

"Anything, Doctor. How can I be of service?"

"My son tells me you have a tape of his *Haftorah*. The complete rendition. With you singing it."

"Certainly. I have a complete tape for every *Haftorah*. But those are for reference, not teaching. The students learn from special instructional tapes, with each phrase broken down so they can learn it. I sing a phrase, they repeat, and so on. I'm sure Howard has told you of our set-up here. Just like the language labs in universities, the latest in technology. A very effective learning method. And more efficient for me, of course." The Cantor had stepped out of his office and taken a couple of steps toward the carrels, extending his arm as if he were trying to sell a new washer/dryer.

Jack kept walking toward his son's carrel, the Cantor accompanying him. Howard scootched his chair sideways to face them.

"Howard has described it to me in detail," Jack said. "A very impressive set-up. Howard says the sound quality is excellent. Could you give me a demonstration in one of these booths? I know this is an imposition, but I rarely get away from the office this early in the day, and I just so happened to have a couple of patients cancel, so thought I might take this opportunity to see things for myself."

"No imposition at all," said the Cantor. "I'd be delighted."

"Here, Dad," said Howard, getting up from his chair and proffering his set of headphones. "Check it out."

"Use mine," said the Cantor, removing his own headphones and handing them to his doctor. "These headphones are the highest quality, professional quality, and it makes a difference. Howard can show you where to plug them in."

"You sure you don't mind?" Jack asked. "I know you're busy."

"Of course not."

"The uninterrupted version I'm referring to," Jack reiterated, laughing. "I would love to hear Howard's *Haftorah* the way a real Cantor sings it. Howard I can hear all the time at home. But a real Cantor like yourself. . . I don't often get the chance."

"It would be my pleasure, Dr. Block. Here. Sit. Give me just a moment to change the tape. And let me make sure everyone else has started."

The Cantor, cheered by the chance to show off both his mechanical and musical prowess, returned to his office with a spring in his step. Jack sat down in the carrel seat, turning the chair so he could keep an eye on the Cantor, and settled the headphones in place. His satchel, which he had snapped open when the Cantor's back was turned, sat expectantly on the floor beside him. Howard stood behind his father, resting one hand on the back of the chair.

The rest of the boys were well into their practicing, except for Stinky who, in Carrel 4, was unable to concentrate on the words and tunes in his ears. He leaned back slightly in his chair to keep an eye on the goings-on two carrels over, the palm of one hand holding his *yarmulke* in place.

Cantor Birenboim removed the tape he had just threaded for Howard, deftly replacing it with a tape he procured from a box on a lower shelf, where he kept all the master tapes. He looked through the window at Dr. Block, who was observing his progress and nodding. The Cantor smiled and nodded back, then depressed the "Play" button. He did not sit down, though, but continued to look out his observation window to see the good doctor's reactions.

Jack listened intently under the watchful eye of the Cantor. He turned up the volume, as Howard had shown him, and cupped both of his hands over the earpieces.

His eyes widened. Eventually, his eyes began to water and he had to remove one hand from his ear to wipe a tear from one eye. He squeezed his son's arm. Watching this, Cantor Birenboim beamed with pride—the operative Yiddish word being *kvelled*. Possessing a fine vocal instrument was one thing, but being able to sell it was another thing altogether. So, was Robert Merrill really such a hot shot? Could the opera star bring good Dr. Block to tears with *Dibre Yirmayahu*?

Jack removed the headphones. Cantor Birenboim stopped the tape and began to rewind. Jack was on his feet and at the door to the office just as the Cantor stopped the rewinding and removed the tape from the spool.

"Cantor. A word with you." He put an arm around the Cantor's shoulder and started to lead him out of the office. The Cantor set the tape on his counter and began walking with him.

Jack continued to address the Cantor in a low, conspiratorial tone, suggesting something to be spoken *not in front of der kinder*. As such, he led him past the carrels, away from the office and toward the far side of the room. He kept his arm on the Cantor's shoulder the entire time, nudging him gently along, as if he were the lead partner in a line dance.

"I just want to thank you, Cantor, for all you've done for my son. Both yourself and Mr. Bettinger. I'm sure it can be difficult for you, with those who are perhaps less observant than they might be, or should be. It is a delicate balance, sometimes. I'm sure you understand what I mean."

"Of course," answered Birenboim. "But sometimes we judge people too much by their outward show. Judging righteousness by an attendance sheet is not always the best criteria."

"I have tried to teach Howard that the most important thing is what you feel in your heart." Jack had already peeked once over his shoulder, and knew it was safe to turn the Cantor around.

They slowly began walking back toward the office. Stinky, keeping a watchful eye on both the movements of Howard as well as his father, quickly buried his head in his carrel and attacked his phrases with renewed dedication and vigor. Howard had had more than enough time to remove the tape from the satchel, sneak into the Cantor's office for the switch, and complete the transfer of the incriminating tape with that of the original *Haftorah* recording. He snapped the satchel shut.

"I could not agree with you more, Dr. Block," said the Cantor, noting with pleasure that Irwin Devinki seemed hard at work for a change.

Howard sat in his chair, feigning impatience.

"I'm ready to get going, Cantor," he said.

"I shouldn't take up any more of your time, Cantor. Thanks again," Jack said. "I can't begin to tell you how much I appreciated this." He reached down for his satchel and turned to Howard. "I'll see you at home tonight, b—" He caught himself and started over.

"I'll see you at home tonight, son."

***

That evening before dinner, using the kitchen phone and within earshot of both his wife and Howard, Jack Block made a call to Martin Oliver, telling him that he was ready to settle. Upon hearing the words, Jeanette froze in the middle of tossing the iceberg lettuce. Howard had been paying attention all along, glued to the side of his father like a secret service agent, prepared for what was coming.

"No, you don't understand, Martin. They're going to settle with *me*! Tomorrow at the office. Just arrange it." He hung up.

"What's going on, Jack?" Jeanette asked.

"Some new information has surfaced."

By tacit agreement, Jeanette was to be kept out of the loop. Given what Howard had done on his own, behind both of their backs, explanations would be complicated, reactions scattershot and profound, ramifications felt for years to come. Howard knew that after his mother's tearful tirades over his deceptions and betrayals, his freedoms—all of them—would be in jeopardy. Life as he knew it, over. Bike riding to Mike's. Sleepovers. Taking the bus to the Plaza. The Schwinn itself. He would be on a 24-hour-a-day Jeanette Watch until college.

The conference, held only moments before the phone call while his father was urinating in the downstairs powder room, had been brief and to the point.

"Mom can't know. She can't."

"You're telling me?"

"It's for her own good."

Jack looked over and gave his son a knowing half-smile while he shook the remaining drops from his penis.

Agenda item completely discussed, the motion was implicitly raised and seconded, and passed unanimously by a silent and internal voice vote of all present. Jack flushed the toilet.

"New information?" Jeanette asked back in the kitchen.

"Yes," said Jack. The tone of his answer expressed a totality, a completeness into itself. "Yes" was his answer, his final answer, and since he wasn't going to say anything else, there was no reason for anyone to waste breath asking.

"That's wonderful!" gushed Jeanette. "I've been putting money in the *pishka* for you, Jack. I knew all along things would work out."

Jack smiled at her and without changing expression turned to face Howard.

"You got any extra change for the blue box, son?"

Howard smiled and reached into his pocket.

Chapter Seventeen

Stinky felt guilty about lying to his best friend. Howard had called, asking to hang out together, but since Mrs. Devinki was specifically dropping her son off at the Plaza to shop for Howard's present, Stinky had to come up with an excuse. Otherwise, he really would have liked to spend that Saturday with Howard. Practically speaking, Stinky could never decide between the cinnamon apples or the popcorn balls at Topsy's, and if Howard had been with him, they could have bought one of each and split them.

His hands sticky from the caramel popcorn ball, Stinky washed them in the bathroom of Putsch's coffee shop before taking a table and ordering a Coke and fries. The big day being a week away, Stinky was nervous for Howard and even more nervous for himself. For some strange reason, the stress was now giving him an appetite. His own moment in the spotlight would come at the beginning of August, and he was trying not to think about it. But what he would think about, as he twirled a French fry in a mound of ketchup, was what kind of gifts he would like to receive over the next couple of months. Nearly anything from Jack Henry's, he decided, lifting his chin and extending his neck to guide the fry into his mouth.

The swanky men's store with its wood-paneled interior was at the opposite end of the social and economic spectrum from Walter's Clothing, its ambiance suggesting an exclusive New England men's club or an English country manor house. In suburban Kansas City, however, it was highly unlikely that a red-jacketed gentleman in jodhpurs would ever make a visit. Nonetheless, the sales staff would be ready for him if he did, and in the meantime they could barely conceal their disappointment with most of their clientele. Jack Henry's employees were oddly protective of their stock, treating cottons and woolens as if they were porcelain or antiques. Patrons and staff all spoke in undertones, as if an actual Mr. Jack Henry were upstairs, an elderly gent under the weather after a difficult hunt and just having taken a sleeping draught. Often the only sounds to be heard were the rhythmic clicking of heels along the highly waxed floor as persons of discretion worked their way between the counters and table displays. Not surprisingly, as an adolescent hang out, Jack Henry's was not a welcoming place, and for most adolescents, the feeling was mutual.

Irwin Devinki—and he always considered himself Irwin when inside the establishment—was a notable exception, his precocious fashion sense accounting for his exuberance whenever he patronized the place. Hands down, it was his favorite shop on the Plaza, excluding places that served food or snacks.

Stinky began by browsing for himself. He slowly advanced along a rack of sport coats, separating and sliding the jackets on the chrome pole with hand and wrist, a few at a time, focused and watchful, like a traffic cop waving cars past while on the lookout for a suspect. He interrupted his rifling to check out the price tag on the sleeve of an especially snappy plaid, raised his eyebrows, and gave a little shudder. Someday. Undeterred, he continued to browse, savoring his communion with natural fibers, custom tailoring, and European styling.

For Anne Huntley, who was holding one of the heavy doors open for her sister, the store was annoying, and she intended to complete her errand in short order.

"Let's get this over with. I know where the ties are," she said, briskly walking toward the tie racks.

Melissa and Anne walked past Stinky, who had picked up a short-sleeved polo shirt from the middle of a meticulously displayed row of shirts and just flagged down the sales clerk lurking nearby. By removing the turquoise shirt, Stinky had left a gap in the arrangement, which the clerk noted with discomfiture. He fought the compulsion to straighten his stock immediately, but controlled himself and waited for resolution. Until the kid moved on or actually bought the shirt— and fat chance of that—he would have to live with the mess.

"Excuse me," said Stinky, "could you tell me if this is one-hundred-percent cotton?"

"Yes," said the clerk, who Stinky immediately recognized as one of the haughtiest workers in the store.

"Is that 'yes' you could tell me? Or 'yes' it's one-hundred-percent cotton?" he persisted.

"'Yes' to both," came the reply. The sales clerk began doing something weird with his lips.

"Cool," said Stinky, thinking indirect flattery was more likely to win the guy over than sassiness and wondering why he had to be stuck with the biggest butt-hole in the place. "I'll keep looking, then," he said, considering size and color selection, using both hands. The sales clerk rolled his eyes, thinking "Why doesn't the pudgeball just ransack the place?"

To make matters worse, another battlefront had opened in neckwear, where a couple of teenage girls were rummaging. Girls were even worse than the boys. The clerk ambled over in their direction, hands clasped behind his back in a death grip.

Anne was running her hands through the hanging ties, as if playing a harp.

"It really doesn't matter, does it?" she was telling herself and her sister. "He can exchange it if he doesn't like it. Get this one, or the other one. I don't really give a shit."

"May I help you?" The sales clerk seemed to step out of nowhere.

"Don't think so," said Anne.

"Thank you, no," said Melissa. "Just a tie for our father."

The sales clerk, who by now deserves a name—which was Lawrence—could have inquired as to whether the tie was to be worn primarily with blue or brown suits or if their father had a preference as to a club pattern versus stripes. He decided against it and retreated instead to the home base behind the counter, a safe haven in the ongoing field of battle.

"I think this one," Melissa said, an orange and blue striped tie draped across her palm.

"Peachy keen," said Anne. "Pay for it. I'm leaving. I hate this place. Meet me at Hartzfeld's." As if she had suffered a grave insult, she turned on her heels and left.

Melissa made her way to the register in the front of the store, Lawrence's register, but Stinky had gotten there first. The clerk and the boy were in the midst of a mild kerfuffle.

"I know my name isn't on the front of the certificates," Stinky was saying, "but he gave them to me. Look—he signed his name on the back of all of them, like endorsing a check."

Stinky was having trouble controlling his irritation. The clerk was stone-faced and looking obstinate, unconvinced.

Stinky continued his explanation. He had to get through to this schmuck.

"Howard Block. He's my best friend. I didn't steal them. He GAVE them to me. He signed his name on the back of every one."

"Howard Block?" Melissa moved from behind Stinky to next to him at the counter.

"You know Howard?" Stinky asked her, surprised. The girl looked familiar, but he couldn't place her. He didn't know her from Indian Hills, he was fairly sure of that. One didn't forget a babe like that, and he was happy to have something in common with her.

"Um. . . yes. Sure, I know Howard."

"I'm surprised we haven't met, then. Since he's my best friend."

The flow of the conversation, the business at hand, was slipping from Lawrence's grasp.

"He didn't give *you* any of his gift certificates as well, did he?" the clerk intruded, his sarcasm devoid of any trace of good-naturedness.

The kids ignored him and continued their own conversation.

"Then you're going to his Bar Mitzvah at B'nai Jeshurun next Saturday?" Stinky asked her. Since this was relevant to his argument, he turned to Lawrence, including him for what he had to say next.

"This shirt, this one right here, is actually a Bar Mitzvah present for Howard. Howard Block."

"You're buying him a gift with one of his own gift certificates?" Lawrence asked.

"I told you!" said Stinky, getting riled again after the soothing encounter with the cute girl standing beside him. "They're mine! I can do whatever I want with them! Let me explain it to you again, okay? Most of the stuff in this store isn't his style, which is why he gave them to me in the first place. But he'll like this polo shirt, I'm sure of it. It's a Countess Mara."

"I'm well aware that it is a Countess Mara," Lawrence replied snippily, now willing to concede the standoff. He was doing the weird thing with his lips again.

"Alright," he said, relenting. "I'll take your word for it this time. But your change will be in store credit. No cash back, is that understood?"

"I'm fine with the credit," said Stinky, pleased to have reached any accommodation.

While Lawrence rang up the purchase, Stinky turned his attention back to Melissa.

"So you're going? It's going to be a mob scene. Dr. Block's son. He'll pack them in like the High Holy Days. The whole town's going to be there."

The girl looked perplexed, which Stinky attributed to his slight overstatement. So he proceeded to clarify, "All the Jews, anyway . . . ."

"I wasn't—"

Stinky interrupted her.

"Did you get him that tie?"

Melissa looked down at the tie in her hand—as if she had forgotten that she was still holding it—and paused.

"Do you think he'd like it?"

"I really like it," said Stinky.

She nodded.

"So when does it start? And where exactly is this place?"

Before Stinky could answer, Lawrence interrupted again. "I suppose you want this in a gift box?" he asked.

"And I'll need one, too," said Melissa.

***

It was Friday night, and Howard needed to set out his clothes for the next morning. He was well aware that the Rabbi and Cantor had expected him and his parents to attend Friday night services, where, at the conclusion, Rabbi Margolis would announce that his Bar Mitzvah was the following day. They hadn't gone. Jack was stuck making late rounds at the hospital anyway, as if he needed an excuse. Besides, they were not *shul* regulars, and that was that. Clearly Howard felt guiltier about missing services than his father did, but the guilt wasn't nearly enough to make him want to go, or suggest that he and his mother could attend by themselves. Maybe like his father, he would outgrow the guilt.

After the adventures of the past few weeks, namely his key involvement in an actual secret mission, Howard just wanted to get his Bar Mitzvah over and done with. The continued influx of checks and gift certificates to Jack Henry's and Woolf Brothers irritated him, salt poured into a wound. Mike kept asking, and Howard kept telling him, that he had not received a single gift card from the Toon Shop.

"What are these people thinking?" Mike had asked.

"I got a couple more thesauruses."

"Unbelievable!"

"And a set of English Leather, cologne and aftershave. . . ."

"Aftershave! What the hell are you going to do with that?"

"You sure you don't need any clothes from Jack Henry's?"

"Jeez, man . . . like I told you a million times. Thanks, but. . . ."

Howard had expected elation after their success. A real spy would celebrate, most likely with a hot babe—maybe even a Playboy bunny—and some sex. Howard wasn't exactly sure of the equivalent for a just-turned thirteen-year-old. Maybe a twenty-five dollar gift certificate to the Toon Shop would have improved things, but probably not. Truth be known, the mission hadn't really been a success after all.

He had made his father proud, though, and that was something. When he had detailed his escapades, Jack's eyes had widened and he had shaken his head in disbelief. Howard had told him everything, including getting mugged by Junior Lee downtown, and even including what he had initially considered glossing over; namely, his crush on Melissa Huntley. A son could rarely tell his father such a phantasmagorical bedtime story. Jack Block had been riveted and amazed by the adventure, and sometimes he had laughed, laughed so hard that he whistled between his teeth. Still, as Howard's father had explained earlier that week, the tape, unfortunately, wasn't exactly something that his lawyer could use.

"But, it certainly casts a new light on things, according to the lawyers," he had said. "It's a start."

"What do you mean, 'It's a start'? You've got him by the short ones, don't you, Dad?" Howard was sitting on the bathroom counter. The meeting had been like the usual bathroom conference, except Jack wasn't reading a journal. Instead, he had been waiting for Howard to appear, sitting on the pot without a journal or pipe in his hand.

"Well—the tape you made. It isn't exactly legal, or admissible in court, as it turns out."

"You mean it isn't hard evidence?"

"As far as I'm concerned it is. But the legal system is different. You know how lawyers are."

"Dad, Mike and I can get the real file! Honest! We can get it!" Howard was animated. And desperate too, not wanting to admit all the effort had been wasted.

"You mean you could steal the file."

"Huntley stole it from the hospital!"

"Howard, I'm grateful for all you've done, but you should let the adults handle things from here. . . ."

"I'm going to be a man in four days!" Howard blurted, to his own disbelief that he had actually said such a thing. What a joke!

Jack smiled, not needing to state the obvious. Howard was a thirteen-year-old kid, Bar Mitzvah or no Bar Mitzvah. The distinction was relevant to a devout Jew, perhaps, but for Howard, an assimilated, non-observant Jew in the Midwest, the whole notion approached absurdity. He barely had any armpit hair!

Jack went on. "You've done more than enough. As for me, I'm grateful and humbled and proud. And I'm vindicated, at least as far as Martin Oliver and those other schmucks are concerned. This is just a nuisance, Howard, nothing more. I just wasn't looking forward to a long, drawn out legal case. I'll get behind on my journals. And any day I'm in court is a day I can't see my patients."

Then he went for the toilet paper.

"You have your own more important business to take care of. What, now? Four days, you said? That's right. Four days."

"I haven't given my Bar Mitzvah much thought lately."

"You'll make us all proud, right? Even if you're not quite sure yourself right now why it's such a big *mishigas?*"

"Sure, Dad." He could pull it off. He could play the game. He could think of it as another mission: go undercover to learn Hebrew, infiltrate a Bar Mitzvah language lab, learn a scripture reading in an ancient tongue, and then perform a fourteenth-century religious ritual in front of a sanctuary full of Jews, most of whom were patients of Dr. Jack Block. For that reason alone, he wouldn't let his father down. He would assume the role of Bar Mitzvah, Son of the Commandments, and he would fulfill his mission. He was Howard Block, Jack Block's son, Bar Mitzvah extraordinaire, and most importantly, Master of Deceit.

"Howard," Jack said, "I couldn't possibly be more proud of you than I am right now."

And then he flushed the toilet.

***

So why wasn't what his Dad had said enough? Why did he still feel so bad?

Asking himself that question, Howard slid open his closet door, removed his Bar Mitzvah suit, and slipped off the plastic. He held it out in front of himself for a good look. A three piece would have been cooler.

He carefully laid the suit over his desk chair and headed over to the bureau for his underwear and socks.

***

Over at the Devinki home, Stinky was at the kitchen table, placing wrapping paper over the Jack Henry box. He had Scotch tape and scissors at the ready.

"You're wrapping Howard's gift yourself?" Phyllis Devinki asked.

"Yep," said Stinky proudly.

"It was so thoughtful of you to buy him a gift with your own allowance money, Irwin. And I'm sure he'll love the shirt."

"It's a Countess Mara."

"That's what you said. But wait—we can put our present in with yours."

Phyllis went into the den, where she had left her purse, and shortly returned holding an envelope. She handed it to Stinky, who immediately spotted the store logo on the upper outer corner.

"A gift certificate?" he asked her.

"Yes," she answered. "Jack Henry's."

Stinky smiled broadly.

"Excellent," he said.

***

Mike Hunsacker was also wrapping a gift. Having scavenged an old cardboard box that accommodated his needs dimensionally, he was affixing the final pieces of cellophane tape to a somewhat clumsily wrapped package, while Yuri watched passively from his cage.

The only appropriate wrapping paper he could find around the house—most of the stuff he came across was girly-themed—had jet planes on it. This he reasoned, was not all that bad, and could have been worse. A hunting pattern, for instance, might be offensive to Jews, a culturally-enlightened Mike rationalized. Jets were neutral, though not overtly religious. But then again, you had to be a man to pilot a jet, right? So there was a connection. The decorative paper, if one thought about it, was practically the perfect Bar Mitzvah gift-wrap.

He had also dug up a gift card from his mother's desk, which he wrote on before tucking it into its envelope. The latter he licked and sealed, and then taped securely onto the package with two long strips of tape. That probably was excessive, since Howard could easily figure out who had sent him the gift once it was opened. Not a thesaurus or worthless men's store gift certificate, that was for damn sure. This was something he could use and appreciate. Already Mike had decided to dispense with a ribbon and bow, which he considered a waste of time and effort, both in terms of putting on and even more so in taking off—it would slow things down considerably, not to mention being too girly anyway.

Mike set the package down, and stepped back to admire his handiwork.

Then, for the final touch, he exchanged his pen for a red Magic Marker and wrote on the wrapping paper, front and back, in large block letters.

***

A different package, more neatly prepared, was being unwrapped at the Huntley house. From the size and shape, it was certainly a tie. Dessert completed, Juanita was clearing off the table. Chadwick paused momentarily from carefully lifting up a taped corner to place one anchoring hand protectively on his tumbler of Scotch. Juanita, knowing better, had no intention of removing the glass. Resuming the unwrapping and setting the used paper aside on the table, Chadwick raised an eye appreciatively at the sight of the Jack Henry box.

"I wonder what this is. . . ." he said with a wry smile. With the appropriate dramatic pause, signaling to the gift buyers that their purchase indeed represented an act of thoughtfulness and generosity, of love, even, and was fully appreciated as such, he opened the box. Until that moment, from his expression of curiosity, one might have thought that he was so stupid that he didn't know it was a tie. But it was a tie. And not just any tie. Another tie.

He slid the tie out from its bed of tissue paper and held it up for all to see.

"Well, isn't this nice," he said. "This will go well with my new gray pinstripe. Indeed it will. Did you girls pick this out all by yourselves?"

Elaine was nodding, silently confirming that the girls were entirely responsible. Anne was also smiling, as if the tie had actually been her choice, or that she had given any real thought to the matter at all. Which left Melissa, unfazed by the compliment to her taste, sitting stone-faced.

***

All the clothes were out, draped over Howard's desk chair or on the chair seat. Like the suit, the shoes and shirt were new. So were the socks, which were the thin black ones with ribbing, mid-calf, like the ones Stinky and his father wore. Howard had removed the white shirt from its packaging and taken out all the cardboard inserts and straight pins. He had gone to his parent's bedroom and picked out one of his father's nicest blue ties. His brand new *tallis*, a gift from Grandpa Block, was crisply folded in a velvet-embroidered case just like his father's, and sat on the desktop. In his suit jacket pocket, Howard placed the creased and folded single sheet of paper, typewritten in single space, the speech written for him by Rabbi Margolis. He had it memorized, of course, and wouldn't need it in front of him, but he would be reassured knowing that it was in his pocket just in case he froze.

In a reflective mood, and too restless to actually accomplish anything, Howard sat on his bed, looking through his father's old war photo album. He found it hard to believe that all the death and destruction had taken place only a few years before he was born; the history and those times seemed so far away, almost incomprehensible in light of his comfortable life, the life his parents had made for him. This sense of distance wasn't the same for his parents, he realized, though they rarely talked about the war or the Holocaust directly. Jack had never talked to him about his war experience, not for want of asking. Jack never had much to say, skirted the questions, and managed to find a way to change the subject. No one in his entire family drove a Volkswagen, though, which was a statement in itself.

A real man served and fought in the war, Howard thought. That should be the mark of manhood, not memorizing a *Haftorah*. He looked at the younger version of his father with fascination, but always found himself drawn to the images of the death camps, the horrendous piles of bones and walking skeletons with sunken eye sockets. His father had taken those pictures, had been there to take them, but Howard didn't know the circumstances. Regardless, Howard thought he could understand why his father had stopped being observant and not bothered to pass on the rituals and traditions to his son, other than in a superficial and somewhat nonsensical way.

A knock on the door was followed by his father entering his bedroom, almost deferentially, as a guest.

"You ready for tomorrow?" Jack asked.

"Uh-huh."

"Nervous?"

"Not too bad."

"You want to run through your speech or *Haftorah* for me?"

"I don't need to, thanks."

Jack recognized the photo album in his son's lap.

"What you got there?" he asked. "Where'd you find it?"

"In a box in the basement. During that last tornado warning we had. Mom and Ada and me were stuck in the basement for over an hour, and I was poking around." He looked up at his father. "You looked pretty good with a moustache," he said.

"I shaved it off when you were born. A bunch of us had a pact not to shave for a while."

"Why was that?"

Jack seemed hesitant to explain, but considered for a moment, and forged ahead. "One time, during something called the Battle of the Bulge, we were surrounded by the Germans. It was cold and snowy, and the Germans would cover themselves with sheets so they could sneak up on us. We actually had to lower our anti-aircraft guns and shoot them across the forest. Those things would just mow down the trees."

His images were confused and disjointed, like the experience itself. He was baffled by his inarticulateness, but then again, he had never attempted to describe what had happened to anyone before. Those involved didn't require tidy exposition and didn't want to talk about it, anyway. They were there, and words could never satisfactorily express what they had gone through. Jack took a deep breath, debating on how far he wanted to go back, how much he wanted to reveal. He decided to cut the story short.

"Basically, the men in my platoon decided that if we survived, we wouldn't ever shave again."

"So you thought you were going to get killed?"

"Or captured, which probably would have amounted to the same thing. I had already thrown away my dog tags just in case."

"Why did you do that?" Howard asked.

"Because of the 'H.' 'H' for Hebrew. If the Nazis saw that, they'd shoot you immediately. Anyway, enough of that. Back to your *Haftorah*."

"What about these?" Howard persisted, turning to a page with photographs of a concentration camp.

His father sat down on the bed beside him and looked at the pictures.

"I took those when we liberated some of the camps. That particular one was Buchenwald. Afterwards, during the occupation, I traveled around trying to track down your cousins."

Howard knew nothing of this. He looked into his father's eyes with anticipation, wanting him to continue without having to ask.

He didn't have to, since Jack went on without prompting.

"We had cousins over there. Your grandfather's two younger brothers, their wives, their children. Ten children altogether. The youngest was named Hillel. I was about fifteen when he was born in Poland, which would have made him about thirteen—your age—in 1943. When he was in some concentration camp somewhere."

"Hillel?" Howard asked. He knew that Jews named their children only after non-living relatives, sometimes just using the same first English letter, if not the exact name. For some reason, Howard was struck by the possibility that Hillel was his namesake.

"We named you after him, Howard," his father confirmed.

"You never told me that."

"I suppose I was waiting for the proper time."

"They all died in the gas chambers?" Howard asked.

Jack nodded solemnly. "All of them." He stood up. "I sometimes wonder if Hillel lived to be thirteen. If he celebrated his Bar Mitzvah in that concentration camp in some small way." He closed his eyes for a few seconds before opening them and continuing. "You never forget, Howard. And you never really forgive, either. But you go on, and you try not to let it poison your life."

Howard found it hard to move.

"You feel more like a Bar Mitzvah now, don't you? All the *mishigas*—when you get beneath all the *mishigas*, then you start to understand what it's all about."

Together, for a few moments, they embraced the silence.

"Maybe I could run through my *Haftorah* one more time," Howard finally said.

"Come downstairs so your mother can hear," said Jack.

Chapter Eighteen

The narrow end hung a good two inches below the wide end in front.

"Crap," Howard muttered, working the Windsor knot out and starting over.

He had already made three previous attempts and still couldn't get it right. At the rate he was going, getting dressed would take all day.

He grabbed either end of his father's tie and slid it back and forth under his collar. He desperately tried to remember the relative lengths of hanging tie he had started with before, so he could adjust accordingly.

Having done so, he started over, the memorized mechanics of hand over hand, under and through. He knew long before he pushed the knot to his neck that he was off again. The wide end hung down so low that he could have tucked it into his pants.

"Crap," said Howard, undoing the knot.

In his parent's bathroom, Jack and Jeanette were sharing the mirror, tilting and sidestepping as required for unimpeded views of themselves. Jack was in his boxer shorts and undershirt and mid-calf socks, shaving, while Jeanette wore a beige nylon slip and was putting on her eye make-up. The preparation was ritual-like, proceeding with a dignity as if they were girding themselves with armor and preparing for battle.

In the other bathroom, Howard had come pretty close this time, with the long end just about two or three inches short of matching the front. Should he leave it be, or try one more time to come even closer?

***

Stinky was so excited for the day's ceremony and subsequent festivities that he awakened long before his alarm had been set to go off and was completely dressed even as both his parents were still sleeping soundly. He had manipulated his tie expertly on his first attempt and admired himself in the full-length mirror that was attached to the inside of his mother's closet door. The door had a noisy latch, but both parents remained asleep during his intrusion into their room and lengthy preening. In his double-breasted suit, he almost looked like a Mafioso. Noting that his gold plated tie clasp was slightly askew, he fixed it. His shirt had French cuffs, and he arranged the cuff links, which matched the tie clasp, until they were perfectly aligned. Stinky relished any opportunity to wear his one shirt with French cuffs, and he intended for his mother to buy him a new one soon, especially for his upcoming Bar Mitzvah.

Stinky closed the closet door without regard to the noise it made; still, his parents didn't stir. Maybe he had jumped the gun a bit. He didn't have to rush the shower. He could have towel dried his hair instead of letting it air dry. But his hair was fine, better than fine. Aided by Vitalis, every hair was in place, and sculpted like a topiary sitting atop his skull. But there was the matter of excess time on his hands. He didn't want to eat breakfast and risk spilling something on his clothes. And he didn't want to sit down for too long and wrinkle his pants. With no other options, Stinky decided that he would just walk around the house for the next couple of hours, pausing before every mirror he passed.

***

Mike Hunsacker, on the other hand, needed an early start, since B'nai Jeshurun was a fairly long haul by bicycle, and his parents had other plans and were unable to drive him. He was reprising the same outfit that he had worn to the abbreviated services the previous week. The sunglasses were unnecessary, of course, at least when he was inside the sanctuary, but he would wear them for the ride over. His hair was slicked back with Brylcreme, but the cowlick was unconquerable. Mike gave up. When you could smell the Brylcreme over the animal smells, you had put on enough.

Yuri was out of his cage and enjoying some free time on the desk. The amount and variety of clutter on the desktop made for a challenging topography, and Yuri could explore the rough terrain as if he were an adventuresome hiker in a national park. But not unsupervised; that had been the recently instituted policy ever since the Wollensak disaster. With his mother as confidante and transporter, Mike had happily arranged for the tape recorder repair without his father ever learning about the incident.

Mike put a final dollop of Brylcreme on his index finger and gently massaged it into the mouse's fur before putting him back in his cage.

"A little dab'll do ya, Yuri," he said.

Mike vigorously wiped the remaining hair cream off his hands on a pair of underpants atop the desk, picked up Howard's present from the seat of the chair, and headed down the two flights of stairs. Since he had learned there was free food after the ceremony, he didn't waste any time on breakfast. He looked at his watch; he needed to allow plenty of travel time, and he wanted a good seat.

Within less than a minute, Mike was on his bike, pedaling away.

***

The Blocks were dressed and readied, the men of the household not so patiently waiting by the stairway door to the garage. Howard patted his jacket pocket to be reassured, yet again, by the crinkling sound of his folded-up speech. He carried his new *tallis* bag in one hand and his *Haftorah* booklet in the other, so he could review it in the car. His father carried his own *tallis* bag, formerly the mission supply bag. It now once again contained a *tallis* and a couple of *yarmulkes*.

"We ready, then?" Jack asked again.

Jeanette went forward in one direction, only to abruptly go in another, a classic misdirection move that was reminiscent of a tight end executing a very complicated pass pattern. She was wide open.

"Do we have everything? Wait—"

Jeanette, clearly the weak link, had been continually adjusting her girdle and patting her dress down. Now she was in the kitchen, ostensibly checking to make sure the burners were off. When she came out, she was predictably holding the blue box.

Howard was already holding out his palm, with an assortment of coins.

"Oh, no, Howard, it wouldn't be right for me to take the money from you. . . not today. Jack?"

Her husband reached into his pocket and came out empty handed, except for his keys. Howard immediately dropped his own change into his father's hand, under Jeanette's watchful eyes.

"It's kosher, Mom," said Howard. "I owe Dad the money. Now it's his. And now he'll give it to you." Not yet a Bar Mitzvah, already his logic was Talmudic.

Jack was looking at the change in his hands and tallying up the total, for no reason that he could explain. Seventy-four cents.

"How much do you need, Jeanette?" he asked.

***

The B'nai Jeshurun parking lot was already beginning to fill up when Mike arrived. He decided that the safest place to leave his bike was against the side of the dumpster. Not surprisingly, his was the only bike to be seen, and the obvious lack of demand explained the absence of a bike rack. Ernie was standing at the top of the back stairwell, leaning on the handrails, taking a break and watching all the worshippers arrive.

"You rode your bike, then," said the janitor, somewhat taken aback but undeterred from maintaining his smile.

"Good *Shabbos*, Ernie," said Mike, nodding and making sure the bicycle was stable.

"And a Good *Shabbos* to you, young man," replied Ernie.

No one was entering the back way, so Mike became part of the clusters of arrivals that were walking around to the front of the building from their parked cars. Worshippers of all ages, all dressed in their finery, were being dropped off, milling about, or entering the front lobby. Mike headed inside and immediately procured a *yarmulke* and a *tallis* for himself from the bin. He had cherry picked one of the better-looking ones from the pile, and like an old pro, brought the prayer shawl to his lips before expertly sweeping it into position around his neck.

Mike and Stinky spotted each other at about the same time. Stinky and his parents were at the opposite side of the lobby from Mike, about to enter the sanctuary. Deserting his parents momentarily, Stinky strode over.

"You want to sit with us?" he asked.

"Thanks, anyway" said Mike. "I prefer this side."

"I'll see you after, then," said Stinky, rushing back to his parents.

No offense was taken, apparently, and it was nothing personal. Mike wanted to sit where he had sat the previous occasion, on the left side near the back, conveniently next to the Cohen family. To his pleasant surprise, they were in the same general area, with an empty seat beside them. He was warmly greeted by Mr. Cohen and managed to get a seat beside young Lael, who had clearly dolled herself up for the Howard Block show. She smiled shyly at Mike, and he returned the favor. He had been too clever by half earlier, with that whole Jewish Field Service business, one of the perils of being a spy. Now he would have to keep up that cover and the accent the whole time. Any future relationship would be complicated right off the starting block, with him having to explain that he was neither Jew nor foreigner, but a liar. There was always a Plan B, he thought, and he would work on it. For the moment he looked over at her and met her eyes, saying nothing. Nothing spoke volumes. Slowly, provocatively, he removed her braces with his eyes.

The buzz of activity and separate conversations echoed in the sanctuary, the typical signs of an eager audience in a theater, waiting for the lights to go down and the performance to start. Mike surveyed the room, looking for anyone he recognized. There were Stinky and his parents, of course, who were sitting near the front. And then he saw Junior Lee with his mother, Ada. Junior was less flamboyantly dressed than was his custom, and his tough guy look was tempered considerably by the Jewish beanie. In the front row, Mike saw Mrs. Block, sitting by what he assumed were both sets of grandparents, and assorted aunts and uncles and cousins. Jeanette kept nervously looking over her shoulder at the arriving crowd, greeting well-wishers with a nod of her head, white-knuckling her purse.

Howard and his father were already sitting on the altar in the throne-like chairs. Mike watched them as they stood to greet the Cantor and Rabbi, who entered though the wrought iron door behind the alter. Both wore long black robes with redundant sleeves, oversized and super fancy *tallises*, and the largest *yarmulkes* he had ever seen. After exchanging stiff pleasantries, the four retreated to their own individual thrones. The Rabbi and Cantor seemed at ease in those straight-backed, ornately carved chairs, settling into them as if they were plopping into their favorite recliner. Howard and Dr. Block, in contrast, sat rigidly and self-consciously.

The Rabbi, Buddha-like, surveyed the sanctuary as it continued to fill. It was going to be a full house. The Rabbi checked his watch. The Cantor checked his watch. Howard and his father pretended not to check their watches, but both managed to sneak peeks.

A few more minutes until show time, thought Mike. It was nearly ten o'clock.

Unseen by Mike, as well as the four observers on stage, a tentative Melissa Huntley stood just inside one of the sanctuary doors, holding a gift-wrapped package, summoning the courage to enter further.

Five more minutes, the Rabbi was thinking.

***

Melissa's father and mother were in their breakfast room. They had finished breakfast and were sharing the morning's "Kansas City Times," which was always skimpy on Saturday mornings. Juanita had cleared the table, and Chadwick was sipping his coffee, Elaine her tea. Other than the occasional directive to Juanita and each other, they had spoken very little. Breakfast at the Huntley's, when the girls weren't around, possessed a peculiar sanctity.

They looked at each other, mildly surprised, upon hearing the garage door. Soon after, Anne entered the kitchen and announced herself.

"I'm back," she said. "Any breakfast left for me?

"I thought you and Melissa were still asleep," said Elaine.

"So did I," Chadwick added, though his focus was back into the paper.

"I had to drive her to that Bar Mitzvah thing. I thought you knew."

Elaine brought the tea to her lips and blew on it softly, but didn't sip, instead saying, "It's the first I've heard about it. Chad?"

Chadwick was not paying attention. "What?" he said, without a trace of curiosity.

Anne turned up the gas burner of indignation. "That little liar," she said. "She made me get up at eight o'clock, and she said you told her I had to take her. And that present she had for him—I assumed you bought it."

"I didn't buy any present," said Elaine.

"And I haven't driven her shopping anywhere," said Anne.

"Whose Bar Mitzvah?"

Anne rolled her eyes. "You know, that weirdo—Howard Block."

Elaine strained to think, and came up empty, which meant it couldn't be someone of any importance or, rather, from a family of any importance.

"I'm not sure I know him," said Elaine.

"That little liar. I can't believe her. You don't know anything about this, do you? Not the Bar Mitzvah, not Howard Block?"

Chadwick had now awoken from Friday's stock market closings.

"Block?"

"He was at the last Young Life Meeting," Anne explained. "So weird. We—I came upstairs during the meeting, and—" At this point, Anne realized she was treading on thin ice, but she thought she could finesse it. "And—and for some reason he was upstairs, in the corridor. By himself in the dark. Sneaking around, like. Weird."

Chadwick was now more than a disinterested participant in the conversation. "You never mentioned that before," he said, putting down the paper without folding it.

"I—I thought, maybe he was just looking for the bathroom, or something."

"Was he in my study?" His voice had reached *forte* without the gradual groundswell of a *crescendo*.

Anne didn't trust her own voice, afraid that it would quaver. She had not intended her whining to elicit an interrogation, especially one taking such a nasty turn. She resorted to a typical teenager shrug.

Chadwick bolted from his chair, bumping the table and rattling Elaine's teacup. Tea sloshed onto the table.

"I'll get it," Juanita piped in reflexively at the sound of the jolt, a kitchen towel already in her hand and under the cold water tap.

From the dining room, Elaine, Anne, and Juanita could hear the study door banging open. They were not there to witness Chadwick's increasingly agitated, and increasingly futile, search of the top drawer of the file cabinet, but couldn't help but hear the bang when he had given up and slammed the drawer shut in such fury that the entire cabinet convulsed backwards, perforating the dry wall behind it.

Puzzled by what had set him off so, especially since he was sober and had given no prior indication of a foul mood, their reactions were varied. Elaine tried not to betray her sense of alarm and, in a transparently poor attempt at nonchalance, continued to sip her tea and pretended to read a suddenly absorbing news article. Juanita, outwardly passive and of a more practical bent, was contemplating the mess she would have to clean up. Anne did nothing to conceal her annoyance and disgust. She was the one who had a real gripe, having been duped into getting up at the ass crack of dawn on a Saturday morning to drive her liar of a sister halfway to hell and back. And what in the world is he looking for, anyway? Weirdo Block was just a nosey little creep—he didn't leave anything in the study. She wasn't at all worried that her father would return with some incriminating evidence, some tangible indication that she and Tripp had made use of his precious office. She was one hundred percent convinced that her father would find nothing, nothing at all.

She was right, of course, since her lying sister had made another middle-of-the-night foray into Chadwick Huntley's private domain with a temporarily purloined cabinet key the previous night. Hannah Stringer's medical chart was no longer in the top drawer of the file cabinet.

Chadwick returned to the breakfast room beyond agitation.

"Where did you take her! Where is this place!" he yelled at his daughter.

Anne, oblivious to any connection, was so completely taken aback by the question that she did not register the answer he was demanding.

"What?"

"Tell me now!"

"Chad, what's going on?" Elaine was now standing and coming to his side to calm him.

"Shut up!" he snapped. "Where did you take Melissa?" he asked again, his frenzy having reached some type of pulsating equilibrium, neither escalating nor diminishing, simply hovering near the boundary of lost control.

"Some synagogue," Anne answered plainly, feeling no need for emotion or confrontation, hers the voice of sanity in all this crazy business. "I don't know the name of it. On 63rd and Rockhill Road. Jeez, what's your problem?"

Chadwick made a lunging move to the door to the garage, as if a bus on the other side were about to take off without him. He was through the door in a flash.

The car door slammed and the engine turned over. But before the garage had fully opened, Elaine was halfway through the door herself.

"Wait!" she screamed. "I'm going with you!"

After another car door slamming, the Lincoln screeched backwards out of the garage. Chadwick, who didn't bother pressing the remote button to close the doors as he pulled recklessly out of the driveway, jolted the vehicle as he shifted into drive before fully stopping and screeched off like a cop on a chase. Juanita calmly walked over to the door and opened it just enough to reach through to the garage door button on the wall. She closed the door as the garage door mechanism started whirring and was back by the kitchen sink as the garage door struck ground with self-assured finality.

"How about a nice French toast, Annie honey?" said Juanita.

Chapter Nineteen

The morning service was about to begin. Nearly everyone was seated, and only a few empty seats were left. At the last minute, moments before Rabbi Margolis extricated himself from his seat, Melissa timidly walked down the aisle past Mike and the Cohen family to take a seat near the front of the sanctuary. Mike only noticed her as she was edging sideways past a couple of worshippers to the only unoccupied seat in the row. She had then looked back at him, clutching the present to her chest and silently communicating the contents. She smoothed out the back of her skirt with her free hand before sitting down, took her designated prayer book, and wriggled into her seat.

Mike bolted upright in his seat the instant he saw her, alert with a single-minded attentiveness. Howard first spotted her a few moments earlier, as she walked down the aisle, and since he was already sitting rigidly in his chair, his postural reaction was less pronounced. Melissa looked at him meaningfully from her seat, slightly lifting with one arm the present that she still cradled in front of her. Howard took his eyes away long enough to look at Mike, who was looking back at him. With that glance they conveyed mutual comprehension of the situation. Melissa was prepared to deliver

Hannah Stringer's chart, gift-wrapped. Now under cover herself as a Jew, she had unexpectedly brought the goods, possibly the best Bar Mitzvah gift of all. Plan C was evidently of her own devising, and the boys had been left in the dark. There had been no need to know, thought Howard. There's always a file, thought Mike.

Howard's heart was thumping. His surroundings became blurry, and the sounds in the sanctuary appeared to come from a distance, muffled, as if his ears were stopped up. He had nearly forgotten where he was, transported to an unknown location in his consciousness by adrenaline and neuronal circuit overload. Jack had noticed, and saw that his son's eyes appeared glazed over, as if he were in a drug-induced trance. What was the diagnosis? Was he freezing up? Jack could break the spell, he thought, if only Howard would look over at him.

The Rabbi stood at the podium, waiting for the silence to become absolute. "We will now begin today's Torah reading," he finally said. "Please rise as we open the Ark."

And thus came the collective sound of the worshippers rising to their feet in a chorus of dull thuds as the cushioned seats flipped into their unburdened, upright position against the seat backs, punctuated by the scattered groans of the elderly. Howard, lost in a confused array of thoughts, was slow off the mark. The Bar Mitzvah boy was the last one to stand.

***

Howard passively observed the goings on in a daze.

The Torah scroll had been uncovered and placed on the altar table. Mr. Federman had joined the distinguished group at the altar, as the designated *Gabbai*. This was the dignitary who oversaw the Torah reading and called up the participants, previously chosen and notified, who would receive the various bit-part honors that were doled out, called "*aliyahs*."

Mr. Federman stood before the microphone and read out the name: "Mr. Yitzak Cohen."

Mr. Cohen, far in the back of the sanctuary, rose from his seat and edged his way past Mike.

"I have the first *aliyah*," he proudly informed Howard Block's young friend in passing.

"Way to go," Mike said appreciatively, pronouncing "way" as if it were "vey."

Mr. Federman wasted no time in reciting the next name on the list.

"Mr. Ronald Dworkin," he said.

Bruce Dworkin's father rose from a group of worshippers, closer to the front, but off the same aisle as Mr. Cohen. He waited at the end of his row for Mr. Cohen to join him, shook his hand, and the two men walked together to the wide aisle traversing the front of the pulpit, crossing to the far side and jauntily climbing the four carpeted steps. They took their places at the altar between the Rabbi and Cantor, directed by the *Gabbai*, who used arm gestures and even a nudge to position them correctly. There was handshaking all round, with Mr. Dworkin even shaking Mr. Cohen's hand a second time.

Mr. Cohen, following the proper religious protocol, sang the blessings, familiar to almost all in the room, which prefaced the Rabbi's reading of a short section from the parchment scroll. Afterwards, there was another round of handshaking, and Mr. Cohen was excused to return to his seat. Walking up the raked aisle back to his seat, a smiling Yitzhak Cohen acknowledged congregation members to the right and left, nodding and mouthing the words "Good *Shabbos*." As Mike greeted his return with a hearty handshake of his own and a "Good job" (with the "job" sounding like "yob"), Mr. Dworkin moved to Mr. Cohen's prior position for recitation, as instructed by Mr. Federman.

Then Mr. Federman turned to Jack Block, still sitting as if there were a rod up his back, instructing him to rise from his ostentatious chair and take up the position at the altar table formerly occupied by Mr. Dworkin. The silent rotation and maneuvering on the altar proceeded deliberatively, without a hitch. Mr. Federman had done this many times before. But had he been directing actual traffic outside on 63rd Street, rather than at the alter, he might have been plowed under by a speeding and weaving Lincoln Continental driven by one Dr. Chadwick Huntley.

Services continued, all a warm-up act for the main attraction, the Bar Mitzvah boy, who was paying no attention at all, except to Melissa. She had the prayer book open, though not on the correct page, and was looking over at English translations and trying to read. Each time she looked up, which was frequently, she would see Howard still staring at her. Then she would look down again, and try to find her place before looking up once again. This behavioral loop had gone on for some time, and never once had Howard's eyes not been upon her. She was pretty enough to watch, of course, but she was also holding the prize, and Howard was keeping his eyes on it as well. Becoming a man was symbolic, but saving his father was real. The praying had become background noise, mere religious *Muzak*. Mike, in the meantime, was shifting his eyes back and forth between the two of them, perched forward on the edge of his seat. What for him represented almost an intolerable crescendo of suspense was interpreted by Mr. Cohen as a manifestation of devotion. The young man, Mr. Cohen observed, was intent upon, even cherishing, every Hebrew word—a veritable Torah scholar. And at such a young age.

Jeanette, from the front row, saw Howard staring intently into the sanctuary, hardly blinking, and thought he looked distinguished. She construed this as his Bar Mitzvah game face, psyching himself up, although she would not have described it in those exact terms. Stinky might have described it that way, though, since Howard's demeanor had not escaped his notice either. He hoped that when his time came, he could sit still like that, without fidgeting or having his stomach growl.

Seeing her son so composed under the stressful circumstances, so regal-like—especially sitting in that incredible chair—Jeanette beamed with pride. Inside she was a wreck, but she knew deep down that Howard would not disappoint, he would pull though with flying colors, just like Frieda Kaplan had done with her hysterectomy. Nearly the entire Jewish community was there as witnesses, so many of Jack's patients, which made the *nachas* all the more satisfying. It never would have occurred to her that her son was undergoing the spiritual transformation from boy to man while fixating on a *shiksa* the entire time. Had Stinky been chosen to weigh in, he might have expressed the opinion that such behavior could very well be a sin.

***

Chadwick Huntley had finally arrived at his destination, an alien house of worship, but was cursing and banging his hand on the steering wheel with exasperation at not being able to find a parking spot.

"You have to tell me what's going on," pleaded Elaine, as she had been pleading to no avail for the entire ride. Chadwick was immersed in his own world and thoughts, seething with anger, and she was invisible to him. Shamefully, she realized that she was now motivated more by a morbid curiosity than any desire on her part to soothe him. She was regressing into the internal dialogue, repeated now and again throughout the years, of "what was I thinking when I married this man?" But it was no longer really about Chadwick, nor had it been from the moment they had left their house—Elaine had her daughter to protect.

Cars were parked in every available space in front of the synagogue on Rockhill Road. Chadwick stopped in the middle of the street, directly in front of the main synagogue entrance beside a parked car, and shifted the Lincoln into "Park," with brutality.

"You stay here!" he ordered Elaine, nearly getting sideswiped by a car trying to go around him as he opened the driver side door. The driver honked. Chadwick was not contrite, nor did he even bother to cast a dirty look or deliver an obscene hand gesture, as men generally reacted when at fault. Instead, he rushed from the double-parked car as if fleeing a burning building, leaving Elaine by herself, sitting there with the engine running.

Cars continued to pass, but none bothered to bleat their horns.

Elaine reached over to turn off the ignition and then removed the car keys. She wasn't the one who would be cited for a parking violation, after all. The car was Chadwick's. And he already had one citation for driving under the influence.

Maybe they'd take his license away. That was the worst that could happen, which wasn't so bad, all things considered. Elaine slid across the seat, since her own door was blocked by the parked blue Oldsmobile on the passenger side, checked for oncoming cars through the side view mirror, and hastened out of the car when the coast was clear. She was composed enough not to slam the door, and didn't bother to lock it. One unreasonable person was enough, and she wasn't going to sit this situation out. That conclusion, which determined her action, bespoke not only her own good sense but internal wiring that had been arranged and rearranged over thousands of years of female human evolution.

Chadwick strode into the lobby of B'nai Jeshurun as if he were entering the pro shop at Indian Hills Golf and Country Club. Clearly he was more dressed for the links than for prayer; in fact, he was scheduled as part of a foursome at the club with an eleven o'clock tee time. Thus, he was wearing a bright green cotton polo shirt and yellow golf slacks, well-fitted to his tanned and sinewy frame. His attire was unavoidably destined to make some sort of citrous, if not ecumenical, statement, even without a *tallis* or *yarmulke*.

His entrance and loop down and around the aisles of the sanctuary made less of a commotion than might have been expected, owing to most attention being focused on the goings-on at the altar and a natural disinclination for rubber-necking during a religious ceremony. Having entered the northern entrance to the sanctuary, Chadwick first stood at the back and scanned the room for his daughter, who was sitting on the opposite side. He might have opted for a retreat and used the other lobby entrance to make a less ostentatious approach to his daughter, but his forward emotional momentum could not tolerate even a momentary redirection.

Thus, he brazenly walked down the right-sided aisle all the way to the front of the sanctuary, crossed directly in front of the altar, and proceeded to the opposite aisle, his passage in clear view of the entire congregation.

Melissa, whose attentions were occupied as previously described, did not notice her father until he was striding across the front of the sanctuary. The instant she did, she jumped to her feet and stumbled passed the worshippers in her row to the aisle and trotted up the incline toward the set of double doors. Chadwick pursued her, increasing the length of his stride. Melissa went even faster toward the exit, slowing only long enough to shove her package into Mike's hands as she passed. Mike was now the bearer of two gifts. He instinctively placed the newly acquired one beneath his own.

Neither Howard nor Mike had seen Chadwick Huntley before in person, but had no trouble determining his identity once they put the stranger's incongruous appearance together with Melissa's panicked response. Jack had recognized Chadwick immediately, of course, and quickly pieced together the situation as best he could, not understanding the significance of the package in Melissa's possession. The entrance and chase happened so fast, and those involved felt so constrained by appropriate decorum, that they were no more capable of responding than if they had witnessed a purse snatching. Only facial expressions could change, into one of worry and puzzlement for Jack, panic for Howard and Mike, and terror for Melissa. Most everyone else maintained their expressions as they were, be they the serenity of prayer or of boredom.

The double doors closed behind Melissa, who was out of harm's way for the moment. Chadwick was not far behind, though, and her frantic hand-off to Mike had not escaped his attention. He slowed down as he menacingly approached Mike's row.

The Torah service, of course, did not stop for such things of this world, and Mr. Federman, incapable of seeing beyond the next *aliyah*, was relentless in his the performance of his duties as the *Gabbai*.

"For the honor of *Hagva*," he announced for all to hear, "Mr. Seymore Weisman."

Mr. Weisman, sitting on the opposite side of the sanctuary from Mike and the Cohens, and also near the back, quickly rose and began working his way across the row to the main aisle.

And, inexplicably, Mike rose with him.

"Give it to me now!" Chadwick Huntley said through gritted teeth.

Mike shoved a package into his hands and pushed past him, scurrying purposefully down the aisle toward the altar, as did Mr. Weisman, in a parallel trajectory down his own aisle.

Object of the pursuit in hand, Chadwick made his exit. In so doing, he missed witnessing the confusion occurring at the altar, where Mr. Weisman and Mike Hunsacker were in discussion with Mr. Federman.

"I thought you called my name," said Mike to the *Gabbai*.

"There's another Seymour Weisman? We have two?"

"I could have sworn you called my name."

The Rabbi stepped over to intercede.

"And who are you, son?" he asked.

"Mike Hunsacker. I'm a friend of Howard's." He looked over to Howard, still in his chair, and smiled. The Rabbi looked over at Howard. Howard was smiling.

"So you're NOT Seymour Weisman." said Mr. Federman.

"Hunsacker," said Mike. "That's what I thought you said. Mike Hunsacker."

Mr. Federman was blinking frequently, which was his manner of twitching.

"Well," said the Rabbi, "you can both share the honor."

"I don't mind," said Seymour Weisman.

"That's real nice of you," said Mike. "Excuse me—I need to get rid of this first." He took a few quick steps over to Howard.

"Here. Hold this," he said, handing him a gift-wrapped package before returning to the altar table.

Shortly thereafter, Mike and Mr. Weisman were jointly holding up the Torah scroll, each grasping one of the carved wooden handles. They held it up high overhead, as the standing congregation chanted. Mike was grinning. So was Howard, clasping the package to his chest. Stinky was wondering how Mike Hunsacker managed to pull off such a neat *aliyah*, when he wasn't even Jewish.

***

Melissa was sobbing uncontrollably in her mother's arms in the lobby.

"I'll deal with you later," Chadwick threatened.

"The hell you will!" said Elaine, stroking her daughter's hair.

Chadwick ignored her and examined the package in his hand. The edges of the package were sharp, obviously a box, of approximately the proper size to hold the chart.

"What is that?" Elaine asked.

"None of your business," snapped Chadwick.

Melissa looked up, her face flushed and eyes swollen. Immediately noticing that the present was wrapped in paper with airplanes all over it, she buried her head back in her mother's arms. She was taking short, gasping breaths, but now she had stopped crying. She turned her head slightly, so she could see with one eye. She couldn't help herself.

Chadwick hadn't bothered with the card, but couldn't help but notice that the gift wrap was odd—a variety of fighter jets on a Bar Mitzvah gift?—and clumsily wrapped. And then there was the big block lettering on the paper, written in red Magic Marker. "Top Secret" it said. He did not recognize the writing, but it certainly wasn't Melissa's.

He ripped off the wrapping paper too quickly for his sense of foreboding to have fully emerged. The box being sealed with scotch tape on all sides, he impatiently ran his thumb under all four edges to free the lid.

Chadwick opened the box and fished his way through tissue paper.

The box did not contain Hannah Stringer's chart. Inside, instead, was a magazine. Specifically, the May, 1963 issue of "Playboy." Had Chadwick bothered to leaf through the pages, which he did not, he might have come across some very enticing articles.

Chadwick closed his eyes. All adrenaline spent, there was no more left, not even enough to open his eyes. His lids had suddenly become extremely heavy, and he wasn't sure he could ever lift them again. He took several slow, deep breaths. He felt his racing heart responding to the pulling of some invisible reins, transitioning from a gallop to a canter, a good sign. And he was still perfectly capable of grinding his teeth. Chadwick knew that he had to get a grip.

"Let's go home," he said to Elaine, as soon as he could see the world again.

"I'm staying for the reception," Melissa said adamantly, wiping her eyes with her forearm.

Outside, a policeman was writing out a citation for a double-parked Lincoln Continental.

Chapter Twenty

Howard stood on the pulpit, chanting his *Haftorah*. Jack, still enthroned, was beaming with pride, smiling and listening, nodding his head to the musical strains of his son's voice. There was no faltering, nothing off pitch, no backing off from the high notes, and no cracking. Jack patted his fingers on the package he was holding in time to the music. Howard, taking a slight detour en route to the alter, had set it down in his lap.

"The chart," was all Howard had said. But by then, Jack had already figured things out for himself.

***

Services had progressed to the Bar Mitzvah speech.

"The *Haftorah* which I read this morning consists of a dramatic chapter about the appointment of Jeremiah as a prophet of the Lord," Howard began, reciting Rabbi Margolis' words effortlessly. "When young Jeremiah heard God calling him to speak to the nations, he was frightened, and he said, 'Ah, Lord God, I cannot speak, for I am a mere child.'"

Rabbi Margolis, back in his seat of honor, was clearly pleased with this passage and the speech in general. He had tried to make the recitation a little special, even a bit longer than the usual speech, since it was for Jack Block's son. Dr. Block was his personal physician, of course, and it was the least he could do. And Howard, so far, had not let him down. He listened carefully to his own meticulously crafted words, expressed in a voice not his own, but nevertheless authoritatively and convincingly. The Rabbi wasn't aware that he was silently mouthing the words to himself.

"Every boy who is called to the *Torah* on the day of his Bar Mitzvah," he surreptitiously lip-synched, "and to do 'a man's job' in the years to come, must be able to learn from these sacred episodes of the Bible, and the first lesson from today's *Haftorah* is that even the greatest man started life by being a boy."

But then the Rabbi's lips movements were out of sync with the spoken words, and it might have been clear, had anyone been taking notice, that Howard had strayed from the script.

"I must admit," said Howard, "that I had found it hard to relate to Jeremiah, even a twelve-year old Jeremiah. I did not see how he could be a model for me and how I am to become a man. But then I began to think about what he must have felt in his heart, not just what he said. Because righteousness and courage begin in the heart. . . ."

Rabbi Margolis, lips no longer moving, found himself listening to a Bar Mitzvah speech that he had not written, an experience he found both unsettling and remarkable.

***

The old basement sanctuary had been transformed for the occasion. The carrels of the language lab had been dismantled by Ernie and set against the wall, and large tables set up for the buffet. Hors d'oeuvres, dominated by a prominent centerpiece of chopped chicken liver, occupied a circular table near the stage; two parallel tables on opposite sides of the room were lined with a variety of hot dishes, like *kugel* and *kasha varnishkes*. Sitting areas were provided by smaller round tables—all covered with white tablecloths and surrounded by folding chairs—that were placed along the periphery of the room, leaving plenty of mingling space in the center. Cakes and sweets, all home made, were on a separate table. The color décor, predictably, was blue and white, although flower arrangements on all the tables provided bursts of a variety of colors. Plates, glasses, cups and saucers, and cutlery were provided by the synagogue; only the paper napkins were distinctive, lined in blue and imprinted with "Howard M. Block, June 22, 1963" in one corner.

Since Howard's mother and aunts didn't keep kosher, they hadn't been allowed to prepare any of the food in their own kitchens. Thus, over the preceding two months, they had regularly come to the synagogue to bake and then transported their kugels and desserts home, keeping them frozen in trays or in plastic bags until needed. By the usual standards, the reception was an elaborate event, since most of the time celebratory victuals were limited to appetizers and sweets, or even just the latter. But for Dr. Block's son, more was expected, and there were a lot of patients to feed. It was a full course buffet.

Howard needed to spend the first part of the reception close to his parents, where he could accept congratulations and good wishes before heading off on his own to actually have some fun. He was in high spirits, relieved that the ceremony was over, of course, but more excited about the gift-wrapped package that his father still sandwiched under his arm. They did not refer to it specifically—ritual taking precedence over business, the spiritual over the worldly—but they knowingly smiled at each other often. Howard looked around for Melissa Huntley in between handshakes and pleasantries, but she was nowhere to be seen, and he assumed she was long gone. And probably in a shit load of trouble, all on his behalf, he thought. She would pay the biggest price of all, perhaps be physically beaten, and while grateful, he felt guilty about her sacrifice.

Rabbi Margolis was the first to pay his respects.

"*Mazel Tov*," he said, smiling broadly and vigorously shaking Howard's hand with both of his own. "Howard, you did a fine job, your parents should be proud."

Howard felt awkward despite the Rabbi's graciousness. He couldn't pretend that nothing had happened, not to a Rabbi. . . .

"Thank you, Rabbi," he said. "I hope you didn't mind that I—"

"The speech," Rabbi Margolis finished for him. "Ah. . . ." He stroked his beard, mainly still black but streaked with white stripes on each side, as if a pair of Siamese skunks were dangling from his chin. "To tell you the truth," he said, "I liked your version better. But don't tell anyone, I wouldn't want it to start a trend."

"I'm sorry that I haven't been as involved with the synagogue as I might have been," Howard said, realizing as he said it that he wasn't actually sure how sorry he was. Still, he felt obliged to apologize and confess. By any standards, his academic performance at Hebrew School and Sunday School had always been sub-par—especially for an "A" student in secular school—and he had frequently been absent over the years. Academically, he had been a religious school under-achiever, and he hoped he had redeemed himself somewhat by nailing his *Haftorah*.

The Rabbi looked at him closely. "Don't apologize. It is the empty kettle that makes the most noise."

Howard was stunned by the remark. He couldn't believe that the Rabbi accepted him for who he was, that he didn't hold things against him, that he somehow understood that Howard couldn't pretend to be someone that he wasn't. Until that very moment, Howard had really not liked Rabbi Margolis very much.

The Rabbi turned to Jack and Jeanette. "I'm sure he will bring you great *nachas*," he said.

"He already has," said Jack. Jeanette was uncharacteristi-cally quiet, perhaps due to the reality of the milestone in her son's life sinking in. She wore a serene smile of contentment. For the moment she had stopped worrying about anything. Maybe that was why she was quiet, Howard thought.

After repetitive conversations with a number of his father's patients and other congregants, Howard excused himself and sought out Stinky, finding him by the chopped liver. Howard quickly filled him in about Melissa Huntley's gift, how their mission had succeeded after all.

"We couldn't have done it without you," he said

Stinky looked down, as if embarrassed by the praise, but internally swelling with pride.

"I was just a pain in the *tuchus*," he said, with self-deprecation.

"That too," said Howard.

Stinky handed Howard a cracker laden with chopped liv-er and made one for himself. They ate quietly, instantaneous-ly comforted by the chopped liver as if it were a fast acting drug. Chopped liver was usually associated with celebrations, good things, the warmth of family and friends. There were no bad connotations surrounding chopped liver, unless you bothered to consider the chickens.

They surveyed the room. Everyone appeared to be having a good time. The noise in the room was getting incrementally louder and more animated. Howard nudged Stinky and pointed over at Mike, who was with Mr. Cohen and family.

Mr. Cohen was addressing his wife.

"Remember? Jewish Field Service. An exchange student." And then, to Mike. "Michael, do they ever call you Moishe? I'd like you to meet my daughter, Lael. . . . "

Junior Lee was hovering near one of the buffet tables, chatting up an attractive black catering employee who was replenishing the table with knishes. Cantor Birenboim was with his wife and small son, for whom he was jovially preparing a plate of food. Yakov Bettinger was nearby with his wife and two small girls. He appeared relaxed, happy, and warm, and was affectionately entertaining his daughters.

"Look at him," said Stinky. "He seems like a nice guy. He has a wife. He has kids. He's smiling. Like he's human or something. He looks so different."

"A lot of things look different," said Howard.

***

When he first saw them, standing by themselves just inside the front double doors, Howard had no idea how long they had been standing there. The bulk of the action—the food action, in any case—was at the other end of the room, where most of the guests were congregated. The crowd became progressively thinner as one headed toward the Cantor's office, and no one else stood by the front doors except for them. The three of them just stood there, expectantly, Chadwick Huntley still holding the already-opened gift in his hand. Elaine was holding Melissa's hand. They were not wearing their party faces.

Likely they were holding back, waiting for Jack to notice them, which he did. He and Jeanette had been separated by different clusters of well-wishers, so no explanation to his wife was required as he headed over to them. Howard saw his father in transit.

"Uh-oh," Stinky said, following Howard's eyes.

Howard shoved the cracker he was eating into his mouth and jogged over for what was likely to be an unpleasant business.

As Howard left, Stinky topped two more crackers. He would munch on them as he watched, near the safety and security of the chopped liver.

**

"Hello." Jack greeted them warily, stopping in his tracks a comfortable distance away.

"We're sorry to have disturbed such a special event," said Elaine. "We want to offer our apologies. All of us. Right, Chad?"

Howard was now beside his father, more winded than he should have been after covering such a short distance. He felt a barely discernable mini-convulsion as a protracteed shiver passed from somewhere below his waist up through and beyond his head. He looked over at Melissa. Neither could manage a smile, and both were extremely anxious about the adult interaction that could no longer be avoided. They were powerless to control, or even influence it.

"Everybody's welcome," said Jack.

"I think you have something that belongs to me," said Chadwick, firing his warning shot across the bow and setting a tone that all of the others hoped might have been avoided.

Jack reflexively clenched his upper arm tighter to his chest, squeezing the package under his armpit. He stared at Chadwick, thinking hard, not sure of how to negotiate his dingy through the troubled waters. He wanted to avoid a fight without backing down.

Elaine interceded.

"You need help, Chad, and don't come home until you get it. I'm so sorry, Jack," she said, starting to leave. "Let's go, Melissa."

But Melissa was glued to the spot. Elaine, who initially had not had the nerve to stay for his response, was obliged to. Chadwick gave her a hard look, making calculations in his head. The equation had changed, the variables not just about Hannah Stringer anymore. Elaine wasn't bluffing. Still, he said nothing.

"I'll help you in any way I can, Chad, " Jack said, adding, "I don't want to make more trouble for you. I have no interest in that."

"Just like that?" Now that he was spared direct communication with his wife, Chadwick could gather his words. "They'll kick me off the staff and you know it. I'll lose my license." These were tangibles, things he could grasp at the moment, simple and straightforward. His marriage, his relationship with his daughters, the demons that gnawed at him—those were more complicated matters.

Jack took a deep breath and exhaled. He had come to his personal crossroads and decided which direction he would go. There would be no turning back.

"No one needs to be the wiser for it. Get yourself some help, and I'll see that doesn't happen. I promise you. You have my word."

Chadwick snorted. "You're willing to just forget the whole thing—"

"I don't forget things, Chad, but I don't dwell on the past, either."

He reached under his arm for the package. He looked down at it, then into Chadwick's eyes, then extended it as an offering.

"You can return this gift. Take it back from where it came. Exchange it for something Howard could really use."

Chadwick took the package, the responsibilities and changes that lay ahead of him falling upon him like a sudden cloudburst. Whether he would be cleansed, or merely soaked, remained unknown. He silently and unconsciously squeezed the package rhythmically, a pulsating heart within his grasp, as if he were anticipating a rubber toy to make a squeak. The only sound was the crinkling of the wrapping paper.

"Howard could use a thesaurus," said Jack, relaxing his face into the semblance of a smile for the first time.

"Dad!" Howard protested.

"Thank you, Jack," said Elaine, Taking her husband's arm and preparing to lead him away. He was now carrying two presents but didn't think to return the "Playboy." "Are you coming, Melissa?"

"I'd like to stay," she said.

"We'll get her home," said Howard, who was no longer tongue-tied in her presence.

Jack stood in place, and watched Elaine and Chadwick Huntley pass through the doors.

"I'm going back to your mother," he said to Howard, nothing more, and walked away.

Howard escorted Melissa to the prime real estate near the chopped liver. Stinky, ever the squatter, was still there. He had witnessed the package exchange, wasn't exactly sure what had transpired, but apparently, at least from the looks on the faces of Howard and Melissa, things had worked out reasonably well.

"This chopped liver is fantastic," said Stinky. "The best."

"My grandma made it," said Howard, before proceeding with the introduction that he thought was needed.

"Melissa, this is my friend Irwin Devinki."

"Hi, Stinky."

"We've already met," said Stinky, prompted by Howard's look of utter astonishment. "You coming to the party tonight?" he asked her.

"I'd love to, if I'm invited."

"You're invited," said Howard.

"A five piece combo, right, Howie?" said Stinky through a mouthful of cracker and liver. "And a *klezmer* band for the adults, am I right?"

"Yeah," replied Howard. "Zvi and the Kugels. They're patients of my Dad's."

"See you later, then," said Stinky heading off, ready to sample the hot dishes at the other table.

"You can try the liver and see if you like it. It's sort of an acquired taste if you aren't Jewish." Howard leaned over to prepare a cracker for her, going light on the spread.

"You really did a good job," she said, taking the cracker. He also handed her one of his personalized napkins, a gesture that verged on showing off.

"Thanks," said Howard.

"Your dad's a special man," she said.

"Thanks. I'd like to be like him when I grow up."

"I think you're like him now."

"Thanks," Howard said, a warmth expanding from deep inside him. He had never received a better compliment.

Howard watched as Melissa nibbled a corner of the cracker. She smacked her lips thoughtfully.

"Not bad," she lied.

***

Jack found Jeanette alone for the moment. He came up to her and waited for her to say something, anything. He knew she would.

"Where's Howard?" she asked, as if he could get into trouble at his own Bar Mitzvah. Perhaps choke on a cantaloupe ball.

"Over there." He pointed at the round hors d'oeuvre table.

"With that girl? She's a doll, isn't she? Just like a little *shiksa*. You know her? One of your patient's daughters?"

Jack shrugged while Jeanette continued.

"They look so cute together. A little *shiksa* and our little *shaygets*."

"Uh-huh."

"Our little *mensch*."

"He's a Bar Mitzvah now, Jeanette," Jack said. "He's a real *mensch*. A *haimaishe mensch*."

Jeanette was still distracted.

"I wonder who she is? Do you know?"

She looked at her husband for an answer.

He raised his eyebrows and shrugged.

"We paid for all this food," he said, "let's get some before it's all gone."

Jack Block slowly led his wife toward the main buffet, all the while looking back at his son Howard.

THE END

Made in the USA
Charleston, SC
14 July 2013